The Cache
and Other Stories

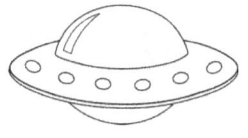

Sherry D. Ramsey

First Published in 2017
Compilation © Sherry D. Ramsey 2017
Cover Artwork © Sherry D. Ramsey 2017
UFO icon by Dale Humphries (www.flaticon.com)

Ramsey, Sherry D., 1963-, author
The Cache and Other Stories / Sherry D. Ramsey

Email: sherrydramsey@gmail.com
Web: www.sherrydramsey.com
Cape Breton, Nova Scotia, Canada

The Cache and Other Stories
Print ISBN: 978-0-9938973-7-5
Ebook ISBN: 978-0-9938973-9-9

"Upload" first appeared in *Aiofe's Kiss*, June 2003

"Ghosts and Dark Objects" first appeared in *Astropoetica*, Winter 2005

"The Cache" first appeared in *Unearthed: The Speculative Elements v. 3*, Third Person Press, Canada, 2012

"ePrayer" first appeared in *Grey Area: 13 Ghost Stories*, Third Person Press, Canada, 2013

"B.R.A.N.E., Inc." first appeared in *Flashpoint: The Speculative Elements v. 4*, Third Person Press, 2014

"Alien Gifts" first appeared in *2016 Young Explorer's Adventure Guide*, Dreaming Robot Press, 2015

"Addicted to Love" first appeared in *Mystery Weekly Magazine*, July 2016

Other Books by Sherry D. Ramsey

The Nearspace Series
One's Aspect to the Sun
Dark Beneath the Moon
Beyond the Sentinel Stars
(forthcoming)

The Seventh Crow

Magica Incognita Series
The Murder Prophet
The Chaos Assassin
(forthcoming)

To Unimagined Shores – Collected Stories

Dedication

For my dear aunt, Mary Hay,
who always encouraged me
to "keep going."

Contents

Acknowledgments

Despite the persistent perception of writing as a lonely pursuit, the acknowledgments section in almost every book lists countless people whom the author recognizes as helping them along their writing journey. This one is no exception.

The stories in this collection unarguably represent many hours spent sitting alone at my desk (or walking at my treadmill desk), and yet they also represent months and years of quiet and unwavering support from my husband, Terry, my children, Emily and Mark, and the rest of my family. Some of these stories would not exist at all without the ongoing encouragement (and occasional prodding) of my dear friends and partners at Third Person Press, Julie Serroul and Nancy Waldman. And these stories often took shape with the help of input and critique from my fellow writers, in groups and at meetings both online and off.

I would also be remiss if I didn't mention the help of my daughter, Emily Ramsey, who assisted me immensely with proofreading and layout of the collection in its final form.

So often alone, yes; but lonely, never.

SDR
June, 2017

The Cache

The GPS beeped. A few feet in front of me, Ricky whooped, startling something small in the underbrush. It skittered away, unseen, through the carpet of dead leaves. The dog immediately shoved his nose under some brush, straining at the leash. I tugged him back.

"Don't drop it!" I yelped, because as usual, the kid seemed unable to keep himself still like a normal human being. I already regretted letting him carry my GPS. He looked ready to dash into the underbrush himself in search of the cache.

"I'm not going to drop it, Danny," he reproached me, holding it out so I could see how tightly he held it, and that the strap was still looped around his wrist. I took his hand and turned it so I could see the screen.

Arriving at Gully's River West. Below that, it displayed the coordinates.

I eased the gadget away from the kid. He relinquished it reluctantly. "Okay, we're here. Now, you're not going to find the cache by jumping up and down like a maniac. This is the part of geocaching where you really have to pay attention and concentrate."

I expected my words to fall on deaf ears, but surprisingly, Ricky stood still.

"So once the GPS says we're here, it's gotta be somewhere close, right?" he asked, peering into the forest around us.

1

"Yeah, but that doesn't mean it's going to be easy to find. It could be up in a tree, or hidden inside a rotted log, or tucked under some bushes in a container covered with camo—"

"How big is it?" Ricky interrupted me.

I sighed. "One second." I punched commands on the GPS and details of the cache came up on the screen. "Hmmm. This might be a tricky one. All it says is, 'Low to the ground, it will be found, you won't need a shovel, but dig around.' It's a container about four inches by five inches."

"How big is that?"

I showed him.

Ricky frowned. "But it's not actually buried."

Duffy, the big lab, must have understood the word "buried" because he started pawing at a spot on the ground. Geez, his paws were muddy enough already from this sorry excuse for a trail—not much more than a path —without having him start an excavation project. My truck would be a mess. I yanked him back. I'd done that so many times already today that my shoulder throbbed. "No, you're not allowed to actually bury geocaches," I said, "because they're usually not on your own land. The idea is not to disturb anything—"

"Okay, Danny, I've got it." He bent down, staring at the ground, taking small slow steps.

I have to admit I was kind of amazed. When Celia suggested I take her dog and her kid geocaching with me, I'd expected a total nightmare. I loved Celia, but I wasn't exactly in love with her dependents. The house always seemed to be full of kids and dogs, even when it was just Ricky and Duffy. I haven't been around a lot of nine-year-olds, so maybe they're all like that, but let's just say if Ricky was twins I would have been out of there long ago, Celia or no Celia.

Duffy whined and pulled at the leash, wanting to follow the kid, so I slipped the clasp loose. He wouldn't stray too far and my shoulder needed a break. He proved me wrong immediately by plunging into the brush where we'd heard the noise earlier. I shut my eyes and sighed.

"Hey, Danny, is this something?"

Ricky had pulled aside a low-hanging pine branch to reveal a discarded water bottle. Mud spattered the outside, so I guess he might have thought something could be hidden inside.

I shook my head. "Naw, that's just garbage. We're looking for a box, remember? And a geocache is going to be closed up tight so that the stuff inside doesn't get wet. That bottle doesn't even have a cap."

The kid let the branch fall back into place. "This is hard."

"We've barely even started looking. Listen, think about where *you* would hide something around here if you wanted to make it kind of hard to find, but not impossible."

Duffy barked, once, and I heard a rumbling whine that could be the motor of an ATV. Geez, even in the woods that dog could find a car to chase. It sounded like he'd managed to get a good distance away in only a minute.

"Duffy, come back, boy," I yelled.

"Here, Duffy, Duffy, Duffy," Ricky hollered, cupping his hands around his mouth.

"Keep to the side of the trail. I thought I heard an ATV coming," I warned him, but no vehicle materialized.

The dog barked again.

"Why'd you let him off the leash, Danny? Mom never does that."

I sighed. "I was asking myself the same thing." I called the dog one more time but there was no sound of him crashing back. "Just keep looking, and we'll get him after we find the cache. He won't go far."

Whoever had hidden this cache was a jerk, because it sure wasn't easy to find. My back was aching in minutes as we looked under every bush and low branch, pushed aside drifts of fallen leaves, and peered into the dark recesses of hollowed-out deadfall. My backpack felt like it held lead weights, not a few sandwiches and hiking supplies. I'd hoped the cache wouldn't be too hard to find and the kid could spot it himself. Then we could eat the lunch Celia had packed for us and be home early with

3

everyone happy. I should have known it wouldn't be that easy.

Duffy barked again and Ricky stood up, stretching on tiptoes to see over a tangle of scrubby bushes. "Duffy sounds like he found something. Maybe it's the cache!"

"It wouldn't be that far from the coordinates," I said, but the kid was right. The dog's barking had taken on an insistent tone. A *come-here-and-look* tone. I stretched a kink out of my back. "But okay, let's go and get him, and then we can concentrate on the cache better. If we go back a bit, I think there was a clearer—"

But Ricky had already pushed into the brush, heedless that there could be thorns or mudholes or insect nests that I'd have to rescue him from. No sense in calling him back, so I shut up and followed him. Duffy's barking was easy to follow, and once through the initial bushes the space opened up a lot, the way it tends to under an evergreen canopy. Brown and orange needles carpeted the ground, which was also sprinkled liberally with pinecones and dotted with lichen-smeared stones. We still couldn't see Duffy.

Typically, Ricky started running, even though the ground was uneven and I figured a half-buried root would send him flying any second. "Slow down. Duffy isn't going anywhere." He didn't stop, though, so I broke into a half-jog to keep him in sight. Celia might forgive me if I lost the dog—might—but not if I lost the kid.

Only a minute or so later I heard Ricky yell, "Duffy!" and then I saw him, too. He ran toward Ricky, then turned and rushed back to whatever he'd found. Mud spattered all up his legs and the underside of his belly, and his golden snout had a generous coating as well. I squeezed my eyes shut for a second, heaved a deep breath, and pressed on.

"Danny, this is so cool!" Ricky hollered back to me. I wondered whether the dog had found a dead bird or an ancient cow bone. The kid would think almost anything was cool.

But as I got closer I saw that it was neither of those things. I couldn't exactly say what it was, either. The dog barked again and Ricky bent down toward the thing. "Don't touch that!" I yelled, and he jumped back.

He glared at me as I caught up to him and the dog. I shook my head. "I just want you to be careful until I see what this is," I said, but he still looked mad. I ignored him and looked at the thing poking out of a muddy hole in the ground.

It looked kind of like an oxygen cylinder you'd use with a cutting torch—a big grey canister, or at least the top half of one. About three feet of it showed above the ground, but I couldn't tell how deep it went. It was about eight inches in diameter, and on the side facing us, a groove with a narrow slot at the centre ran the length of the thing. It was too dark inside the slot to see anything. On top of the cylinder, instead of pressure gauges and regulators, a ring of dark glass surrounded something that resembled a small solar panel. I walked all the way around it. On the far side, a little hatch stood open, revealing an LCD-type screen about three inches square. The strangest thing about it was that despite sprouting out of the muddy ground like some weird plant, there wasn't a speck of mud on it.

"Is it the geocache?" Ricky asked, breathless.

"No way," I said. "It's nothing like the description and it's nothing like any cache I've ever seen."

"Maybe it's a bomb."

My heart gave a big bang in my chest because although I hadn't thought of that, it did kind of look like some kind of missile. After a second I shook my head. "I don't think so. Who the hell—the heck—would put a bomb out here? There's nothing to blow up except a bunch of trees."

"Well, what is it?"

I squatted down and put out a tentative hand to touch it. It was cold enough that the air close to it felt noticeably chill. When my fingertips got within about two inches of the surface, it beeped one strident, high-pitched note, and blue-white light flashed from the glass ring at the top. Startled, I tried to stand and jump back at the same time and ended up falling on my butt in the mud.

5

Ricky burst out laughing and I bit down on a word Celia wouldn't have liked.

"We'd better get out of here and leave this thing alone," I said. I wasn't going to tell Ricky, but the thing had me sort of spooked. I shook my hand. My fingertips tingled with cold, even though I hadn't actually touched the cylinder. There had to be a logical explanation for it, but it gave me a vibe I didn't like.

"Aw, Danny, it's cool," Ricky protested. He walked around it, peering at it like I had. He stopped on the side bearing the screen and squinted. "Maybe this is something to do with the cache," he said. "These look like more cordates."

"Coordinates," I corrected him, but went around to the other side to look again. I hadn't noticed it before, but he was right—the screen showed numbers that could easily stand for latitude, longitude, and elevation. Underneath those, a row of symbols I couldn't read crawled across the screen.

"Didn't you say that sometimes a cache has two or three parts, and it's like following a treasure map? You have to get one part to get the co-or-din-ates for the next part?" He pronounced *coordinates* very slowly, but he got it right. Apparently he sometimes did listen to what I told him.

I pulled out the GPS. "Yeah, but they're supposed to say if they're part of a series." I pulled up the map of the area. It showed only two caches, the one we'd been looking for and another about half a mile to the south. "I don't think that's it."

"Put the numbers in and see where they lead," Ricky said. "You can do that, right?"

"They probably don't lead anywhere. They might not be the right kind of numbers."

"Come on, Danny, just try it, please?"

"Why don't we go back and find the cache we're actually looking for? We were probably just about to find it when Duffy started barking."

"Come on, please? Maybe this is a secret one that nobody knows about."

I wiped a hand across my face, mainly to stop myself from explaining that a geocache no-one knows about kind of defeats the purpose. It wouldn't do any good. Once the kid had an idea in his head it was hard to dislodge it. Easier just to humour him.

"Okay, okay. Put the leash back on Doofus while I do this."

"Haha," he said, but he took the leash and secured the troublemaking dog.

I punched the numbers from the little screen into the GPS and was only half-surprised when it did plot a course from our current position to the point the numbers indicated.

Ricky must have read something on my face. "Can we see where it goes?"

"It's probably just some kind of survey equipment. Not likely it leads anywhere interesting. If we go back to the other cache there'll be cool things in it and you can pick something to keep. Remember I told you, people leave little treasures to swap."

"I know, but this is more exciting. It's a mystery." And I knew that, in his mind, the lure of a dollar-store toy or a keychain couldn't compare to this.

I squinted up through the trees at the sun. I couldn't use the weather or the time as an excuse to say no. "Okay, it says it's about a hundred meters away...that's about three hundred feet. I guess it's not that far out of our way."

"That doesn't sound very far at all."

"Yeah, if there's any kind of path between here and there. We're not going crashing through a ton of underbrush. I'll make you a deal. We'll start out, but if the going is too hard we give it up, okay?"

"Deal."

Stifling a sigh, I hitched my backpack up higher on my shoulders and pointed him in the direction the GPS laid out. Celia's lunch would have to wait a little longer.

The GPS route led us back to the path we'd followed earlier in the day and it looked like we could continue to follow it. Duffy wasn't too happy about being back on the leash, and strained ahead until I thought my arm was going to pull out of the socket. He had his nose down like he'd caught a scent, but luckily if I let the leash out long enough that he could walk ahead of me, beside Ricky, he eased off a little.

Normally, I love being in the woods. The shady quiet, broken only by the sound of your own footsteps on the path and a few birds and small animals. The warm, moldery scent of pine and earth and bark and leaves. The cool air giving way to warm spots when the sun breaks through the overhead canopy of greenery. It was one place where I felt at peace, and I usually only wanted the company of a good friend or two, if I wanted any at all. Ricky and the dog—well, they were here with me today on sufferance, but I had to admit that it hadn't been all bad. It was obvious that Ricky appreciated the forest, so that gave us something we could relate on, even if I still thought he was mostly a little pain-in-the-butt.

Since we'd found the cylinder, though, the walk wasn't the same. My fingers continued, weirdly, to tingle and ache with that burning cold. The woods were too quiet now, as if every bird and animal that normally lived here had fled. Ricky was too excited by the adventure to pick up on anything. The dog seemed intent on following something only he could scent on the air.

Once again, I thought I heard an ATV somewhere nearby and tugged on the collar of Ricky's jacket to nudge him off the path, but no vehicle came into sight. There must be a network of trails in the area.

We got to a bend in the path where it skewed left but our destination showed off to the right—only about twenty meters away now. "Okay, kid, this is it. Pretty open here so I think we can leave the path again. But go slow, and be careful."

Duffy already had his nose pointed in that direction. I wondered what he smelled. Anyway, I didn't need the GPS after we left the path because damned if that dog didn't lead us straight to another grey canister, identical to the first one.

Identical, except for a little clump of dark earth and

green moss sitting on top of the solar panel-thing. Otherwise it was pristine. Duffy got to within a few feet of the cylinder and stood sniffing the air, growling intermittently. He took care not to get too close and I wondered if he'd got a noseful of super-cold air back at the first one. I took a stick and knocked the earthy clump down, then picked it up. The soil was soft and moist, as if it had only recently been dislodged from the forest floor. Thin ice crystals, jagged and translucent, clung to some of the root tendrils.

Ricky squatted beside me as I examined it. "It's like that thing just pushed up out of the ground, isn't it?" he asked.

Goosebumps prickled my skin. I'd been struck by the same thought, but I wasn't going to say anything because of course that was impossible. For one thing, if that was the case, it should be covered with dirt and mud.

"Nah," I told Ricky. "I know it looks like that, but I don't think so. It wouldn't really make sense."

He looked skeptical but stood and walked around it. "This one's got numbers, too. There must be more!"

"Okay, but are we really going to spend all day doing this? We've found two and they're both the same. I don't think we need to do it again."

He looked at me over the top of the canister. "Don't you want to know what they are? It told you, it's a mystery! We have to solve it."

The only mystery to me was what time I was finally going to make it home today. "They're just survey markers or something," I said. "But if you want to find one more, we'll do that. Then have lunch and head home, okay?"

"Got the GPS ready?" He read the numbers to me. I noticed that he didn't actually agree that one more would do it.

The next one was, predictably, about the same distance away as the last one, but off in the general direction where the path had been leading when it headed left.

The trail had deteriorated to something more like a

cow path, and I was starting to think it would run out any time. To tell the truth, I hoped it would. But suddenly it opened up at a stream and I realized I'd been hearing the hiss and gurgle of the water for the past few minutes without noticing it. A haphazard line of half-submerged stones offered the only obvious bridge to the other side.

I looked at Ricky with raised eyebrows.

"We can make it across that, easy," he said.

"The dog's going to get wet for sure. And if you slip, your feet will be soaked. We'll have to go back anyway then, because hiking in wet shoes will give you wicked blisters."

"I'm not going to slip, and Duffy's feet will dry off," he argued. "Anyway, it'll wash some of the mud off him."

I shrugged. "Okay, we'll give it a try. I'll go first and you come behind me. Hold my hand and step exactly where I step."

He put his hand in mine confidently. I let the dog out to the extent of his leash to fend for himself. Honestly, the crossing didn't look that bad, so long as the stones were steady, and I had my good waterproof hiking boots on. A slip wouldn't be that bad for me.

We went slowly. The sun had disappeared behind a skiff of clouds and a chill breeze blew straight down the stream, raising goosebumps on my arms and back. The dog was on the other shore by the time we were about halfway across. I heard the now-familiar ATV engine rumble and Duffy barked, shattering our concentration and the otherwise eerie silence. The kid jumped and skittered on the stones, one toe skimming the surface of the water. He shrieked and caught at my arm with his free hand. A clutch of birds flushed out of the tree branches above us with a rush of wings, startling him further, and he almost went in.

Luckily, I had a solid footing on two stones and managed to help Ricky catch his balance. I pretty much pulled him along the last few steps, figuring we'd be better off getting across in a hurry. Once there, he leaned forward with his hands on his knees, panting a little.

"Stupid dog," he muttered, and I had to agree.

"You okay?"

He nodded.

We set off again, although the path shrank even further and low-hanging branches barred the way every few steps. We walked in silence, concentrating on the quickly-disappearing trail.

"You want some water?" I asked Ricky, and my voice sounded strangely loud. The kid jumped at the sound of it and then giggled nervously.

"Sure."

We stopped and each had a swig from the water bottles I'd insisted we take, and Ricky cupped his hands while I poured some into them for the dog to slurp. He dried his hands on his jeans when Duffy decided he'd had enough and turned his nose to the trail again. Once more, we had to leave the path to find the actual spot, but now that we knew what to look for I spotted the cylinder before we'd gone more than a few feet from the trail.

It held no surprises. Exactly like the others. Even Ricky gave it only a cursory glance before going around to the back to check for a screen. I pulled the flashlight from my pack and tried to peer inside the narrow slot that ran the length of the side groove, but I couldn't really make out anything inside—maybe a shadowy hint of some mechanism, but that was all. I was careful not to lean in close enough to feel the intensity of the cold or set off the light and alarm. Ricky read off the numbers without even asking me if we could find another one. I felt a twinge of annoyance but shrugged it off and plugged them into the GPS. What the hell. He'd tell Celia all about it and I'd look like a hero. And I admit I was getting curious about how many of the damned things there could be.

When the new destination popped up on the screen I looked at it for a long moment and then wordlessly showed it to Ricky. I'd marked the locations of the three cylinders we'd found already with little flags.

"We're going in a circle," he said.

I nodded. "That's what I thought. So there might not be many more. They've all been about the same distance apart. I'm betting one more after this one, and then those coordinates will lead us back to the first one. I'll bet five will be it." *And then we can go the hell home.*

Ricky looked a little disappointed, but still determined to see if my prediction was right. We set out again, Ricky walking beside me this time. The sun was still high in the sky but now seemed pale and watery, clouds drifting between it and us. After a few minutes Ricky reached up and took my hand. He'd never done that before. Usually, it might have irritated me, but right now, his hand felt warm against my still strangely-cold skin, and I didn't mind at all. We walked in silence, letting the path and the GPS guide us.

I thought we were almost there when Duffy stopped in his tracks and whined, low in his throat. Ricky looked at me, frowning. I shrugged my shoulders. The dog glanced around and then shook his head vigorously. I took a few steps and tugged at the leash and he came along, but he carried his tail low, almost between his legs, and sniffed the air constantly. A couple of times, he stopped to lower his head and swipe at his ears with a clumsy paw.

"Not far now, boy," I told him, although it was more to reassure the kid than the dog. Duffy didn't look at me but answered with a whine and a growl, although he kept pace with us. He shook his head again, ears flapping.

"Do you hear that?" Ricky asked me, glancing around us.

"What?"

He wrinkled his brow. "I don't know. It's like a whistle or something, coming from far away."

I hadn't noticed anything, but when I concentrated, a high-pitched humming registered with me, just on the edge of my hearing. It was a little like the earlier alarm, but continuous instead of a beep. The sound must be the source of Duffy's agitation. It made sense that the dog would hear it first, then Ricky.

"I hear it now, but I don't know what it is. We're almost at the coordinates, though."

The fourth cylinder came into sight as expected. The hum or whine droned steadily, although it didn't get any

12

louder. It didn't seem to come from the cylinder, but from all around us, like white noise—but more annoying. Checking the cylinders had become routine now. Duffy sniffed around it cautiously. Ricky ran around to the side away from the path while I attempted to see if there was any detail that made this one different from its fellows. I didn't see it. The kid read the coordinates off to me, I put them into the GPS, and we left.

The lassitude that had overtaken us a few minutes ago dissipated now that we were heading for the fifth, and probably last, cylinder. Ricky almost ran along the path ahead of me while I strode to keep him in sight. The path was still barely visible, but I'd given up warning him to watch his step. Duffy ranged as far ahead of me as the leash would allow.

I caught up with Ricky easily when he stopped short and put his hands on his hips in a gesture that reminded me of Celia. He stood, staring at the fifth cylinder, which looked exactly like the other four. The background noise seemed a little more intense, and Duffy must have thought so, too, the way he pawed intermittently at his ears. Otherwise everything was just the same. Ricky sauntered over to check the back of the cylinder for the expected screen, but his disappointment was palpable. He'd expected this last cylinder to hold the answer to the puzzle.

He read me the coordinates and when I entered them, it was obvious they'd lead us back to the first cylinder. I showed him the screen. "I guess that's it."

Ricky stared at it for a moment longer and said, "I guess so." He frowned up at me. "Didn't you think we'd—I dunno—find out what they were for, or something?"

I shrugged. "I didn't really know. Like I said, they probably have some purpose we just don't know about. They could be monitoring the weather or something."

He looked back at the screen, then looked back at the cylinder. "That noise is getting louder, isn't it?"

I looked around. It still seemed to come from everywhere and nowhere, but the kid was right. Duffy whimpered. A gust of wind set the leaves overhead shivering.

"Maybe we should get out of here," I said. Not for the first time since we'd found the cylinders, I felt uncomfortable. The forest seemed oppressive, the sunlight paled to a wan half-light and the hairs on the back of my neck prickled.

"Hey!" Ricky shouted. He snatched the GPS from my hand. "They're in a circle, right? Maybe there's something in the *middle* of the circle! Come on, Danny!"

He turned and ran past the cylinder, into the area that —he was right—would be encircled by the five cylinders. Duffy lunged after him, jerking the leash from my hand.

The pervasive whine in the air ramped up and I felt a tremor in the ground under my feet. That didn't make sense—we didn't live anywhere near earthquake country. "Ricky! Come back," I yelled. But he'd plunged into the underbrush and out of my sight almost immediately. He must have heard me—I could hear him and the dog crashing through branches—but he didn't answer or turn back. I swore and took off after him, slapping branches out of my way.

There was no question about it now, the earth trembled under my feet as I ran. Branches and leaves around me and overhead shook, so much that I flashed back to watching *Jurassic Park* years ago. Not that I thought a T-Rex was about to come smashing through the trees. But that was what it looked like.

A big tremor sent me reeling and I stumbled but kept going. Duffy barked in a non-stop frenzy, and I homed in on the sound. The forest's odd silence had shattered. Trees groaned, limbs crashed, and the background hum had risen to a roar. Something terrible was happening, and I'd let Ricky get caught right in the middle of it. My heart banged around in my chest like a pea in a pressure cooker. I could only breathe in deep gasps.

How had Ricky gotten so far ahead of me?

Then something erupted out of the earth just off to my right. A long rail, it looked like, maybe eight inches wide, running parallel to my stumbling path into the centre of the area ringed by the cylinders. A few small trees toppled, their grip on the earth completely dislodged by the emergence of the rail, but luckily they fell away from me. The narrow rail rose slowly, inexorably, clods of earth tumbling, networks of roots pulling and snapping, showering me with sprays of dirt. I blinked and shielded my eyes. The creak and groan of metal under strain filled the air.

When I realized I had stopped running, I barrelled forward again. Duffy sounded close now. I broke through some underbrush and almost ran headlong into a wave of spilling earth and bushes. It cascaded from a slowly-rising circular platform, easily thirty feet across, already a few feet off the ground. Five of the narrow rails, each coming from one of the cylinders, connected to the platform like the spokes of a wheel. As the rails rose out of the ground, they lifted the platform. Its laborious ascent slowly dislodged the layer of earth that had covered it. A slim birch tree slid from the centre of the platform toward the edge in a shower of soil as I watched, and I dove left as it pitched toward me. Branches brushed my back as its crown crashed to earth.

"Danny!"

I looked up to see Ricky's terrified, dirt-streaked face peering over the lip of the platform. Frozen in place, he gripped the unstable earth as the platform shook and ground its way upward. Duffy raced back and forth under the platform, barking as his boy was carried further and further away.

It hit me. He hadn't screamed, "Danny." He'd said "*Daddy.*"

"Jump!" I yelled, "I'll catch you!" But I knew it was useless. He was too frightened to move.

The lower half of the fallen birch tree still rested on the platform, roots tangled in the soil. It wasn't much of a ladder, but it was all I had. I shucked off the backpack and started to clamber up the tree. It wasn't easy. The notches where branches attach to the trunk are great for climbing an upright tree, but they're slippery and inconvenient when you're going the other way. The trunk shook and shuddered as the platform moved inexorably upward.

At least my movement jolted Ricky into action. When he saw me coming, he crawled toward the upended roots of the birch and tried to hold them steady. The whole thing slipped sideways just as I reached the edge, but I managed to heave myself over the lip just before the trunk crashed sideways.

So now we were both in trouble. Duffy, below us, went berserk barking. The platform continued to rise, shaking more violently now. Dislodged earth bounced and vibrated toward the edge, raining over it. Bare patches showed grey metal like the cylinders, pristine even though it had been buried only moments before.

"What—" Ricky started, his voice shaky, but I cut him off.

"I don't know. We just have to get down."

I shimmied close to the edge and peered over. We were ten, maybe twelve feet off the ground. Still low enough to escape with nothing more than maybe a turned ankle if we moved fast. If *I* moved fast. I turned back to Ricky. His eyes were huge, and fixed on mine. Scared but trusting.

"Climb on my back."

"Huh?" he said, but then he did as he was told. He slid his arms around my neck and clung tight. His legs wrapped around my waist.

"Whatever happens, don't let go." I cleared earth and debris from the edge. The smooth, slick metal offered no appreciable lip to hold on to, but I had no choice. I lay on my belly, stuck my palms on the surface near the edge and carefully slid my legs over. The roar increased in volume and the platform vibrated roughly. The muscles in my arms and shoulders—especially the one already sore from hauling the damn dog around—trembled and screamed as I levered us over the edge and as slowly as I could, lowered us down until we hung from my fingertips. Ricky stayed silent and still, just hanging on.

The platform jittered up, and I let go. I tried to bend my knees and roll into the impact as my feet hit the ground, but I had to try and protect Ricky, too, so I took the brunt of it. Sharp pain lanced up my left leg and I swore as a blast of heat from the underside of the platform hit me. Ricky slipped off and I rolled over onto my back. The platform, supported only by the five rails, hung suspended above us, the rails tilted upward now like the frame of a teepee. The heat came from some kind of engine on the underside. As I stared up at it, the whole thing began a lazy rotation.

The pain in my leg gnawed at my brain for a minute and then I realized that Ricky was hauling on my arm, trying to pull me out from under the thing. "Come on," he grunted. "Can you walk?"

"Are you okay?" I answered, and he nodded. With his help, I managed to get to my feet. I tested weight on the left leg. Not broken, I thought, but not in great shape. With Ricky supporting me, we hobbled as fast as we could away from the platform. The back of my jacket felt warm, and I knew the heat from the thing was increasing. We might not be out of danger yet, and I tried to push the pain down and move as fast as I could. Duffy barked up at the thing non-stop as he backed away from it.

"Ricky, run ahead. Get as far away as you can."

He didn't say a word, just shook his head and tightened his grip around my waist. I wanted to scream at the pain in my leg, but I gritted my teeth and moved faster. If he wouldn't leave me, then I had to get us both out of there. The roar behind us reached a crescendo and pain flared in my ears. Duffy yelped and I felt Ricky catch his breath. *Whatever is about to happen must be close.*

Just then we came in sight of a stream—another bend of the one we'd crossed earlier. Not much in the way of a bank and it wasn't very deep, but it would be better than nothing.

"In the water!" I ordered. "Just keep your head out for now, and if we need to, maybe we can duck underneath." I pictured a wall of flame spurting out from the thing behind us, charring everything in its path. The water could save us. Ricky seemed to stumble as he got to the bank, but he didn't fall.

The water was so icy I could barely force myself into it, but it took my mind off my leg for a minute. Ricky and I lay down in its chill embrace, panting, teeth chattering. The dog splashed in beside us. In the direction of the platform, the trees danced wildly now, telling me that the slow rotation we'd seen starting must now be creating a wash like a helicopter's rotors.

"Ricky, thanks for your help back there. You did good."

He stared at me for a second, then grinned and shouted back. "No problem, Danny." The grin faded as the roar from the platform stopped abruptly. Trees still whipped around in the gale, but even with the wind it felt like silence by comparison.

I should have made us both duck under the water right then, but I was too mesmerized to think of it. In place of the roar, a whirring like a million bees in flight filled the air, and the platform rose above the treetops, spinning like a flywheel.

Ricky breathed a word I'm pretty sure his mother doesn't even know he knows. I echoed it.

Lucky for us, the heat I'd expected didn't come. The underside of the spinning platform hung above the trees, and pulsed an eerie blue-yellow for a minute, like the heart of a match flame. Then it flew straight up like a pebble from a slingshot, too fast to really see movement before it vanished. The downdraft stopped abruptly, and within a minute the trees had settled. That now-familiar hum like the motor of an ATV came through the trees, but I didn't expect a vehicle anymore. I thought I knew what was happening. The rails, the cylinders were probably retracting back into the earth, disappearing without a trace.

I realized I didn't really care.

We were both panting and shivering. We limped slowly out of the water, teeth chattering harder than ever as icy water ran off us in rivulets. The dog shook all over us and Ricky squealed—a nice, normal sound. The sun picked that moment to slide out from behind the clouds, and I ordered Ricky to strip down to his underwear while I did the same. Hobbling, I retrieved the backpack, found the matches and we gathered enough dry wood to get a little fire going.

"Should we get out of here?" Ricky asked, when our shivers had finally stopped.

I shrugged.

"Maybe so, but I think—I think it's gone. Whatever it was. I think we're better off getting dry as we can before we try to hike out." My leg throbbed. It was going to be a tough walk.

He looked up, to where the platform—*I might as well start calling it a ship,* I thought—had disappeared into the clouds. "What do you think it was?"

I hesitated. It was the hesitation of not being sure, and of not being sure how your thoughts might be received. Suddenly it mattered what Ricky thought of me, more than it ever had before. I took the coward's route.

"What do *you* think it was?"

He shrugged and frowned. "I think it was something from aliens. Some kind of UFO."

Apparently that sort of cowardice is not a concern for nine-year-olds. I nodded. "That's what I was thinking. That metal wasn't like anything I've ever seen. Heck, none of it was like anything I've ever seen." I shook my fingers, still a bit tingly from the cold that had bitten them, although the sensation was fading.

Ricky hunkered down and poked another stick into the fire. "You think they were watching us or something?"

"Maybe. For some reason I didn't get the feeling there were actual aliens there. It might have been a probe or something, gathering information."

"It must have been there for a long time, because of all the trees that were growing on it."

"Exactly," I said. "So the chances that there were any kind of creatures in it—"

"Yeah, I doubt it. I wonder what they were looking for?"

It was my turn to shrug. "No idea. Maybe just studying the earth or something. Not many people out here to study."

"Except us." He flashed me a grin.

"Ha, yeah."

We fed a few more twigs into the flames, the growing heat casting a welcome warming radius. "Are we going to tell anyone about this?" he asked me after a few minutes.

I looked at him. "Do you think we should?"

He pulled a deep breath. "I think it might be better if we didn't."

I nodded. "Me too." I fished sandwiches out of the backpack and passed him one.

He unwrapped the plastic and bit into a mashed peanut butter and jam. "But what are we going to tell Mom?"

He had a point. I was going to have a limp for a while, and it would be pretty obvious that we'd been drenched. I squinted into the sun for a second, then looked at him as I bit into my own sandwich. "That I twisted my ankle on a rock?" I suggested.

He nodded wisely. "And then we slipped and fell in the stream coming back, since it was hard for you to walk. 'Cause it would be nice if she let us go geocaching again sometime," he said around bites of sandwich.

"When I get a new GPS," I said. "I have no idea what happened to it."

He threw me a grin. Getting up, he walked to the spot where I thought he'd stumbled as we ran for the water. He pulled the GPS out from under a rock. "I thought it shouldn't get wet," he said, proffering it to me. "And we might need it to get out of here."

I grinned back at him. "Yeah, we might. But you carry it," I told him. "I think you can handle it. Maybe next time we'll bring your mom along too."

"Next time," he said. "I like the sound of that. But I don't think I want to come back here."

I chuckled. "Me neither. But there's lots of other places we could go."

"I never did get to find a real geocache," he said, pushing a button on the GPS experimentally.

Kids. They're never satisfied.

But it struck me that maybe I am.

ePrayer

"Hello?"

Larry jumped as the voice sounded in his headset, his index finger reflexively clicking the mouse button and accidentally closing the document he had open. *Damn.* He hadn't even realized the line was ringing. He glanced at the opening of his cubicle, but fortunately no-one was watching him.

Recovering, he launched into the answering protocol. "Hello, and thank you for calling ePrayer, where we care about your Life...and your Afterlife. My name is Larry. How can I help you today?"

Silence. Then, "ePrayer?" the voice asked hesitantly.

"That's right," Larry said smoothly, re-opening the file showing the day's preset patter. "The world's largest provider of spoken electronic prayer services. You picked an auspicious day to call ePrayer, sir, because today we're offering new customers a special package. Any two prayers from your chosen religion or belief system, plus a new prayer for world peace, for one low monthly rate. They'll be offered up daily in your name by our dedicated servers—"

"I'm...I'm already a customer," the man's voice said.

"Wonderful," Larry said, quickly switching mental gears—and patter. "Then you might be interested in our new buy-one-month, get-one-month free offer. It applies to any prayer of your choice, any religion, and it will be repeated as many times as you specify, daily for the full two-month period. This is really an unbeatable—"

"Did you say your name was Larry?"

"Yes, sir, and I'm here to—"

"Larry, could you just be quiet for a minute?"

Larry took a breath and bit his lip. That was...unusual. He pursed his lips and clicked to the "Dissatisfied Customers" protocol. A glance down the list didn't reveal anything helpful. The voice wasn't angry, crying, or offended, hadn't demanded anything, wasn't asking to speak to his supervisor, didn't seem to be a crank.

"Uh, sure," he said quietly.

After a moment's silence, the voice said, "Okay, Larry, can you look up my file for me?"

Well, that was something he could handle. "No problem, sir. Your name?"

"Henry Rutherford."

Larry's fingers skittered across the keyboard as he input the data. "I show five Henry Rutherfords on file, sir. Middle initial?"

"V."

"Thank you, sir. Code word?"

The voice hesitated again. "Phoenix."

"Thank you. Okay, I have your file open, Mr. Rutherford. What can I do to help you?" Now maybe this weird call would get on track.

"Can you tell me what prayers I've paid for in the past, Larry?" When Larry didn't answer right away, the voice chuckled. "Old men have short memories sometimes."

"Uh, sure. Our servers recited six months of 'Prayers for Departed Loved Ones' on your behalf just over two years ago, and we've been doing 'Supplications to Cure Illness' for the past year. And I show a non-standard special prayer that you must have written yourself, which we've been incanting twice daily for two months now."

"That would be the *I-don't-want-to-die* prayer," Mr. Rutherford said.

"Uh...if you say so, Mr. Rutherford. I don't have the specifics here in this file." Larry glanced at the cubicle "doorway" again, this time wishing one of the supervisors *would* be there.

"Well, I guess it worked—sort of."

The incoming call signal beeped in Larry's headset and his red line light lit up. He frowned at it. There was no way he should be getting another call when he was already dealing with a client. He decided to ignore it.

"You'd better get that, Larry," Mr. Rutherford said. "I can wait."

Huh? There was also no way the client would be able to hear the signal from another call. Then Larry noticed that no line glowed red for Mr. Rutherford's call. Double weird. Hoping for the best, Larry pressed the "hold" button and took the new call.

He made it only halfway through the answering protocol when a woman's voice interrupted, said she had a wrong number, and hung up abruptly. He sighed and looked down at his phone, wondering how to go back to Mr. Rutherford since none of the lines seemed to be active. He hoped he hadn't cut the old guy off. That would look bad.

"Everything okay, Lawrence?"

Larry's supervisor, Andrea, had a soft voice and an even softer step. He whirled in his chair, feeling his face prickle with heat. He hadn't heard her outside his cubicle.

The last thing Larry wanted was to look bad in front of Andrea, who had dark brown hair, eyes to match, and a smile that haunted his dreams. He forced a rueful smile and tried to banish his blush by pure force of will.

"Sure, just a wrong number. They didn't even give me a chance to finish my intro!"

Andrea returned his smile with her own, the one that always made his heart secretly melt in his chest. "Better luck next time!"

While Larry mentally dithered, wondering if this would be a good time to ask her out for coffee, she gave him a little wave and moved on down the row of cubicles. He closed his eyes and sagged in his chair. Too late off the mark again.

ePrayer had no restrictions about employees dating—Larry had checked. The only restriction he kept running into was the one that kept his brain from engaging his mouth like a normal human when Andrea was around.

He suddenly remembered Henry and frowned at his phone. Experimentally, he pressed the "hold" button again.

"I'm still here, Larry."

"Oh, great!" Larry leaned back in his chair. "So did you want to renew your subscription, sir, or can I start a new prayer cycle for you?"

"Hmmm. Neither, Larry. I don't think I'll be needing any more prayers at all."

"We'd hate to lose you as a customer, sir. Is there anything—"

Mr. Rutherford cut him off again, just like the wrong number lady. The old guy had an annoying habit of doing that. "Oh, you won't be losing me, Larry," he said with the ghost of a chuckle. "I think I'll let you go now, but I'll call again. Thanks for your help. Have a good day."

There was no click or signal that the connection had been broken, but Larry felt a strange certainty that Mr. Rutherford had left the conversation. He heaved a deep sigh. Hopefully that one hadn't been recorded for quality control. He had no idea if he'd handled it correctly or not. With luck, the man would get a different associate if he did call back.

When Larry arrived at work the next morning, he had to detour from his usual route through the ePrayer building because they were still waxing some of the floors. It meant he had to pass the server rooms, which he usually tried to avoid. As soon as he entered the hallway, the stilted muttering of text-to-speech electronic voices filled the air. He always wished they could soundproof the rooms, but of course that wouldn't make much sense—the point of the voices was to be heard, right? *Then again, couldn't God hear through a soundproofed wall?* Eventually he'd stopped thinking about it because it made his head hurt. Usually he just took the long way around to the elevators.

Today, though, he couldn't avoid the voices. The din really didn't sound terribly devotional. Cacophonous was more like it, with hundreds of computers intoning different prayers, in different languages, at the same time. ePrayer tried hard to walk the line between catering to the requirements of each religion and being inclusive; they didn't keep separate rooms for different faith denomination servers. Part of that was practical use of space. They did, however, observe niceties like geographical orientations and the use of various prayer paraphernalia for faith-dedicated servers. Some of the servers bore holographic stickers of stylized religious symbols, which flashed in the overhead lights as Larry passed.

The voices battered against Larry's ears as he passed the rooms. Clients had many options to make sure their prayers were intoned just as they'd like: male or female voices, over sixty languages, hundreds of accents and dialects. Only a word here and there rang clearly over the devotional tumult.

"—peace to all—"

"—grant us humility—"

"—ease our suffering—"

"—multitude of blessings—"

The server room was separated from the hallway by a long wall that was mostly windows. An ePrayer employee in a cleansuit moved among the racks of machines, collecting last night's backup discs for shipping offsite and loading up the new ones. Larry couldn't imagine how loud the noise must be right inside the room. Miniature multicolored prayer flags fluttered here and there in the breeze from the cooling system.

He suppressed an urge to run to get out of earshot and steeled himself to a normal, measured pace. Somehow, the voices always sounded reproachful. Maybe because even though he worked here, he had his doubts about the efficacy of computer-generated prayers. He shook himself. *What's wrong with me?* They were computers, inanimate

25

objects, simply doing what they were programmed to do. They had no idea of his existence, let alone that he was passing through the hallway.

Still, he pulled in a deep breath and huffed it out in relief when he settled into his desk chair and slid on his headset.

"Good morning, Larry," said Henry Rutherford's voice in his ears before Larry's workstation had even finished booting up.

Larry almost jumped up from his chair, but managed to limit himself to grabbing the armrests for support. He didn't want to attract any attention by having his head suddenly pop up above his cubicle walls. "Mr. Rutherford?" he answered, just above a whisper.

A low chuckle. "Yep, it's me. I've been waiting for you to come in."

Larry's phone console lay dark, no red lights blinking. "Where are you, sir?" he asked slowly. None of this made sense. "My computer's not even fully on yet."

"That's actually a very good question, Larry, and one I'm not sure I can answer myself. I seem to be in your system."

Larry frowned. "You're tapped into the ePrayer system? You mean, like, the phone lines are crossed or something?"

"Not exactly."

"You—you hacked us? That shouldn't be possible. We're a closed internal network." Why would anyone hack an electronic prayer service anyway? Unless he was some kind of nut, but Mr. Rutherford didn't sound unbalanced.

He did sound slightly exasperated. "I wouldn't know how to hack a peanut butter sandwich, son. I mean actually *in* the system. Larry, could you open up my file again?"

The computer had finished its boot cycle and sat waiting for him to enter something. Still bemused, he called up the file in question. "Okay, I have it."

"Would you check the billing information for me, Larry?"

"Sure." Larry clicked to the billing screen and his

frown deepened. "This is weird."

"What does it say?"

"There's a termination notice set for about a month's time..."

"Anything else?"

Larry swallowed. "Until then there's just one active request—another round of 'Prayers for Departed Loved Ones,' but—"

"They're for me this time, aren't they, Larry? It's okay. I had pretty much figured out that I must be dead."

Larry tore off the headset and dropped it on the desk as if it were a snake.

"Lawrence? Something wrong?"

Andrea again. Her face showed concern, her clear brown eyes puzzled as she glanced at the headset on the desk.

Yeah, there's a ghost in the system. But he couldn't say that. He didn't even believe it, not really. Sweat prickled his forehead and he felt his face begin another slow burn as he picked up his headset and tried to cover it with a chuckle. "Sure. Fine," he said. "Got some kind of...some kind of shock from the headset, that's all." He frowned at it and pretended to examine the wires.

Andrea frowned. "That's strange. Better requisition a replacement," she said. "Has that happened before?"

"No." He shook his head. "I'll see if this one will last the shift, anyway." Mentally he kicked himself. She was never going to go out with him if he impressed her as a troublemaker.

"Okay, let me know if it keeps acting up," she told him. "Have a good day."

"You too," he said, trying to look distracted by the headset. As soon as she disappeared around the corner he carefully put the headset down on his desk and stared at it.

The red line light flashed on and he almost jumped again. Larry closed his eyes and shook his head. *Get hold of yourself, man. You're imagining stuff. Or this is some kind of prank. No such thing as ghosts. If you don't take calls you're going to get fired, or at least get Andrea mad at you.*

He forced himself to reach out and pick up the headset again, although his hand trembled a bit. He slipped it on, and blew out a sigh of relief when it stayed silent. Henry —or whoever it was—seemed to be gone again. He closed Henry Rutherford's file, pulled up the days' script, and punched the button to take the call. He also surreptitiously glanced around his cubicle, trying to spot a hidden camera. Was a video of him tearing off the headset going to show up on YouTube?

"Hello, and thank you for calling ePrayer, where we care about your Life...and your Afterlife. My name is Larry. How can I help you today?"

Don't be Henry, don't be Henry, don't be Henry—

It wasn't Henry. It was a lovely, polite elderly lady who wanted to set up an account to say prayers for her while she had surgery. The normalcy of the whole thing felt wonderful, and Larry felt the knots in his stomach relaxing as he set up her file, took her credit card information, and put her on the email list for special prayer offers. By the time the call ended, the tension between his shoulder blades had almost completely disappeared.

Larry slid the headphones off so they hung around his neck, and rubbed a hand across his face. The whole Henry thing had to be some kind of elaborate prank. The problem was, he didn't know anyone who seemed at all likely to do such a thing.

I'm sorry. The letters sprang up on his screen, in the notepad window he always kept running in the sidebar for quick notes. *I truly did not mean to upset you, Larry. But I do think I need some help, and I trust you. Let me know when we can talk again. Henry R.*

Somehow the note was much less unnerving than the voice in his headphones, even though there was no way it should be just writing itself when no-one was even touching his keyboard. He wondered fleetingly if it could still be the result of a prank, but in his heart he knew it wasn't.

He closed the notepad so anyone walking past

wouldn't see it, took the headphones off altogether and put his phone into "AFK" mode. He had ten minutes to get back to his desk before the break expired. His first stop was the bathroom, where he splashed cool water on his face and stared in the mirror for thirty seconds. He didn't look crazy. Then he visited the break room, poured up a travel mug full of hot coffee and added cream and sugar, just the way he liked it. By the time he got back to his desk and took a sip of coffee, he felt better. He slid the headphones on and reactivated his phone, but until his line lit up, he was free.

He restored the notepad and looked at the message for a moment, then took a deep breath and typed, *What kind of help do you need, Henry?*

The delay in the answer wasn't more than five seconds. *I seem to be stuck in the ePrayer servers, and I want to get out of here.*

Fair enough. But you are dead, right, Henry? You are— whatever is left of Henry V. Rutherford, some part that has somehow survived death. A...ghost?

I wouldn't like to say that for sure, Henry answered, *but I'm sure not in Kansas anymore. :)*

Larry actually caught himself chuckling. The old guy had a sense of humour, anyway. Apparently God did, too. The old guy hadn't wanted to die, so he was still around...sort of.

Any idea how I could get you out?

Seems to be a closed system in here. No network or Internet access. I've been all through it.

Larry nodded, then remembered that Henry couldn't see him. Or, at least, he figured Henry couldn't see him. He hoped not. That would make things all the more creepy and unbelievable.

Security, Larry said. *The prayer servers are a closed loop. No chance someone who doesn't like us can hack in and mess up people's prayers.*

I wonder if I'd fit on a USB stick?

Larry laughed out loud, then quickly put a hand over his mouth and looked around guiltily. He hoped no-one— especially Andrea—had heard that and thought he was laughing at a client.

The red line light pulsed to life.

I have to take a call, Henry, Larry typed, *but tomorrow I'll bring one and we'll see what happens, okay?*

Appreciate it, Larry. Talk later. And Henry was gone again.

It wasn't until he got home that night that Larry remembered he wasn't permitted to bring a USB stick to work, as part of the security protocols for protecting the ePrayer system. However, security was actually pretty lax —it wasn't like anyone ever searched pockets or bags. He shrugged. It would be a minor breach, and he figured he could do it without getting caught. Now that he believed Henry's story, he couldn't bring himself to leave the old guy stuck in the system without at least trying to help him.

He tucked the stick into his lunch bag in preparation for the next morning. Hopefully four gigabytes of space would be enough.

Despite his efforts to convince himself that taking the USB stick in to work was no big deal, Larry found himself sweating uncomfortably as he entered the ePrayer building the next morning. Chuck, the security guard, looked up and greeted Larry with his customary nod and grunt. Larry thought Chuck's eyes lingered on the lunch bag, but of course that was silly. It was the same lunch bag he brought to work every single day. There was no reason for Chuck to take any special notice of it today.

Larry sighed inwardly when Chuck turned his gaze back to his magazine without another word. *Past the first checkpoint.* He reached his cubicle without further incident and sank into his chair, setting the lunch bag on the floor near his feet. All he had to do was watch for his chance, sneak Henry onto the USB, and get out safely at the end of the day. No big deal.

He hoped. As his computer finished its startup routine and he slipped on the headphones, a note popped up on his screen. *Larry?*

All set, Larry answered hurriedly. *Just going to watch for a good opportunity.*

I'll be here. The window disappeared again. The line light went red, and Larry answered his first call of the day.

The perfect opportunity to try to rescue Henry came at break time. It was Saria's birthday, apparently, and someone had brought a cake. No-one in his unit would notice his absence, though. When he heard them start to sing at her cubicle on the other side of the room, he glanced around to make sure he was alone, and slipped the USB stick out of his bag. He had to unplug his mouse to open a port for it, so he opened the note window first.

Henry, you there? I'm plugging in now, he typed.

I see it, came the reply.

A blue light blinked on the stick, indicating that it was active, but it went on so long that Larry felt sweat trickle along his spine. The singing had stopped and now all he heard was general chatter as people shared out cake and made jokes about getting older.

"Not at the party, Lawrence?" came a voice from his cubicle opening.

Andrea. He managed not to jump, and twirled his chair so that his body might block the blinking USB stick. "I'm trying to eat a little healthier," he said with what he hoped was a charming smile, and patted his stomach. At least she couldn't see how it roiled in fear of being discovered. "No cake for you, either?"

She smiled and held up an icing-stained napkin. "I had a half piece. The store-bought variety is a little too sweet for me. But it's bad luck not to eat birthday cake, you know."

Wish I'd known that earlier, Larry thought. He had to get rid of her before she noticed the blinking blue light. "I'll remember that next time," he said lamely.

"Headset working okay now?" she asked, leaning lightly against one of the precarious cubicle walls.

"Oh! Yeah, fine," he said. *Why would she pick right now to hang around?* He prayed that Henry didn't start messaging him on the screen. There was no way she'd miss that.

Andrea glanced down the cubicle hallway, then back at Larry. She looked down at her napkin quickly again, chewing her lower lip. She wanted to say something, Larry could see, but what? She was pretty straightforward when it came to work issues. Was it really that big a deal that he hadn't joined the others for cake?

She obviously came to some kind of decision, because she looked back up, smiled, and said, "Well, see you later," then walked off quickly.

Larry slumped in his chair, the perspiration on his back suddenly cold. He shivered. He swung around and saw that the blue light had gone dark.

Henry?

They hadn't made a plan for how Henry would communicate with him if he'd made it onto the USB stick. He slipped on the headset and said "Henry?" in a low voice.

"*File too large*," came Henry's voice, punctuated with a sigh. "I couldn't fit. It was like trying to pour a bottle of vodka into a shot glass. Guess we need another idea, Larry."

Dammit. "I'll try another one tomorrow, Henry. One with more space. Are you going to be okay until then?"

"I'll be fine," Henry said. "In fact, I discovered something rather interesting last night."

"Something in the system?"

"Lawrence? Who are you talking to?" Andrea's voice sounded behind him, puzzled and suspicious.

Double dammit. He hadn't heard her come back. He spun his chair slowly to face her, slipping the headset off and hoping she hadn't noticed the USB, which still stuck out of his mouse port. Her face seemed colder as she looked at him. Personal calls were strictly forbidden on the incoming lines. There were phones in the locker room for employees to use, and almost everyone had a cell phone these days, anyway, although they were supposed to leave the building to use them so as not to risk any interference with the prayers.

"It's...er, sorry," he stammered. "I...um, my uncle called...he's kind of senile. He didn't realize it wasn't allowed. I was just getting him off the line." He smiled weakly at her.

The wrinkles of concern in her forehead didn't smooth. If anything, she looked more suspicious. "He called you? What are the chances he'd actually get *you* to answer instead of someone else?"

Larry forced a weak chuckle. "Heh, I know. Crazy coincidence, huh?" *Please don't notice the USB stick.* If she saw that, he couldn't talk himself out of trouble.

She put her hands on her hips, her look changing to sorrowful. "You know we have a zero tolerance policy, Lawrence," she said. "I have to report this."

"I know you *should*," Larry agreed. "But it was only a few seconds, honestly. I mean, you know that, you were just here and I wasn't on the phone then."

She pursed her lips and looked down. She still held the balled-up napkin from her piece of cake. "That's true," she admitted.

"I'll make sure it doesn't happen again." He hated the pleading note in his voice, but he couldn't help it. He didn't think he'd get fired for one little infraction of the rules, but he didn't want a black mark or warning on his record.

"Okay, just this once," she said with a sigh. "I can't do anything if it happens again."

"Thanks," he said, relief flooding him. He smiled at her with genuine appreciation. "I really appreciate this."

She didn't return the smile, just nodded once and turned away from the cubicle. As soon as she was gone, Larry yanked the USB stick out of the port without bothering to properly eject it, and stuffed it into his pocket. He plugged his mouse back in and collapsed back into his chair, running a hand over his face. *That was close.*

It wasn't until then that he wondered what Andrea had come back to say.

A message popped up on his notepad window. *Sorry. I heard all that through the headset.*

Don't worry about it, Larry typed. *We'll figure something out.*

He just wasn't sure what. And he hoped it wasn't going to cost him his job.

Larry shook off a feeling of dread as he slipped a sixteen-gigabyte USB stick into his pocket the next morning. It was the biggest one the local computer store had in stock, so he hoped it would be enough. How big was a human consciousness? He really wanted to help Henry, but he couldn't keep taking risks that could cost him his job. And his chances to date Andrea... If that opportunity hasn't already evaporated, he thought glumly.

He made it past the security desk and Chuck's customary grunt and nod, feeling—ridiculously—like the tiny stick made a huge, noticeable bulge in his pocket. He reached his cubicle and collapsed into the chair with a palpable feeling of relief. Today, he'd have to be more careful. He couldn't afford to get caught doing anything out of the ordinary. But if he could get the job done, get Henry out, at least it would be over with.

This time he decided not to wait until break—he was just going to do it now. Get it over with. He took a quick glance around to assure himself that he was unobserved, then slid the USB stick out and switched it for his mouse again. He took up the headset.

"Henry?" he murmured.

"Good morning, Larry. I'm here."

"Second try," Larry said.

"Okay, hang on."

The new USB had a red light, which began to pulse rhythmically. Larry hastily angled a couple of things on his desk to try and block the glow, which seemed brighter than the blue had been. He realized he was holding his breath. With luck, this would take under a minute, and Henry would be safe—

"Lawrence?"

Larry whirled in his chair, startled, to find Andrea staring at him in obvious disappointment. Dan Chalmers stood beside her, clutching his ever-present data tablet to his chest and frowning.

Larry tried to recover, holding up one finger as if he was on an incoming call, but Dan's eyes had locked in on the tiny pulse of red light from the USB. Andrea stared at the dangling, disconnected mouse cord, which Larry had neglected to conceal. He felt his chest clench tightly as he knew no amount of explanation was going to help.

The game, as they say, was up.

Dan took a step into the cubicle, leaned over, and pulled the USB stick from the port. Larry almost yelped—what if Henry had been half-transferred?

"What's this, Lawrence?" he asked in that smarmy tone of voice, as if he didn't know exactly what it was.

"Well, it's a USB data stick," Larry said, trying to stay calm.

"Larry?" Henry's whisper sounded in his headset. "I'm okay. It was too small again."

Larry's muscles went weak with relief, but the feeling didn't last.

"And may I ask," Dan said through lips taut with anger, "what you were doing with it?"

"It's blank!" Larry managed. They couldn't accuse him of trying to sabotage the servers with a blank data stick.

Dan and Andrea stared at him wordlessly.

"I mean, I wasn't doing anything bad," he stammered. "I was just—I was just—"

"Getting a personal file," Henry suggested.

"Getting a personal file," Larry repeated, improvising as he went along. "It's just something I work on when I'm waiting for calls. When there's nothing else I should be doing. Some people play games," he added defensively. "No-one has a problem with that."

Andrea frowned. "What kind of thing is it?"

Larry blanked again, terrified of saying the wrong thing.

"Tell her it's a novel, " Henry hissed.

"It's—it's a novel," Larry said, a red flush heating up his cheeks. Good, maybe that would make this more convincing. "A ghost story...sort of, a mystery. I just wanted to take it home to make a backup."

"You know you shouldn't have a USB stick in here, Lawrence," Andrea said, her voice tinged with disappointment.

Dan waggled the stick at him. "So is this supposed novel on here?"

Larry shook his head. "There wasn't time—I'd just put it in when—"

"It's called *'Ghost in the Machine'*," Henry said suddenly in his ear.

"Well. Sorry we interrupted you," Dan said in a completely unconvincing tone of voice. He jerked his head to indicate that Larry should get up, and Dan sat in his chair instead. Larry had to slide off the headset to be able to stand up straight, but he kept it dangling from one hand.

Dan plugged the USB stick back in to the port and said, "So, Lawrence, what's the name of this *novel?*" He used the cursor keys to open a file listing.

"*Ghost in the Machine*," Larry blurted, trying desperately to think of a way out of this. "But for all I know, you might have corrupted the file when you pulled out the stick. It might not even be—"

He broke off as Dan leaned back in the chair, folding his arms across his chest. "Humpf," he said, sounding reluctantly surprised.

Larry's eyes found the file in the list. *GhostinMachine_ms.rtf*, it read. He couldn't believe what he was seeing. *Henry.* Somehow Henry must have been able to create a fake file—

Dan highlighted the file and hit *enter* to open it, and Larry smothered a gasp. How was he going to explain that his "novel" was nothing more than an empty file?

But...it wasn't. *Chapter One: An Unpleasant Discovery* headed the first page, and paragraphs of text scrolled away beneath it. Larry didn't have a chance to read any of it before Dan had closed it with a contemptuous click of keys.

He stood up and glared at Larry. "All right. I guess you were telling the truth. But that doesn't excuse your blatant disregard for the rules. There will be consequences," he promised, waggling a finger at Larry as if he were a naughty child. "Put your file on that stick and give it to Andrea to hold until the end of the day. Erase it from this computer. And I'll see you in my office later." Tablet held close to his chest once more, Dan stormed away from the cubicle.

Andrea said nothing, just stood quietly in the opening while Larry copied the file, ejected the USB stick, and handed it over to her. Then she gave Larry one sorrowful, angry look and walked after Dan.

Larry blew out a sigh so deep it almost made tears start to his eyes. He slipped the headset back on.

"Sorry, Larry," Henry said immediately. "Now you're in big trouble, and it's all my fault."

Larry shook his head. "No, it's not, and you're still stuck in there," he said. "I'll come up with something else, though, don't worry."

"I know you will."

After a minute, Larry said, "How'd you do that, anyway? With the novel? The *supposed* novel," he added with a hint of a smile.

Henry chuckled. "Things move pretty fast in here, Larry," he said. "And I've been thinking about that novel for a long time. They say everyone's got a book inside them, right?"

"Maybe so, but I don't think one has ever come out that fast before."

Henry snorted. "Well, it was only the first six chapters. Just enough to make it believable."

Larry grinned. "Is it any good?"

"I have no idea," Henry said. "You'll have to read it sometime and let me know."

"Yeah," Larry said, as his call light blinked and he switched over to take what he hoped would be a normal call. *If we get out of this mess, Henry, old buddy.*

Thou kind Lord! This gathering turns to Thee—
Larry pulled a server—a computer case about the size

of DVD player—out of the rack and ran a duster over it morosely, then slotted it back into place. Like most servers, they had no need for peripherals like monitors, keyboards, or mice, but the ePrayer servers all had small, built-in speakers that allowed the digitally-intoned prayers and supplications to drift heavenwards. He was trying, with little success, to block out the voices all around him. He squeezed his eyes shut for a moment, trying to ease the headache that had started knocking on the inside of his skull.

Through thy gift of nature, O Goddess—

He'd been working in the server room for just over an hour.

This was the "consequence" Dan had promised. After arriving at work this morning Larry had been informed that he'd been suspended from the active phone lines while his case was reviewed, and put on server room detail. He'd had to strip off his clothes and don a cleansuit before entering. Eleanor, the steely-eyed head of IT, had given him quick instructions on the cleaning ritual, long-winded admonitions of everything he should not, under any circumstances, touch or disturb, and set him to work.

There is no god but He—

Larry knew that Dan couldn't possibly know how much the server room bothered him, but it still felt like cruel and unusual punishment.

Gururbramha gururvishnu gururdevo maheswarah.

"Larry?"

Through the cacophony of computer voices raised in prayer, Henry's voice came to his ears, low but recognizable. Larry moved toward the voice, down the server racks a few feet. He pulled out a server and applied the duster. Luckily, Eleanor was nowhere to be seen.

"Henry?" he whispered, realizing even as he spoke that there was no input device here for Henry to be able to hear him. But Henry must have sensed his presence somehow.

"Larry, I can't hear you, but I know you're there," Henry continued, his voice coming tinnily from the speaker. "Look, I hate to put more pressure on you, but I think something's happening to me in here. I feel like I'm...degrading somehow, and I think it's from being in this closed system."

Larry continued his duster ministrations on the next server.

"And that's not all," Henry continued. "I'm not alone in —" Henry's voice broke off abruptly as Eleanor rounded the corner.

Lord God, Giver of Life, Source of all healing—

Larry dusted busily. Eleanor peered in to see how he was doing.

"Good job," she said shortly. "Keep it up. When you finish this aisle, come and find me. I've got to switch out some cabling, and I could use another pair of hands."

Larry nodded and watched her depart, but Henry's voice didn't come again. "Henry?" Larry whispered, although he knew it was futile. There was no way Henry could hear him in here, with no headsets even anywhere close. He dusted slowly, mechanically, thinking. What had Henry been about to say? Something about not being alone? What did that mean?

How in the world am I going to get Henry out of here now?

Around him, the voices droned on. Lost in thought and worry, Larry was at last able to ignore them.

That night, Larry lay awake a long time, trying to make a plan. He'd learned something critical that afternoon, after helping Eleanor with the cable task, but he had to figure out how to use it to help Henry.

By late in the day, he'd worked his way around about half the racks, ending up near Eleanor's workstation. He was amazed that the voices had faded from his awareness now, becoming a background, white noise. He still heard the odd word now and again, but he'd quickly become used to the buzz of sound.

Eleanor had her back to him, keying in commands, when he saw her do an amazing thing. She picked up an ethernet cable connected to her workstation, plugged the other end into a server in the nearest rack, and ran a brief program. After about thirty seconds, she unplugged it again.

"What's that for?" Larry asked her, dusting nearby and trying to sound casual.

"Just uploading the day's requests," she told him, "and taking another backup." Her gruff demeanor had mellowed over the course of the day, sort of like the voices. "Everything that happens up in the call center gets funneled into my station, then I send it all to the servers at once."

"Security," Larry said.

She nodded. "Mine's the only system that actually hooks into the prayer servers, and it only happens at this one time every day." She plugged a different cable into her workstation, opened another program, and ran it. "Now I'm sending the soft backup to the off-site storage center. We'll ship the hard copy discs off later."

"Cool," Larry said carelessly, sliding the last server back into place after dusting it carefully. Inside, his heart pounded and his stomach did flips.

For a few seconds every day, there was a stepping-stone bridge from the prayer servers to the internet. If Henry could make it into Eleanor's workstation when she uploaded the requests, then he could wait until she sent the backup off-site, and go with it. He'd be free!

But how could he get that information to Henry? As long as he was suspended from the call center, he couldn't connect with the ghost. He'd be noticed if he tried to slip into his cubicle, and there was no-one else he could trust to try and contact Henry for him.

The only idea he could come up with, as he tossed and turned, was to try and access Eleanor's computer when she wasn't around. If he plugged it into the server systems and typed a note to Henry, would he get it? The ghost did seem to know where Larry was when he was in the server room, but either he hadn't noticed the brief internet connection, or he had, but didn't think he could make it across quickly enough.

Larry rolled over, throwing off the sheets in frustration. Eleanor never seemed to leave the room. She even ate lunch at her workstation. He couldn't imagine when he'd get an opportunity to go near it.

The worries piled up. He didn't know how long the suspension was going to last, or what might happen at the end. He could be fired and never get a chance to contact Henry again. And what Henry had started to say about degrading—it didn't sound good. Larry couldn't just wait around to see what happened.

But when the first hint of pink lightened the horizon outside Larry's window, he wasn't any further ahead.

The day went about the same as the previous one. Larry knew damn well that Dan was toying with him, stalling on the "review" of Larry's case, but he tried to push that thought to the back of his mind. He pulled out servers and dusted them, able to ignore most of the praying voices now except for a word here and there. There was some excitement when a humidity sensor sounded an alarm and he helped Eleanor investigate.

"Seems like you should always have a helper in here," Larry told her as they crawled around in a wiring closet.

"Tell that to the folks upstairs," she said, inspecting a relay. "Most of the time, I have to do everything else and clean, too." She grinned at him. "I wish more people screwed up in the call center and got sent my way for a stint."

Larry returned the grin ruefully.

He was finishing up for the day when he realized that Henry hadn't spoken to him once all day. Guilt washed over him. Why hadn't he noticed before this? And what did it mean? Was Henry's degradation progressing so fast that now he couldn't communicate with him? Larry had to get him out of here, fast.

The plan flashed into his mind fully-formed as he was about to leave. He'd pretend he was leaving, hide in the wiring closet until Eleanor and everyone else had gone, then sneak out and make the transfer. "See you,

Eleanor!" he called. She was finishing up the install of a new server at the other end of the room, so she couldn't see him.

"Later, Larry!" came her voice.

Larry slipped into the wiring closet. It was dark, not terribly comfortable, and a tangle of cables looped out every place he wanted to put a hand or foot, but he could stand it for a little while.

Of course, once he was settled inside with nothing to do but wait, he started to worry. What if Eleanor came to this closet when she was done with the server? What if she noticed his street clothes were still in the spare locker he'd been using? What if he couldn't get out of the server room once she left? He'd have to spend the night in here and pretend to have come early in the morning. Sweat pricked his scalp and trickled down his back as he listened for Eleanor moving around in the room outside. The cooling system didn't have much effect in here. The clamour of computer voices lifted in prayer grew loud again now, blocking out everything else he wished he could hear.

Breathing deeply to calm himself, Larry closed his eyes and tried to let the voices wash over him, lulling him into a peaceful, trance-like state while he waited to be sure everyone else had gone home. It worked...a little. He was still sweating, but he didn't think it was from fear any more, just being locked in a dark, airless closet with hundreds of feet of cable coiling everywhere around him. He wasn't wearing a watch and of course his cell phone was in his locker, but he counted slowly to a thousand, then two thousand, then three thousand for good measure. Surely everyone would be gone home by now.

Slowly, holding his breath, he eased the closet door open just a crack. The lights in the server room had dimmed, which he took as a good sign. The voices chanted their never-ending supplications just as loudly as ever, but he couldn't hear any sound of Eleanor, and the hallway outside the glass wall of the room was dark, too. He left the closet with a grateful sigh, leaving the door open in case he had to duck back in. He lifted his face to the breeze from the cooling fans. Now that the coast was clear, he wasted no time crossing to Eleanor's workstation and booting it up.

"Larry, you're here!" Henry's voice came from a speaker in the first rack of servers next to Eleanor's computer. Larry looked around for a headset, but of course Eleanor would have no use for one in here.

"Is he going to get us all out?"

The voice made Larry jump and whirl around. The woman's voice seemed to come from the same place as Henry's, but that couldn't be right. *Could it?* The room behind him lay empty, belying his sudden fear that someone else was in here with him.

So, if not with him...then, with Henry?

He had to communicate with Henry, to let him know the plan. Down the hall was a tech supply room; there'd be spare headsets there. Moving as quickly and quietly as he could, he tiptoed down the hallway and tried the door. Mercifully, it wasn't locked, and Larry found what he needed in the second cabinet he tried.

Back in the server room, he slid a server out of a rack and fumbled around the back of it. It had a sound card to run the speaker, so it should have a jack for the headset —

"Lawrence?"

The headset plug slid into the jack as Larry lifted his head to find Andrea glaring at him with angry puzzlement. She carried her lunch bag, and her sweater draped over her shoulders. Larry felt the last of his hopes to go out with her shrivel up and drift away. He started to slump inside his cleansuit, but meeting her green eyes, he straightened. This was his last chance—obviously his *very* last chance—to help Henry. Maybe he could turn her into his ally instead of his enemy. And if she thought he was crazy and reported him...well, at least Henry would be free. He pushed the server back into place in the rack.

"You're working late," he said wryly.

She nodded. "And I don't think you are," she said, crossing her arms.

He took a deep breath. There was no point in lying.

"No, I'm not."

She studied him, still frowning. "I should call security."

He nodded. "You probably should. And I won't try to stop you. But...I'm trying to help someone, and I'm not hurting ePrayer. Will you give me a chance to explain?"

"I trusted you, Lawrence. I already gave you a chance." The anger made her eyes so hard he could almost feel their glare. Anger, and something else. Hurt. "I *liked* you."

Liked. Past tense. Larry took a deep breath. "You can still trust me. I'm just asking for five minutes."

"To do what? I'm guessing Eleanor doesn't know you're still here?"

He ignored the second question. "Like I said, I'm trying to help someone," he said, and lifted the headset microphone to his lips.

"Henry?" Larry said. "Henry, I'm here, and so is Andrea. Would you say hello to her?"

Only silence answered his words. He glanced at Andrea and saw confusion and mistrust in her face. She raised an eyebrow skeptically.

"Only the computers talk in here," she said. "And they only say what they're programmed to say."

He didn't answer her. "Henry," he said again, louder. "I know you might not trust Andrea, but I do. I know she'll help if she knows what's going on!"

He won't answer while she's here, Larry thought, a sick certainty forming in the pit of his stomach. *Or maybe I took too long, and now he can't—*

"Hello, Andrea." Henry's voice sounded tentative but strong, emerging from the speaker. "I hope Larry's right about you."

Larry turned to see how Andrea would react. Her mouth hung open and her eyes were wide.

"It sounds kind of crazy, I know," Henry went on, "but I—what's left of me—I'm trapped in your system here. Larry's just trying to help me get out."

Andrea's eyes narrowed as she looked back to Larry. "What kind of trick is this? You can't be messing around with the system—"

"It's not a trick, Andrea," came another voice, female this time. The one Larry had heard earlier. "It's not just Henry. There are more of us in here and we're—we just want to get out. Most of us didn't think there was any way to do it, but Larry has a way."

Andrea shook her head as if trying to clear it. "What—who are they?"

Larry took a deep breath. "As far as I can tell—they're ghosts," he said. "Or something like ghosts," he added quickly as Andrea's eyes narrowed again. "Henry was a customer—maybe the others were, too. Call them whatever you want—consciousness, souls, ghosts, I don't know exactly. But they're real, and they're trapped, and I'm trying to help them."

"It's true," Henry piped up. "Larry's been trying to help me for days, but it's only now that he's figured out how to make it work."

"There are ghosts in the ePrayer server network," Andrea said, crossing her arms again and staring at Larry. Her voice was steady, but skeptical. "And you have a way to set them free."

It wasn't really a question, but Larry hurried to explain. "I tried to get Henry off on the USB stick," he said, "but he wouldn't fit—there was too much data. Now what I want to do is just connect Eleanor's computer to the system long enough for Henry—and the others, I guess—to cross over. Then I'll disconnect from the network, and connect to the Internet, and they can go. Please," he added when the stony coldness didn't seem to soften in Andrea's eyes, "you can watch me the whole time to make sure I don't do anything else. And then you can call security if you want. I won't make a fuss."

"Please, Andrea, let him help us," Henry added.

"Yes, please," the woman's voice chimed in.

And then other voices joined them, too many to count, all emanating from the speakers nearest where they stood, a chorus that threatened to drown out even the ongoing din of prayers. The voices of the ghosts were easy to tell apart from the computer voices. They called Larry and Andrea by name. They sounded real, individual, authentic—*alive.*

Andrea held Larry's eyes for a long moment, and he knew that common sense and anger and betrayal were fighting with the very real evidence of what her ears were telling her. Finally she took a deep breath and blew it out, then nodded.

"I must be crazy, but—go ahead."

Larry plugged in the cable and said, "Okay, guys, the path is open," then stepped back.

"On our way," came Henry's voice.

A minute passed, then two, then it seemed to go on forever, Larry and Andrea standing in the server room, staring at the workstation and the rack of servers next to it.

"How will you know if it worked?"

"I'm not sure."

A notepad program window popped open on the screen and a message appeared, one letter at a time.

We're through! Close the connection.

Larry unplugged the cable and switched it over to connect the workstation to the Internet. He swallowed hard, a lump forming in his throat. He hadn't thought to say goodbye.

Thank you, Larry. The words appeared slowly on the screen. *I'll be the last one out. Andrea, thank you for listening. Larry's risked a lot for me—for us. He deserves his job back.*

Larry sat down at the workstation and typed, *You're welcome, Henry. Goodbye, and...have a good afterlife. :)*

See you when you least expect it, Henry typed, and then the notepad program closed.

Larry waited a minute or two, then looked at Andrea, who watched him with an unreadable expression on her face. "Do you think that's long enough?" he asked.

"Why don't we leave it until you get changed," she said slowly. "Wouldn't want to...cut anybody off."

Larry nodded and went to change out of his cleansuit, not daring to say anything else. When he came back, Andrea stood where he'd left her, watching the rainbow of prayer flags flutter next to some of the servers. He unplugged the cable and shut down the workstation, then turned to her.

"So. What now?"

She tilted her head to one side and regarded him. Her eyes had finally lost that hard-edged anger. "Now," she said, "You take me out for coffee, and tell me the whole story from beginning to end. Deal?"

Larry grinned. "Deal."

Chapter Seven of *Ghost in the Machine* showed up on Larry's home computer three days later, when he logged in to check his email before taking Andrea out for dinner. He grinned and opened a notepad window.

I'm thinking we should call the sequel, "On a Wing and an ePrayer," he typed.

Deal, said Henry.

B.R.A.N.E., Inc.

The first odd thing I noticed was the pale blue sticky note pasted on the bottom of his shoe. He knelt in front of the dark, silent copier and had already removed an access panel without saying more than "Good morning" to me with a brief nod and a not-quite-smile when he arrived at the office. The embroidered badge on his limp cotton shirt read *Leonard* and he was cute in a grim, planes-and-angles sort of way. Hadn't even asked me yet exactly what the trouble was with the copier. I debated whether to explain the problem or tell him about the paper stuck to his shoe as I surreptitiously checked my hair with my phone camera.

When he shifted his weight to reach inside the guts of the machine, I saw the bottom of his other shoe—and the blue square of paper there, too. I squinted. They looked like sticky notes, but they were held in place with packing tape. So I figured that a) he must know about them and b) I might as well just explain about the copier, even though he hadn't asked.

"It was fine yesterday afternoon, but then this morning when I went to print out the dailies, I just got gibberish," I told his back, repeating what I'd said to a bored-sounding dispatcher over the phone.

He didn't turn around, just nodded, his hand still deep inside the copier.

"I turned it off and then on again a few times, and I

unhooked it from the network, and then I tried again, but I got the same thing," I added, because for some reason I wanted him to know that I wasn't the type of girl who just throws up her hands when a machine or piece of tech screws up.

He sat back on his heels and glanced at me over his shoulder. A smudge of something dark marred the back of his shirt, as if he'd brushed up against something dusty. "You still have what it printed?"

"Sure." I retrieved some sheets out of the recycling bin and showed them to him. Each page bore just a couple of illegible lines. "But like I said, you can't read it. I don't even know what font this is." The characters were printed in a weird symbol font I didn't recognize.

He glanced at the pages and his back stiffened. Suddenly the office felt very still.

"What was it you were trying to print?"

I shrugged. "Just the dailies—blank timesheets, schedules, appointment lists. I do it every morning, before everyone else comes in. I send them direct from my computer." *Just the first of the day's usually mind-numbing tasks,* I added silently.

"How long have you had this copier? About two months?"

I thought for a second, nodded. "Yeah, it's about that."

He nodded. "I think you might have gotten the wrong model, by mistake. Anything strange ever happen with it before?" Now he was looking at me—really noticing me for the first time, I thought. He hadn't even looked at my tattoos before, which most guys do, whether they like them or not—they still notice. Sure enough, now his eyes did linger over the new ink on my forearms—some cool symbols I'd found on the Internet. He had pushed his ball cap way back on his head and damp dark curls peeked out from under its brim. Why was he sweating? The office AC hummed along just fine. I noticed that his eyes were mismatched—one dark hazel green, one deep amber. It was oddly attractive.

You're the weirdest thing so far, I thought, but I only shook my head. "Folks will start arriving in about half an hour. Do you think you can fix it by then?"

"Do my best," he said, getting slowly to his feet. He stared at the copier for a minute, like he was thinking over his next move. Finally he said, "I have to get some equipment from the truck. Don't let anyone else in here until I come back, okay? And you should probably stay away from the copier now that it's open. Maybe over at your desk."

This got stranger and stranger, but I wasn't getting a bad vibe from the guy, just a weird one. "Sure."

I went and sat at my desk when he went out, but I couldn't settle in to any work. The exposed inside of the copier looked dark and deep, and even though he'd unplugged it, an intermittent yellowish light flickered within. I turned to my computer and started checking email, deftly deleting the overnight spam, but my eyes kept straying back to that oddly-lit blackness.

Leonard came back, lugging a rivet-covered silver toolbox. He bumped the door shut behind him with his hip and set the box down about five feet from the copier.

"What's your name?" he asked me. Not in an *I'd-like-to-ask-for-your-number* kind of way, but more like an *I-need-to-call-you-something* kind of way.

"Nicole."

"Okay, Nicole, I'm going to need your help." His mismatched eyes caught and held mine, looking very serious. "I called the office from my truck, but I don't have time to wait for backup and we want to have everything straightened away before anyone else gets here, right?"

Backup? Copier repairmen had backup? "Uh, sure," I said, although I didn't understand. No-one would miss the dailies for once, and it wasn't like having a repairman in the office was going to freak anyone out.

He put his hands on his hips and considered me. I felt his gaze flicker again over my ink and piercings, but it lingered longest on my eyes. "I'm going to be straight with you, because I think you can take it. There's something living in your copier. Now, that's not bad news in itself—"

I resisted a sudden urge to pull my feet up off the floor.

"What? What lives inside copiers?" Images of spiders, cockroaches, and various other many-legged horrors skittered through my brain.

Leonard took a deep breath and blew it out through pursed lips. "Brownies."

I squinted at him, trying to decide what game he was playing. It didn't seem like a joke, though. "Brownies?"

He nodded, his eyes serious. "You know I don't mean the kind you eat, right?"

"Well, duh. I might think you're crazy, but I don't think you're suggesting the existence of sentient baked goods. You mean, like, fairies."

"Best not to call them that," he cautioned with a grimace and a shushing motion. "They really don't like it."

"Right." I stood up from my desk. "So, supposing for a minute that I grant you the existence of brownies, why would they be in my copier?"

"Well, they live in a lot of copiers. That's not the problem," Leonard said. "The problem is, you've also got a flashpoint indicator, which is why I'm probably going to need your help."

He didn't say what a flashpoint indicator was, but it didn't sound good. He knelt down and flipped up the catches on the metal box, opened the lid and took out what looked like a pair of 3-D glasses. The old-school, one-red-lens-and-one-blue-lens kind, but the lens colours matched his eyes, green and amber. He slipped them on and scanned my printouts from this morning. "*Skítkarl,*" he breathed, and although the word was foreign to me, it sure sounded like cussing.

The phone rang, and I jumped. "Schneider and Ali, how may I help you?"

"You called this morning about trouble with your copier?"

"Yes." I thought I recognized the bored-sounding dispatcher. She still sounded bored, and now her voice was tired, too, as if it had taken all her current energy reserves just to call me back.

"I'm sorry, but we won't be able to get anyone out there

until at least noon." She didn't sound all that sorry.

I frowned at Leonard. "You can't send anyone to fix the copier until noon?" I repeated back to her slowly, for his benefit.

His eyes widened behind the absurd green and amber lenses and he shook his head. He stabbed at the paper with his forefinger.

"Okay," I said into the receiver. "We'll wait." When I hung up I put my hands on my hips and glared at him.

"We monitor calls when the readings in a certain area get unusually high," he explained. He pulled another pair of glasses out of the metal box and handed them to me. I put them on and looked over the printout. Sure enough, the strange symbols resolved into words.

FLASHPOINT ALERT. Portal breach imminent at coordinates 3514.259.4158.SWCNA

I looked up at him and pulled the glasses down on my nose. "You know what, Leonard? My mood has been pretty much going down the toilet since I came in this morning, but I have a little bit of patience left. About five minutes' worth. That's how long you have to explain all of this to me."

He swallowed. Maybe he was used to people just accepting it when he came barging into their offices to announce that their equipment was full of imaginary creatures, but I didn't get to be office manager at twenty-five by being a sucker. And I wasn't about to lose that job, boring as it might be, at the hands of some whacked-out repairman with a few pairs of funky glasses.

Even if he was cute.

I tapped my foot a couple of times to let him know his five minutes were ticking down.

Leonard glanced at the copier and sighed. "Okay, long story short. I think this copier shouldn't be here at all. We had some shipping mistakes a few months ago—"

"Who's 'we'?" I interrupted.

"Oh, we're brain," he said.

"Brain?"

"B.R.A.N.E., Inc.," he spelled out. "It stands for Bureau of Realms and Netherworlds Enforcement. Anyway, as I was saying, some of the units meant for our field offices went to mundane operations, like yours. Unfortunately we've had a hard time tracking all of them down."

"And these 'special' copiers have 'brownies' living in them?"

He nodded, apparently oblivious to the sarcasm. "They're not all copiers, but yeah. See, brownies like to live in houses and offices. They do little chores in return for a roof over their heads. They seem to like big copiers especially—I don't know why. Maybe the warmth. You notice the office is a lot tidier since you got this copier? Cleaners seem to be doing a better job? Maybe people are picking up after themselves more?"

I frowned and thought back over the past two months. He could be right, although I'd thought it was just a result of my nagging people not to be such slobs. I shrugged, not ready to buy into his story just yet. "Maybe. So what's with the gibberish printouts and this 'portal breach' stuff?"

He knelt to the metal box again and rummaged inside. "Brownies are especially sensitive to the links between worlds," he said, "particularly between Earth and the faerie realm, the demon planes, and the ethereal realm. Earth is like a way-station or hub connecting them all. Which unfortunately also means it's full of potential flashpoints. Brownies can sense these. Think of them as an early warning system. They tried to send a message about it, but since the copier is in the wrong office, you got it instead of one of the team."

I blinked. "So you want me to buy into the idea of brownies, other faeries, demons, *and* other worlds? Just because my copier is futzed?"

Leonard found what he was looking for and held out two items that looked almost like a motorcycle helmet and a gun. Almost. "In a couple more minutes, if we don't move to contain the breach, you're going to have a lot more to worry about than a busted copier."

When I didn't move to take the objects, he juggled them into one hand and pulled out his own sort-of motorcycle helmet with the other. Both of them bore an odd logo I didn't recognize: colourful strands woven together in a circle. He slid one over his head, then stood up again and stared at me intently. The effect was somewhat diluted by the green and yellow lenses of the glasses he still wore. "Are you going to help me, or is it all too much for you?"

I snatched the things out of his hands. He might not have convinced me of all this ridiculous stuff, but I wasn't going to have him think I was some vapid keyboard bunny about to cower, snivelling, under my desk. "If whatever goes down here costs me my job, you're going to hear about it," I muttered, slamming the helmet on. So much for the hot rollers I'd spent twenty minutes on this morning. It was comfortable and light for its bulk, though, and I quickly forgot that I was even wearing it. I pulled off my shoes and kicked them under my desk, too. I didn't think heels were going to be appropriate footwear in the next little while.

"So where's this breach going to happen?" I asked him. "Right here in the office? 'Cause I've never been aware of any kind of portals in here, except the normal kind of, you know, *doors*."

Leonard shook his head and glanced down at another gadget he'd pulled out of the box. It looked a little like a tricorder from *Star Trek*. "Not here in the office, but nearby," he said. "Up on the roof, I think. It's actually pretty lucky that the copier ended up in this building by accident. This must be a new portal, just opening up."

Yeah, I feel really lucky. I held up the gun-like thing. "All right, show me how this works."

"You hold it like a gun, point and shoot at the target," he said. "But we call it an equalizer."

"That's original."

He shook his head. "No, not like that, because it's not a gun—no bullets are going to come out of it."

"So, like, a force-field or something?" I asked, pointing it around experimentally. "I think I'll just call it a gun, okay?"

"Sure." He studied the readout on his gadget without looking up. I pointed the gun at him for just a second to see if he'd notice. He didn't seem to. That struck me as pretty trusting, considering we'd only met about twenty minutes ago. I pointed it at the copier.

"Don't do that," he said. "Makes the brownies nervous."

I swung the gun away, but really—I hadn't even seen these hypothetical brownies yet.

"It's definitely the roof," Leonard said, holstering the gadget in his belt and pulling another gun-thing out of the box. His was bigger than mine. *Men.* "Do you have access to the roof directly from this office?"

I shook my head. "Nope. There's just one staircase at each end of the building, as far as I know. If you turn right from here, the closest one is at the end of the hallway."

"We'll have to deal, then." He knelt in front of the copier and held a low-voiced conversation with the putative brownies. It occurred to me that if he was just some nut, I was going to feel mighty silly when everyone else arrived for the morning and found me wearing a not-quite-motorcycle helmet while some guy talked to the copier. However, since it looked like we were going up to the roof, I took the opportunity to dig my sneakers out from under the desk and slip them on. I have to walk a block to the bus, and I don't do that in heels.

Leonard turned from the copier and dug inside the metal box again. He tossed me a small baggie and said, "Stick these on the soles of your shoes."

They looked just like the squares of blue paper I'd noticed on the bottoms of his own shoes, but when I took these out of the bag they each bore a thin film that peeled off to reveal an adhesive. I applied them and they stuck extremely tightly at the slightest touch. I hoped they didn't have to be straight, but he hadn't mentioned that. And his own were only attached with packing tape.

When I looked up from having stuck on the blue things and tied my laces, I was glad I'd sat down. A group of small beings, the tallest maybe six inches high, was in the process of jumping one at a time out of the open access panel of the copier. They reminded me of garden gnomes, although less rotund. Most of them did have pointed hats. Hair colour varied, but their skin was uniformly a deep-tan brown. Pointed ears stretched as high as the tops of their heads, and ended in fluffy tufts of hair. Their faces were, for the most part, fine-featured and a bit pouty. They wore a varied assortment of pants, jackets, and tiny boots in earth tones, except for one rebel who sported a miniature motorcycle jacket in black leather and a blue do-rag knotted at the back of his head. Most of them ignored me, but the biker-type regarded me with an extremely cranky frown. I wondered if I'd been somehow mistreating the copier. Or maybe he didn't approve of some of the jokes I'd copied last week.

Leonard looked over at me and I snapped my jaw shut. "They can help us, but we have to get them up on the roof, and we can't let anyone else see them. They're already annoyed that they have to expose themselves to you."

"Let's hope *that* won't be necessary," I muttered. Louder, I said, "There's hardly anyone around this time of the morning—I get here early because the next bus makes me too late. They can probably just walk."

The brownies started shaking their heads before I finished talking. Leonard did the same. "They won't take a chance," he said. "It's a big deal for them to be out of the copier at all when anyone's around."

I glanced around the office. "Well, there's this," I said, grabbing my oversized purse off the back of my chair. I'd brought my pink and white "Hello Bunny" bag, because I'd been feeling sort of whimsical when I left the house this morning. The cranky brownie looked aghast and I felt a pleasurable surge of vindictiveness. "They'd fit," I pointed out.

Leonard seemed to be trying hard to smother a grin. "They would," he said seriously. "And it would make good camouflage. That thing is huge. I think you could even get the equalizer in there."

The brownies exchanged glances and one started to protest, but the tallest one—not the rebel brownie, but one with a flowing white beard and tiny glasses perched on a bulbous nose—held up a hand. Apparently the decision had been made. I put the gun inside, then set the purse on the floor on its side and held it open. With as much dignity as they could manage, the brownies marched in. I scooped the purse up gently and swung it over my shoulder with care. "Okay, Leonard," I said. "Let's do this thing, whatever it is."

He nodded and closed up the metal box. After a quick press of a button on one end, the whole thing contracted until it was about half as big as before, and he tucked it up under one arm. With the other hand he picked up his toolbag. "Lead the way."

The hallway outside the office was deserted, so Leonard gave me a low-voiced briefing as we walked.

"When the flashpoint portal starts to open, we'll have about a minute and a half to shut it down before it stabilizes enough for anything to pass through," he said. "That should be plenty of time, because with both of us and the brownies working together, we'll be able to hit it with a concentrated amount of anti-thaumatter."

I almost chuckled. If Leonard was making this all up or delusional, he'd thought it through.

"Anti-thaumatter. Right," I said. "Where do we get that?"

"It's what comes out of your equalizer," he said. "That's why we call them that. A portal can only open when the thaumic force on one side of the brane becomes greater than on the other side, and stabilizes that way. The equalizer exerts thaumic force to compensate for the other side's attempts to thin it on their side."

"So it's not like antimatter, then," I said, trying to make it sound like I understood. Most of my notions about antimatter came from old *Star Trek* episodes. "We don't have to worry about particles colliding and cancelling each other out and destroying the world or anything."

"Um, no," he said. "That would only happen if two thaumically identical but opposite things from different sides of the portal came in contact with each other. I don't think even that would destroy the world. It could

THE CACHE AND OTHER STORIES

destroy the two things, I suppose." He kept his voice low but walked faster. "Anyway, all the equalizer will do is re-stabilize the portal so it can't open. And those blue squares you put on your shoes? They're anti-thaumatter grounds, to keep you from being sucked through the portal when it's unstable."

I was glad they'd stuck so tightly. But I frowned. "Seems like portals could be opening all the time if you weren't there to catch them."

Leonard shook his head. "They can only initiate at a place where the brane between the planes is weak to begin with—we call them flashpoints," he explained. "Luckily, there are relatively few places like that. That's why we monitor them. Although," he added, his voice sounding tired, "there seem to be more weak places developing all the time. We're spread really thin trying to cover them all. But once we deal with this attempt, we'll get a team in here to try and patch up the thin portion of the brane as soon as possible, so it won't happen again," he added.

We'd reached the end of the hallway and I pushed open the door that led to the stairs. "Why are they happening more frequently? What's causing the change?" I asked him.

"No-one's sure," he said. "But we're working on it." He didn't sound all that hopeful.

"Humans," a voice said from behind me, and I jumped and whirled. The hallway lay empty.

A chuckle came from inside my Hello Bunny bag, followed quickly by a *shhhhhhh!* I felt a hot wave wash over my face. *Damn brownies.* I'd forgotten about them for a moment.

"We don't know that," Leonard argued, and I had the distinct impression that this was a conversation he'd had before.

"Humans are weakening every other aspect of the Earth," said the same voice, and I realized the voice was female. "Why look any further for an explanation for this weakening as well?"

Leonard threw me an exasperated look and rolled his

eyes.

"But still you're helping us," I threw over my shoulder at the bag.

Someone snorted a tiny snort. "It's our world, too," said the brownie. "We know you humans think you have some kind of superior claim to it just because you've spread your nasty—"

Whatever else the brownie was going to say was cut off by an even louder *shhhhh!* and lost in a burbling noise that sounded like someone had clapped a tiny hand over someone else's tiny mouth.

That little exchange got us up to the top of the stairwell, and I slid back the bolt that secured the door leading to the roof. Before I pushed it open, though, Leonard laid a hand on my arm. His skin was cool, and just a little clammy. It was reassuring that he felt a bit nervous. I was doing my best to ignore the butterflies careening around in my stomach and the tightness in my chest, and I felt glad that I wasn't the only one.

"All you have to do up here is follow my lead," he said, looking intently into my eyes with his mismatched ones. I couldn't help thinking again that the difference was intriguing. "Point where I point, shoot when I shoot or tell you to shoot. Stop when I say it's okay."

I nodded. "Got it."

"You think you can hold your aim steady? The area of the portal should be at least a couple of feet in diameter, so you don't have to hit a really small target."

"I've played laser tag and paintball with my brothers," I said. "Neither one had the fate of the world hanging on it, but we're pretty competitive."

He flashed me a rare grin. "You'll do great."

"When should I let the...er...brownies out of the bag?"

Leonard consulted his gadget. "I think we'll have at least a minute or two once we're on the roof," he said. "The levels haven't reached critical yet. After we close the door we'll look for a spot with some cover, I'll transmit the actual coordinates of the flashpoint, and you can set them down then. No sense making them run further than they have to, since their legs are short."

"We heard that," said the voice from the bag.

"No offense," Leonard said. "But you can't say it isn't true."

When the brownie didn't seem to have a retort for that, Leonard pushed the crash bar down and swung the door open. The sun hadn't been up all that long, but it burst into the gloomy stairwell with a searing brilliance. My eyes watered and I blinked as I followed Leonard through.

The rooftop was typical office-building style, with physical plant intakes and outflows, tin-plated sheds and stacks and other things whose purpose I couldn't identify. Any one of them would have afforded us some cover, but we didn't have time to take two steps toward them because obviously Leonard's gadget was wrong. A three-foot wide, shimmering grey globe with a mercury-like sheen hung in the air about twenty feet from us, spitting tiny forks of black lightning.

Leonard swore and dropped to one knee, scrabbling with the metal box.

"What's wrong? Let us out!" yelled a brownie, and something sharp stabbed into my back, just below my shoulder blade.

I yelped. The Hello Bunny bag slid off my shoulder and slipped out of my sweaty grasp. The bag plopped to the pebbly rooftop with a *thunk*. Brownies grunted and groaned and spilled out of the bag, muttering what I assumed were brownie curse-words.

I knelt and pulled the equalizer out of the bag once the little creatures were out of my way. "Should I shoot it?" I breathed at Leonard.

"Yes!" he snapped. "It's already worse—"

A clear calm washed over me as I raised the equalizer and took aim. This was going to be easy. As a target, the globe was huge compared to the skinny frames of my brothers. I squeezed the trigger.

Nothing happened. I released it and looked at Leonard.

"Keep shooting!" he yelped.

I aimed and shot again, but I still couldn't see or feel any effect. Keeping my aim steady at the globe and my finger pressed on the trigger, I said, "Is anything happening?"

"Yes, you just can't see it," he said, fumbling with the box. He opened the lid and did something inside. "Come on, boot up," he muttered.

"You could have *told* me that."

Meanwhile, the brownies seemed to have taken up a formation utilizing my legs as their cover. They peeked around my ankles and over the tops of my shoes, gripping tiny versions of my equalizer that they had produced from somewhere. They all pointed and presumably shot at the crackling globe, but it was disconcerting that there was no visible indication that anything at all was happening.

If this were a movie, I thought, *there'd be some kind of cool beam or light or something.* Like the spitting, crackling energy beams in *Ghostbusters.* I mean, you *knew* something was happening when you engaged a proton pack. With the absolute lack of feedback from the equalizers, I couldn't even tell if I was hitting the target or not. Nothing on the globe gave any sign that our actions were affecting it at all.

Leonard continued clicking buttons inside the box.

"Is this working?" I demanded.

"No," he said curtly. "Don't stop, though," he yelped, as I let my hand start to drop. "You're slowing it down— maybe even holding it steady—but it's not enough to close it."

"Would you consider helping, then?" I tried to bite down on the sarcasm in my voice, but it came through loud and clear. The weirdest part was how quiet all this was. The globe was virtually silent, except for the sharp pops of the lightning crackles, and the weapons made no sound at all. I wondered if the globe could be some kind of hologram and this could still turn out to be an elaborate prank.

I glanced down at the brownies clustered around my feet and dismissed that thought. They were damn real. One had his forearms braced firmly on my instep.

"I'm trying," Leonard said. "I don't think my equalizer is going to make the difference we need, so I'm trying to tap into the global net, see if I can pull in energy from anywhere else. Trouble is..." he broke off and I heard the stutter of keyboard typing, "...the presence of the portal is disrupting my signal."

"What about other—agents, or whatever you are?" I asked him. "You said there wasn't time to call for backup, but maybe there's someone else in the area already. Can you check on that?"

My arms felt heavy. The equalizer wasn't much of a weight, but the strain of holding my arms out and steady would soon start affecting my aim.

His lips pressed together in a pessimistic line. "I can try—"

Whooomph! Without warning the globe expanded, growing from three feet wide to six in a single burst. It was like someone had forced high-pressure air into a balloon. I actually felt the air displacement hit me, and staggered back a step. Leonard swore.

The air slapped my face, fiery hot and smelling like a compost heap, the heat and stink making me blink watering eyes. My aim faltered for a second, and wavered away from the target despite its increased size. Without the invisible field of anti-thaumatter pouring into it—or onto it, or however it worked—the globe shifted from silvery grey to translucent, and I glimpsed what lay on the other side of the portal. I had three impressions: glowing yellow eyes, a jagged-clawed hand, and tattered black wings. And—definitely more than one. A scorched, burnt-meat scent tickled my nostrils.

I twitched the equalizer back on target and the globe shuddered and greyed out again. It didn't shrink at all. My trigger finger was starting to go numb from squeezing so hard. I had an unwelcome thought.

"Is this thing going to run out of—anything? Energy, or whatever?"

"Eventually, yes," Leonard said. "Look, we'd better switch. I'll take both equalizers and you try to get us some help."

"But I don't know—"

"I'll tell you what to do." He stood from the box,

levelled his equalizer one-handed at the globe, and depressed the trigger. The globe shuddered again, and shrank back a bit, losing maybe a foot or so of its diameter.

Leonard held out his other hand and waggled his fingers for my gun, and I carefully eased it into his grasp, keeping the trigger depressed until his own finger closed over it. I let go with relief, quickly flexing my hands to try and get some feeling back into them. The brownies skittered away from my feet as I moved over and knelt at the box. Inside was an industrial-looking laptop computer, with a standard keyboard and an overlaid skin of weird symbols. A program resembling an Internet browser displayed on the screen, with a bunch of tabs open across the top. Relief washed over me. A computer, I could deal with.

"Press the F7 key," a voice instructed from my left, and I realized that the cranky rebel brownie had clambered up the side of the box. She was also the owner of the female voice I'd heard earlier. She'd passed her weapon off to one of her comrades and had come over to help guide me through whatever I was going to do here. The tone of her voice hadn't softened any, but I was glad of the assistance. I did as she said.

More of the weird symbol font from the printouts scrolled up the screen. I felt in my pocket for the 3D glasses and slipped them on, and the characters resolved into something I could read.

Unfortunately, not something I could understand. It was just a bunch of numbers, and I had no idea what they referenced.

The cranky brownie frowned and shook her head. "That's just data on the portal strength," she said, "and the available energy flux in the area. If we're looking for backup, we want F12."

I duly pressed F12 and another window popped open, displaying a map that I recognized after a moment as the city core. I used the arrow keys to home in on our block.

"Chaltos-A for nearby agents," the brownie directed.

"Well, if I knew which one of these symbols was

chaltos, that might be helpful," I said.

"For Mab's sake, you've got one on your arm!" The brownie snorted and pointed to a key with a two-pronged curlicue.

I froze, startled. She was right—part of the new tattoo was a sigil that looked identical to the one inscribed on the key. The globe crackled as a finger of electricity raced across its surface, and I shook myself. Whatever the coincidence meant or didn't mean, I didn't have time to worry about it just now. I pressed the curlicue and the A key together. Two purple dots appeared on the screen, one that I figured must be Leonard himself since it was exactly where I thought our building would be, and another one very close. I moved the cursor and clicked the nearby dot, and a dialogue box opened up.

"That's for sending a message," the brownie said. "Do it quick!"

"What do I say?" I asked, but I started typing the first thing that came to me. *Portal opening. Request immediate assistance.*

"Keep it short. Something like, 'Portal opening. Request immediate assistance'," Leonard said.

I clicked *send.* "Now what?"

"Better come and take back your equalizer. My arms are burning."

As I stood, he slid one foot toward me so I could reach my equalizer better. In the still-eerie silence, broken only by the globe's intermittent crackling, I heard a faint ripping-peeling noise. Leonard seemed to hear it, too, and we both realized in the same instant what it was.

The sound of one of his jury-rigged anti-thaumatter grounds peeling off the sole of his shoe on the uneven rooftop.

He had just time to meet my eyes in a horrified glance before the force of the destabilized portal pulled him a few stumbling steps toward it. I grabbed for my equalizer, but his finger slipped off the trigger before I could get mine on, and the globe surged again. Worse, with Leonard trying to resist the pull of the globe, his aim wavered, and there was a moment once again when the globe gained power, turned translucent, and gave me another look at the world beyond.

I gulped.

This time, since the globe was bigger, I saw more of the other side. The creature I had only glimpsed before was much taller than I had realized. Taller—and even more terrifying. The ultimate stereotypical devil-type demon— with the addition of an extra set of horns, more teeth, more muscles, and a few assorted tentacles. Some additional clawed fingers and a set of blade-tipped wings. *That's* who was knocking at the door.

I grabbed desperately and caught Leonard's hand with one of mine, while I brought the equalizer to bear on the globe and squeezed the trigger. An opaque skin slid over the surface of the globe, but it didn't shrink. The black lightning bolts streaking across its surface seemed to have grown, too, and one sizzled out and hit the pebbled surface below it. Dirt particles flared and smoked.

The force drawing Leonard toward the globe was incredible. He leaned back, trying to counterbalance it, and I tightened my grip on his hand. It was as if he hung suspended over a gorge, as gravity dragged at him. My arm ached already with the strain of trying to hold him back. There was no way we could do this alone.

"Any reply?" I yelled to the cranky brownie.

"Nothing."

"We have to get Leonard's weapon back on target," I told her. Leonard was still trying to aim and shoot, but he couldn't get a steady bead while he fought to keep from being dragged closer to the globe. It seemed to have grown again, although it remained opaque. I was thankful for small mercies. The eyes of that creature on the other side promised things I didn't want to think about.

"What the heck is going on here?"

The voice came from behind me, and I threw a quick glance back over my shoulder. A girl stood beside the box holding the computer, hands on her hips and a disapproving glare taking in me, Leonard, the globe, and the brownies all at once.

No, not a girl, I realized. Well, female, but not human. I saw upswept, pointed eartips poking through long, straight hair—blonde hair, but oddly tinted with green overtones. Her eyes, large and cornflower blue, tilted up at the outer edges, lending her a puckish look belied by the glare. Her legs and arms were a little too thin, her torso a little too long. All tiny things, but they added up to decidedly not human.

I tilted my head down so I could look over the tops of the 3D glasses I still wore—an instinctive action since I wasn't used to wearing glasses and it just seemed that I should be able to see her better without them. I may not have seen her *better*, but I certainly saw her differently.

Without the benefit of the special lenses, she looked like a perfectly human, perfectly cute, perfectly stylish young woman.

"Amber!" Leonard shouted. He hadn't looked around at her, his attention being quite fully taken up with trying to aim his equalizer and battle the attractive force of the globe at the same time, so he must have recognized her voice.

I felt a weird twinge of…something. Jealousy?

"I hope you're here to help," I said. "As you can see, we're in some trouble."

"Who's your *friend*, Len?" she asked, ignoring me. "Here, let me do that," she said to the cranky brownie, brushing her away from the keyboard rudely. Granted, the brownie's small size hindered her efforts to call for more help, since every key on the keyboard was as big as one of her hands.

Leonard slid a foot closer to the globe, his feet skittering across the rough pebbles underfoot. I had a momentary fear that his other anti-thaumatter grounding pad would be scraped off.

I was about to yell at "Amber" to come and lend a hand, but she beat me to it. "I'm sending out a global emergency call, and trying to suck down some extra-thaumic energy," she said. "I don't really have any upper body strength on this plane, so I can't help keep Leonard back from the portal. I'll bet one of his grounding pads came off, didn't it? Did you tell the human girl, Len, how I kept telling you to get them fixed or get new ones, and you kept telling me how they were 'just fine for now'?"

To do her credit, her thin fingers were flying over the keyboard as she spoke; she wasn't just scolding Leonard, she really did seem to be trying to help.

"I don't think this is the time—" he started, but his words cut off abruptly as the globe enlarged like a balloon being blown up, and both his feet slipped out from under him. I lost my grip on him and his equalizer flew out of his hand and bounced across the gravel. He went down hard on his back.

He flipped himself over and clawed for purchase on the ground, but slid inexorably toward the globe.

I didn't think. I dropped my own equalizer, grabbed his hands, and braced myself, careful to keep my own feet flat on the ground.

It worked. To an extent.

Leonard stopped sliding toward the globe. Some of the brownies swarmed toward his feet, and I saw that they carried his lost grounding pad. If they could stick it back on, maybe we could salvage this yet. I pulled against the force even harder, to give them time to work.

However, with both equalizers off the target, the globe burst suddenly to a full seven feet in diameter, turned completely transparent, and sent a flurry of black-tentacled lightning strikes toward the ground. They caught and held like living mooring ropes, sizzling and hissing.

And the demon stepped through.

I heard Amber swear in that weird language. I knew without a doubt that it had to be a curse. No one in their right mind would say anything else at that moment.

The brownies scurried back towards us as the pull against Leonard abruptly ceased. I fell backwards, half-pulling him over on top of me, and pain shot up my back and down my arms as I landed hard. I felt, rather than heard, his breath whoosh out in a rush, and behind it a wave of fetid heat from the portal. The brownies had fixed Leonard's anti-thaumatter ground. Once he'd fallen down, they could get to the soles of his feet.

Well, that was ironic, because the demon—or whatever it was—was through now, anyway.

It looked around, and its massively muscled chest rose and fell as it took a deep breath. I wondered crazily if it felt fresh and cool after the heat of the plane it had come from, or unpleasantly cold. It didn't seem to mind, anyway, because the first thing it did was reach down, pick up Leonard's dropped equalizer, and casually crush it in one fist.

That can't be good.

I struggled to my feet, because if I had to face some creature from another plane, I wasn't going to do it sitting down. Leonard tried to help me, but it was more the other way around. He'd fallen hard, too, and held one arm as if it really, really hurt to move it.

"Amber," Leonard half-hissed, although the demon was standing right there and could no doubt hear perfectly well, "Amber, do we have anyone—anyone at all?"

To her credit, Amber had apparently just kept on working as the portal opened and the denizen from the other side stepped through. "Help is on the way," she hissed back, although for all I knew it could have been a bluff for the demon's sake. Leonard seemed to stand a little taller, anyway, so I guess what she said gave him some hope. He was probably thinking we just had to contain things for a couple more minutes on our own.

Me, I wasn't thinking that way. Maybe I'm just not one to put my faith in other people, or last-minute rescues or *deus ex machina.* I was sizing up that crimson sucker and wondering where his weaknesses might be.

He stood a good seven feet tall, now that I could see him clearly and we stood on the same level. Crimson skin, covered in rune-like markings that could have been tattoos of some kind, or possibly were naturally-occurring marks, like demon birthmarks or something. Some of them looked familiar. In fact, I recognized a two-pronged curlicue that matched the one on the keyboard—and my arm. A chill like a slow trickle of icy water skittered down my back. What could that mean?

"What do the runes mean?" I hissed at Leonard, because if we were going to pretend the demon couldn't hear us, I could go along with that. Maybe it could hear us, but not understand English. It still hadn't made a move beyond crushing the gun, surveying us with slitted, lizard-like eyes, as if wondering whose head it was going to rip off first. Yeah, that kind of look.

"What runes?" he whispered back, even though he was staring at the demon just like I was.

"The ones covering his hide," I said impatiently. "I don't know, maybe you guys call them something else. Symbols? Sigils?"

Leonard shook his head. "I don't see them."

That freaked me out for a second, because I started wondering if it even looked like a demon to anyone else (the way Amber looked different with or without the glasses). I realized I was still wearing my glasses, but Leonard had lost his when he fell. I lowered my head and peered over the top of the lenses, like a gimlet-eyed librarian when your book's three weeks overdue. Huh. He looked exactly the same, except for—no runes.

"Greetings," he said finally, breaking the awkward silence. His voice sounded like stones slithering over each other in the bottom of a streambed. "If you care to try and bargain with me, I'll hear your pleas now."

That definitely didn't sound good. At. All.

Leonard chose that moment to stand up to the guy, maybe still thinking that help was only seconds away. He took a deep breath and stepped slightly in front of Amber and the brownies and me, and squared his shoulders. "You are neither welcome nor permitted on this plane. You are in violation of the Inter-Planal Reciprocal Exclusivity charter, and as a recognized agent of B.R.A.N.E., I demand you return to your own plane at once."

I had to admit he sounded pretty official and serious and threatening. If it were me, I would have scatted back to my own plane pretty quick.

However, the demon was not me. He regarded Leonard

though narrowed eyes for a moment and then burst into laughter. The streambed rocks were now granite boulders, tumbling down a scree-littered slope and crashing into each other. It was actually painful. I barely stopped myself from covering my ears with my hands, but I somehow thought the creature would like that and I didn't want to give it the satisfaction.

He glanced over at me, still chuckling. I felt his hot gaze flick over me, assessing and dismissing. Instinctively, I took a step closer to Leonard and moved my arm just a little behind his, so the creature wouldn't see my tattoos. Then he seemed to really notice Amber.

His eyes narrowed to even-more-unfriendly slits and he hissed, "Shifter."

I tore my gaze from the demon to see her reaction, just in time to catch her—unbelievably—glance up at the extraplanar horror and flip her middle finger at him.

"Natural enemies," Leonard whispered to me.

"I got that," I whispered back.

I wasn't sure how she did it, but Amber returned her gaze to the keyboard in such a way that it was a deliberate insult to the demon. She also kept typing, and spoke to him without looking up again.

"You heard my colleague," she said. "This isn't going to work; you might as well go back."

He crossed to her in a few quick strides and swung his clawed fist in a wide arc. I gasped, certain he was going to decapitate her in one strike, but instead he batted the laptop. It sailed away from Amber in a shallow arc and hit the pebbled roof fifteen feet away. Miraculously it didn't smash into a million pieces, but I seriously doubted it would still be in working order if one of us managed to retrieve it.

Amber leapt to her feet and hissed something in that odd language. Then she was gone. The demon whirled to watch as a long-haired blonde cat—with an oddly greenish tint to its fur—darted between his legs and toward the crackling black fingers of electricity anchoring the globe.

I took advantage of the distraction to grab Leonard's

glasses off the ground and jam them onto his face. I wanted to be sure he could see everything I was seeing.

"Runes," I told him, sticking my arm in front of his face. "*Runes.* What do they mean?"

I'd noticed that it wasn't just the two-pronged curlicue on the demon that matched both the symbol Leonard had called "chaltos" and part of my new tattoo. The rest of my tattoo—an oval with a wavy line through it and a squiggle that looked like some Greek letter whose name I could never remember—were also replicated on the demon's crimson hide. The three ran together in a line across his midriff in exactly the same configuration as on my forearm.

Leonard's eyes widened as he glanced from the demon to my arm and back again. "*Theros, chaltos, lunata,*" he said. "They—match. I don't understand." He shook his head as if trying to clear it, pain making his eyes dull and unfocused.

The demon roared, making both of us jump, and Leonard hissed in pain at the jolt to his arm. The demon swiped at the cat, missing her tawny hide by mere inches as she bolted through the spitting electricity below the globe. I gasped, expecting her to be injured, electrocuted, or sizzled on the spot, but instead the bolt she touched retracted into the globe for a moment. As soon as she was clear, though, another spiked down to take its place.

"Where are the brownies?" Leonard asked distractedly.

Good question. I hadn't noticed them since they'd helped get Leonard back on his feet. I hoped they hadn't been inside the case when the demon had sent the laptop flying.

Dull red light flashed and the globe shuddered, going opaque for a moment before clearing again. I looked down to see that the brownies had gathered around our feet again, and had all their equalizers trained on the globe. It was a nice gesture, but I knew it was futile. Theirs and ours together hadn't been enough to stop it, so I didn't see how theirs alone had much of a chance.

A clatter and clang from behind the physical plant marked Amber's progress as the demon chased her.

"Psst!" It was the rebel brownie, standing on my right instep and gesturing frantically for me to pick her up. I knelt quickly and scooped her into my palm. As I straightened, she scampered up my arm and onto my shoulder with an agility I never would have guessed at. In the next instant she was pulling painfully on my earlobe.

"Ow! What?" I couldn't turn my head to look at her for fear of knocking her off my shoulder.

"You have to do something!"

Amber flashed into view again. Now she bore the shape of an agile, lizard-like thing with pale, green-tinted scales. The demon was still on her heels but she skidded to a stop, whirled, and breathed a jet of blue flame toward him.

"Look," I said, "I'm with you. But what can I do?"

She tugged on my earlobe again. "You have to stop him!"

"Ow! Stop doing that!" Leonard seemed to be going into shock, sagging against me with more and more of his weight. I didn't know how much longer I could keep him upright, or how much longer the demon would be distracted by Amber's antics. Where was that backup she'd supposedly called for?

I tried to give Leonard a little shake, although it was difficult to shake him and support him at the same time. "Leonard, come on!" I urged him. "What should I do? How do we fix this?"

He turned to look at me, pupils dilated behind lids he struggled to keep open. "Can't...think," he managed. "But the runes—"

And then he slumped toward the pebbled rooftop, my arms finally giving out.

"Watch out!" I yelled at the brownies, and they scattered out from under his descending form. The one on my shoulder caught hold of my collar with one hand and my earlobe with the other, and held fast.

"What did he mean, 'runes'?" she asked.

"Well, that thing is covered with them," I snapped, fighting the urge to swat her away like a bug.

"I can see that," she answered me, no less snappishly.

"But what can we *do* about it?"

"Aren't you the experts?" I hissed at her. The instinct for self-preservation was the only thing that stopped me from yelling, because I knew that attracting the attention of the demon would be worse than anything I had to put up with from a snippy little brownie in combat boots.

"We don't get into the field very often," she admitted in a whisper. "We're usually on the other side of the operation."

And that's when Leonard's earlier words came back to me with the force of a blow to the solar plexus. If two thaumically opposite things from different sides of the portal came in contact with each other...it could destroy the two things.

The demon's runes. My tattoos. They were the same, but different...from two different sides of the portal. Were they thaumically opposite? Did that follow? Would bringing them together eradicate the demon...and me with it?

I had no idea. But it was suddenly, blindingly, obvious to me that I had to try. That thing couldn't be allowed to stay on this side of the brane.

I take an inordinate amount of pleasure in the fact that the demon never saw it coming. I'd seen him dismiss me as inconsequential. He didn't even really look at me when I approached him. Amber had shifted this time into a creature I didn't recognize, which, on reflection, is fine by me. I really wouldn't want to live in a world where something that big, with leathery wings and so many claws and that evil-looking hooked beak is easily recognizable. The only thing that kept me from fainting at the mere sight of it was the fact that its hide was a pale blonde colour, with greenish accents, so I knew it had to be Amber.

And, I suppose it was slightly less terrifying than the demon itself.

Anyway, Amber was dive-bombing the demon and it was batting at her in return with its long, wicked-looking claws. She'd managed to open a pair of deep, parallel gashes in the demon's right shoulder; in exchange she sported a fresh, ragged tear in the leathery skin of one wing. It didn't seem to be stopping her, though. I wondered briefly if shapeshifters could regenerate and heal injuries when they shifted. Too bad I probably wouldn't be around long enough to find out.

So the demon wasn't looking at me as I stole up beside him, threw my arm out to the side with my tattoos facing his runes, lined them up as well as I could, and smacked my forearm into his midriff.

His flesh was hot—not hot enough to burn, but like a really high fever. It wasn't enough to make me scream, but the pain that l anced through my arm, beginning where the runes had touched and radiating all the way up to my shoulder and down through my fingers—yeah, *that* made me scream, and wrench my arm instinctively away from the excruciating contact.

Except it wouldn't come away. My arm was stuck fast where the sigils had connected.

To my shock, the demon screamed, too. Truthfully, his was more of a roar, but it tended toward a scream. Pain more than rage. Not that the rage wasn't there. But it was —overshadowed.

So, this was a big mistake, I had time to think. At that point, a fiery conflagration that immolated both of us might have been a bit of a relief. Instead, the demon picked me up, turned around, and ran for the globe.

Oh no. Not the world I'd glimpsed on the other side of that portal. Fiery conflagration looked better every second. The pain in my arm increased, and so did the heat emanating from the conjoined symbols. I felt certain that we would burst into flames at any second.

But when I twisted my head reflexively to see where we were going, the globe was blessedly grey again. I spotted Leonard on the ground where I'd left him. He'd come around, somehow, and found my equalizer. The brownies were arrayed alongside him. All of them had their equalizers pointed at the globe. Leonard's face was grey with fatigue and pain, but his aim was unwavering.

The demon skidded to a stop in front of the globe and swiped it with a claw. His hand passed right through.

"NO!" The demon snarled and tried again to push my arm away from his midriff. His hands were hotter now, clamped over my shoulder and wrist, and I wondered which would happen first—my shoulder would dislocate, followed quickly by my arm being torn completely off my body, or all the flesh would simply peel off it as he ripped me away. I couldn't quite feel bones being crushed yet, but it felt imminent. My arm would not budge, although the skin stretched alarmingly. The matched runes and tattoos would not let go of each other.

The heat coming off his body was intense now, as if I were standing much too close to an open fire. Waves rolled over me, stinging my skin and blistering my cheeks. *How can there be this much heat without any smoke?* I wondered hysterically.

The demon changed tactics, turning back to the globe and trying to thrust me inside it. Where his hand had passed through it, it remained solid against me, like a medicine ball at my back. I could feel the curve of the sphere as the demon shoved me against it and my spine bent painfully to match. At least the globe was a cool counterpoint to the heat blasting from the demon, which seemed to intensify with every passing second. I couldn't believe my hair wasn't smoking by now.

Still, I preferred going up in flames to passing through to the world I'd glimpsed on the other side of that portal. Bracing against the unyielding, steady globe at my back, I pushed my rune-inked arm harder against the maddened demon's midriff. And without even thinking about it, I repeated the names Leonard had given the runes.

"*Theros, chaltos, lunata,*" I said through gritted teeth. "How do you like that, you big ugly bas—"

I wouldn't have thought it possible, but the demon's face turned an even brighter shade of crimson. The yellowish sclera of his eyeballs bulged, tiny red veins arcing through them in a weird echo of the black lighting below the globe. And the world exploded in blazing white and crimson, and then blessed, blessed, darkness.

Being dead was nothing like I'd ever expected. I mean, I didn't anticipate any kind of conscious thought at all— just a deep, never-ending sleep in which awareness didn't enter into the picture. But there was definitely an unaccustomed weight on my chest, something uncomfortable digging into my back, something strangely cool and comforting on my face, and something else that seemed to be trying to pull my head off. So maybe there was a chance that I wasn't dead after all.

With a supreme effort, I opened one eye. Leonard's mismatched green and amber ones hovered over me, beneath a brow furrowed in concern.

"She's back!" he yelled, and the faces of Amber and the rebel brownie joined his, all wearing similar expressions of relief. He finished slipping the not-quite-motorcycle helmet off my head.

"Give the crazy girl some air, would you?" I muttered, trying to wave them back. My right arm wouldn't move at all, but I managed to lift my left one and bat ineffectively at Leonard's shoulder.

The faces pulled back slightly, and Leonard pulled a cool cloth from my cheeks.

"Put that back," I ordered, and he did. I noticed that his injured arm seemed fine now.

"Are you okay?" he asked.

"There's a stone digging into my spine, and my chest feels heavy," I said. I felt too weak to actually raise my head and take an inventory of myself.

"Oops," the rebel brownie said sheepishly, and scampered off my chest and onto Leonard's shoulder.

Leonard slipped a hand under my back and found the offending pebble, flicking it out of the way.

"Much better," I said. "What about you?"

He flexed his arm. "Amber healed it. A little stiff, but it'll be fine."

I wondered if and when the prickly shapeshifter might get around to healing me. Then I had to know. "What about the—"

"Gone," Amber answered with a smirk. "You killed that sucker good, human girl."

A residual tension I hadn't even recognized fled, and my body felt limp enough to sink into the gravelled rooftop, where I'd realized I still lay.

"I'm curious, though," she continued.

"Shhh," Leonard told her, but she ignored him. "How'd you know to use the runes, and say the spell?"

I closed my eyes. "Good question," I admitted. "Sadly, I don't have a good answer. I took a guess. Dumb luck?"

"Or fate?" Leonard suggested. "Not anyone could have done that, you know. It wouldn't have worked if you didn't have...something...unusual, in your blood."

Leonard set the helmet down next to me and I could see that it was blackened and smoking. Runes that hadn't been visible before now glowed eerily on its surface.

Leonard saw me looking at it and nodded. "Probably saved your life," he said. "Once you and the demon were —connected, it was the only thing stopping you from crossing the portal."

I shivered. If the demon had realized that, he could have just wrenched it off my head and—

Rebel brownie piped up and said, "Well, we owe you one. You were the only thing that stopped this from being a major incursion." She patted my arm with a tiny hand.

Amber looked like she was about to argue the point, but closed her mouth without saying anything.

"Yeah, there's usually a reward for saving the world, isn't there?" I joked. I managed to move my right arm where I could see it, bracing myself for the sight of burnt and ruined flesh. It was, however, intact. My tattoos were still there, and there was no evidence that the appendage had come close to combustion just a few moments before.

No, scratch that. The tattoos now held a sheen, a faint glimmer, that they hadn't had before. Almost like an internal glow, as if they'd taken some of that unbearable heat and absorbed it. They were completely healed.

Leonard looked sheepish. "I don't have much to offer," he said, "except maybe...a job? Ever considered flashpoint patrol as a career?"

"I didn't even know there was such a job an hour ago,"

I said, struggling to prop myself up on my elbows. The rest of the brownies huddled beside Amber, watching me and quietly whispering among themselves. The tall brownie still held his equalizer loosely in one hand, glasses pulled low on his nose, watching me over the tops of them. Expectantly. Everyone was waiting to see what I was going to say.

I smiled at Leonard. His mismatched eyes were warm and hopeful. "Hell, that's the most interesting morning I've had at work in a long time," I said. "I'm in."

"Excellent." He grinned, and the others cheered. He reached out to help me up, but I stopped him with a palm.

"As long as someone fixes the photocopier before I leave," I added. "If things don't work out, a girl's got to have good references."

Ghosts and Dark Objects

Cosmic smudges on deep-sky tableaux
ghostly reflections
in spirit photographs
unveiled by our electronic eyes
as infant galaxies
diffuse and secretive

Ancient youngsters swaddled
in faint baryon glow
progeny of shadow particles
embraced by dark-matter nursemaids
phantom ancestors
of worlds yet to be

But slow, slow;
evolution at the brink of the event horizon.

Eons hence,
their dark planet inhabitants
point strange technology eyes back at us
faint dying yellow swirls
smudges
on their image of the universe

Depleted embers
of once-bright star spirals

bereft of essential particles
waste of half the universe
ghostly remains
of galaxies birthed and dying

Too fast, too fast;
evolution at the unforgiving speed of light.

Alien Gifts

Shallie woke, remembered what day it was, kicked off the thin microfiber sheets and rolled out of bed. Through the sleep pod's skylight, a sulky trickle of orange sunlight outlined the silent computer and the metal footlocker holding Shallie's clothes. Those things and the bed just about filled the pod. She flicked on the computer and set the screen to mirror mode so she could scrape her dark hair into a neat topknot. She pulled a clean excursion overall out of the footlocker and slipped it on, practically dancing with anticipation.

Today was the day she'd finally get to meet the aliens.

Her parents had already emerged from their own sleep pod and sat at the tiny table in the middle of the living pod, eating breakfast.

The inflated pod walls undulated slightly, giving under what must be a brisk wind outside on the planet's surface. The place seemed prone to wind and dust storms. They didn't last long, but this part of the planet was covered with such deep dust—regolith, her mother called it—that sometimes the landscape could change dramatically during a storm. Shallie hoped nothing big would blow in today.

"Breakfast is ready," Shallie's father said with a smile, squeezing food paste from three different tubes onto Shallie's plate and adding a few spoonfuls of water. He passed it under the heating lamp and the paste squirmed and reconfigured itself into more solid-looking mounds of nourishment. Some people liked to watch while their meal went through this transformation, but Shallie didn't. The long wriggles of paste reminded her of colorful worms.

It had been a long time since Shallie had actually seen a worm, back home on Earth—a hundred and six years, in fact. Of course, she'd spent a hundred and five of those years in cold sleep, so it really felt like less than a year. Ten months on the ship, two weeks on the planet, preparing. Still, even a year was a long time, and there was something about just *knowing* it had been more than a hundred years, even if she hadn't experienced them, that made it feel indescribably long.

"Is everyone else ready?" she asked her mother, spooning a bite of "waffle" into her mouth. It tasted a little like waffles, Shallie thought, but mostly not.

Shallie's mother didn't look up from her screen— probably reading another report. Sometimes Shallie wondered how there could possibly be so many topics requiring reports, but her mother was the mission leader, so Shallie guessed she had to know about absolutely everything.

"Reports look good," her mother said. "The rest of the team is on track, and word from the Others says they're ready, too."

"Will I be able to talk to any of the kids?" Shallie asked.

Her father chuckled. "I don't know about *talking*," he said, stirring more sugar powder into what he called his almost-coffee.

"None of us are doing more than very basic communicating with the Others yet. But you should have a chance to interact with Other children, yes." He reached out and tweaked her topknot. "That's why we brought you a hundred years from home, right?"

She grinned. "Right." She opened her screen and brought up the rudimentary communication symbols they'd worked out with the Others, even though she was certain she had them memorized. For today, she had to be sure.

Tlik'chik woke, remembered what day it was, detached from the sleeping-mesh and tumbled out of the darknest. She blinked in the orange sunlight pouring in through the bignest's light panels and padded to the wash chamber, where her parents lingered over their morning wash. Joining them in the thin trickle of water, barely enough to wet her feathers, Tlik'chik shivered in the cold as the family preened and washed each other. Then Tlik'chik's father braided her hair and curled it around her head in his own special way, pinning it tightly, while her mother heated foodpods in the warmer. Finally Tlik'chik scooted away from her father's fussing, snatched up a couple of foodpods and took them to the biggest window with a view of the planet's surface. She squirted breakfast into her mouth, barely tasting it.

Today was the day she'd finally get to meet the aliens.

Tlik'chik dialed down the opacity of the light panel so she could look outside without squinting. Even after quite a few cycles on this planet, the orange sun's light always felt a little too bright, a little too strange, and sometimes it made her head ache. She wondered if the aliens found it uncomfortable, too. She'd read all the data about their home planet, so she knew their own sun was even brighter, hotter and yellower than this one. Tlik'chik took another squirt of breakfast and tried to imagine it, but failed. She wondered what the aliens would think of her own planet's sun, its beautiful dark-red glow so much gentler than this one. A strong wind had picked up outside, swirling tall cones of pale dust into the air and sending them dancing around the bignests of the rest of the duty clan.

"Are you ready to meet the aliens?" Tlik'chik's mother chirped, her short fingers flying over the touchscreen, checking the data. The pads on her fingers made soft bumping noises in the quiet bignest.

Tlik'chik turned from the window and threw the empty foodpod into the recycler, dropping the other one into her pocket. Tlik'chik's father was fastening his honor tabs onto the front of his uniform.

She felt a sudden surge of pride that he'd been selected to lead the contact mission.

"Definitely! I want to know what their kids are like. Do you think they'll want to play itri-sticks with me?"

Her mother looked up from the touchscreen and smiled. "It might take a while to teach them how to play, since we don't have much of a common language yet," she said, "But that's why we're here, after all. I think itri-sticks would be a great idea."

Tlik'chik rummaged in her bag of belongings until she found the long box of polished, brightly-colored wooden sticks, and slipped it into her pocket. She might play itri-sticks with an alien! It was going to be an amazing day.

Halfway between the human camp and the alien one, a weirdly-twisting tree thrust gnarled branches toward the planet's greenish sky. The tree bore a full, rustling cover of pale yellow leaves, and beneath its canopy was the spot where the two missions had decided to meet. Until now, they'd communicated only by simple messages, each trying to learn as much as possible about the other side. Shallie had seen a picture of the meeting place, taken by an observation flyer, but she hadn't been there herself— no one had, yet. Secretly, Shallie wondered why they didn't just get together from the beginning—surely it couldn't be any more difficult than learning a new language on Earth, which lots of people did every day.

But, no, her mother said. This was so much more important than just learning a language; the very first meeting with beings from another planet. And although it seemed both sides wanted only friendship, they had to be very careful. If they didn't know enough about the other culture, someone could make a terrible mistake by accident—make a rude gesture without realizing it, or use a word in an offensive way, and then who knew what might happen?

Shallie thought the grown-ups were probably being too

careful—grown-ups often did that—but there wasn't anything she could do about it. She'd made a point of learning everything she could for herself, though. If anyone was going to make a terrible mistake today, it wasn't going to be her.

The pod walls swayed to one side and then snapped upright again. A small hissing, almost like rain but with a harder edge, filled the pod as dust peppered the outside.

"The wind's really picking up out there," her mother said, worry evident in her voice. "I wonder if we should try to postpone the meeting?"

"No!" Shallie almost shouted. She'd been waiting for this moment. "If I have to wait another day to meet the aliens, I think I'll *die!*"

Her father smiled indulgently at her. "I don't think it will be quite that serious," he said. He went to one of the pod windows and peered out. "It's windy, and there's some dust blowing around, but I doubt it's going to get any worse than this. If we wait for a day with no wind, we'll never meet them!"

"Let's see what Tomaso thinks," her mother muttered, and pulled out her communicator. She held a low-voiced conversation with her second-in-command as Shallie gathered up the drawings she'd sketched as a gift for the alien children. They were all scenes of Earth as she remembered it; their house, her school, the park where they liked to camp. Dogs, cats, horses, other earth animals. Flowers, trees, cars and airplanes. Shallie had carefully printed the names of everything at the bottom of the pictures. She hoped they'd like them as she put them carefully into the envelope she'd brought along, and slid some blank pages and coloring sticks into the envelope, too. If she could manage it, she'd ask them to draw her some things from their world.

"Okay, we're going ahead," her mother announced, slipping her communicator back into her pocket. "Inspection outside in ten minutes."

Shallie stood by the door, tapping her foot impatiently as her parents gathered up the things they were taking as meeting-gifts and finally led them outside the pod. Nearby stood three more pods, identical to theirs, where the rest of the mission crew lived. There should have been four, but one family had not come out of the cold sleep when the rest of them had awoken. It had been the other family with a child; all three had died sometime during the voyage, which Shallie thought privately was actually just as well. The deaths hit everyone else in the mission hard, but she thought it would have been worse if only one or two had not awoken. Imagine being the one left? She shook her head. She didn't want to think sad thoughts now. They were actually going to meet the aliens!

The other mission members emerged and drifted toward them, chatting nervously and checking equipment as they walked.

A gust of wind scudded into her, and tiny bits of dust and sand stung her cheeks. The envelope twisted in her hand, almost flying out of her grasp. She blinked, turning away. "Ow!"

Her father was at her side, shielding her from the wind. "Here, walk beside me," he said, and she took his hand as they turned their steps toward the meeting place.

Tlik'chik and her family and the rest of the duty clan arrived at the meeting place just a little ahead of the aliens. She was happy about that—it would be so exciting to watch the aliens come into view, walking on their long, skinny legs. One of the first things both sides had done, long ago when communication had been established, was to exchange pictures so each would know what the others looked like. Tlik'chik had studied them diligently, wondering over the aliens' flat, bare faces, lack of feathers, and long, thin limbs.

They weren't ugly, she'd decided long ago, although some of the duty clan thought they were. They were just different in an interesting way. She liked that they had hair on their heads, like her people did. It made them a little less strange.

Tlik'chik's mother leaned close. "Are you excited? Not

frightened, are you?"

Tlik'chik held up three fingers and shook them, *no*. "Of course I'm not afraid! This is the most exciting thing ever!"

Her mother smiled and rested a hand on her shoulder for a moment. "Good girl."

The wind whistled and snapped the leaves of the tree over their heads, whipping even taller cones of dancing dust to life. Tlik'chik reluctantly closed her inner eyelid to protect her vision, hating the way it made the scene before her a little unfocused. Still, she'd see even less with her eyes full of dust.

And here they came!

The aliens crested the top of a low rise, all dressed in similar, one-piece clothing of different colors. They did not seem to march in any ceremonial way but formed a loose group. One smaller alien detached itself from a taller one as they came into view. Tlik'chik thought the shorter one must be the alien child—there was only one among them, just as she was the only one in her duty clan.

She fingered the itri-sticks in her tunic pocket nervously, her mouth suddenly gone dry. She hoped the alien child wouldn't think they were stupid.

As the aliens grew closer, Tlik'chik was relieved to see they weren't all *that* much taller than her people. Her father stepped forward and held up a hand in the traditional greeting.

One of the alien females—Tlik'chik knew how to distinguish them, from the pictures—stepped forward and mimicked the gesture, then made one of her own, holding out her hand for Tlik'chik's father to grasp. Although both sides had prepared the other for what would happen, Tlik'chik felt as if all her feathers were sticking straight out from her body. They touched! They clasped hands! For the first time, two entirely different peoples had come together. Tlik'chik grinned widely and hugged herself.

The leaders began a laborious process of communicating their prepared messages, and Tlik'chik quickly lost interest in what the adults were saying. Her eyes sought and found the alien child—a girl, she realized —who had her eyes fixed on Tlik'chik. The alien girl smiled and pointed to a thin packet she held, then pointed to Tlik'chik.

This is for you, Tlik'chik understood the gesture to mean.

Her heart felt like a stone in her chest. She hadn't brought a gift for the alien girl! Her hand went automatically to her pocket, and she realized, over a tiny pang of regret, that it would be all right. She'd give her the itri-sticks, not just teach her to play the game! Her father would understand, and he'd help her make a new set.

Tlik'chik glanced at her father and the other adults— they were entirely engrossed with the aliens, just as the alien adults seemed to be with them. The initial greetings were over, and the two groups moved closer together, exchanging ceremonial items and trying out their halting knowledge of each other's language. Tlik'chik looked back to the alien girl, who jerked her head to the side. *Let's go over there,* she seemed to be saying. Tlik'chik inclined her head forward, which she'd learned, for the aliens, meant *agreement* or *yes.*

Together they sidled away from the adults, unnoticed, and stopped under another nearby tree, shorter and less impressive but still whipped by the wind. The alien girl had small eyes, the color of bingi flowers. She stood about a head taller than Tlik'chik. She tapped herself on the chest and said, "Shallie."

This wasn't a word in the agreed-upon communication exchange, so Tlik'chik thought it must be the girl's name. She tapped herself likewise and said, "Tlik'chik."

The other girl's eyes opened wider and she tried it out. It didn't sound quite right, but close enough, Tlik'chik decided. She inclined her head again and then tried out the girl's name. It didn't sound right to her own ears, but Shallie smiled, so it must have been acceptable.

The tree above them shuddered in a huge gust of wind, its dark-leaved branches creaking. Shallie squealed and put her arms up to cover her head against the harsh peppering of dust the wind lashed into them. When she did, the thin packet whipped out of her fingers and sailed away from them on the gale.

Instinctively, Tlik'chik jumped to catch the packet, and she felt the wind sweep her up and away.

Shallie flailed her arms after the envelope, trying to catch it, even though she knew it was already too far away. She felt a burst of hope when the alien girl leapt for it—but hope quickly turned to fear as she saw the rising wind sweep Tlik'chik off her feet and carry her away.

They must have very light bones, like birds, Shallie heard the scientific side of her mind think. Then after only a brief, startled moment, she ran after the helpless alien. The wind had knocked Tlik'chik down and was tumbling her over the ground like a discarded toy. Even as Shallie ran, the wind whipped and tugged at her coverall with frenzied strength. They hadn't seen a windstorm this strong since they'd been on the planet, and none had blown in so quickly. A gust pounded against her back and almost sent her stumbling, just as Tlik'chik squealed and coughed, clutching at the ground in an effort to halt her momentum. The alien girl rolled through the swirling dust a couple of times—

—and disappeared.

"No!" Shallie gasped, almost choking on the dust-filled air. Behind her, she heard faint shouts. She glanced over her shoulder and gasped. A towering red-grey wall of wind-whipped dust bore down on her parents and the others. It looked like a monster, tumbling and swirling, about to swallow them up. She saw her mother, hands cupped around her mouth to call after Shallie, disappear into the dust-monster.

Shocked and stumbling, Shallie sensed the drop-off before she saw it. But not in time to stop her feet from pounding over the edge into nothingness...

It seemed a long time later when Shallie opened her eyes to dim, filtered light. Reddish-grey dust danced and drifted in the sparse beams. She pushed herself to a sitting position, wincing at the pain in her shoulder and hip. She coughed reflexively, feeling half-choked on the dust.

"Oh!" said a voice nearby, and Shallie startled at the dark, hunched shape to her left. She tried to scramble to her feet but fell sideways, her head spinning.

"Tlik'chik! Tlik'chik!" the voice said, and the alien crept over to her, putting one small hand gently on her arm. "Shallie?"

Shallie could have cried with relief. She nodded and patted the alien girl's hand. "I'm okay, I think," she said, then realized the girl probably didn't understand. She met Tlik'chik's eyes and smiled and nodded, patting her own chest. "Okay."

Tlik'chik held up a finger and flicked it up and down, which Shallie knew meant *yes* for the aliens. Then Tlik'chik held out Shallie's envelope, now slightly crinkled and smudged with dust. "Okay!" she said, beaming.

Shallie took it. It must have blown over the same drop-off she and Tlik'chik had tumbled into, and the alien girl had found it. Carefully, slowly, Shallie stood up and looked around. This seemed to be a natural cavern, but the light came from a long way above them. It looked like hundreds of dust storms had drifted piles of soft sand and dust into the pit, so neither of them had been seriously injured in the fall.

Unfortunately, the mounds of dust didn't reach nearly high enough for them to be able to climb out.

They stared up at the opening. The distant roar of the wind and the dust still sifting down through the air told them the storm continued to rage on the planet's surface, even though the cavern lay quiet and still. Shallie wasn't sure how far she'd run before she fell into the pit. Would their parents be able to find any trace of their footprints? Or even tell which way they'd gone? How bad would the storm become? It had descended so fast and fiercely—she imagined their tents being torn to shreds. She pulled her mind quickly away from that thought.

Tlik'chik tapped her on the arm, and when Shallie

turned to her, the alien girl motioned a thin limb around them. She said something Shallie didn't understand, but she thought she knew what the girl was saying. They should look around the cavern, see if there was another way out, or anything to help them. Shallie nodded and pointed to the left.

"I'll look over here."

Tlik'chik nodded and pointed to the right. They moved in opposite directions, stepping carefully in the faint illumination from above.

It didn't take long. The cavern was probably thirty feet long and a bit wider, starting from the end where they'd fallen in. A few fist-sized rocks were scattered randomly on the floor, along with a rare dead tree branch or two and a few odd tangles of twigs that reminded Shallie of tumbleweeds. She and Tlik'chik met at the far end of the cavern, where a narrow opening in the stone suggested a dark passageway beyond. The girls looked at it together. It wasn't wide enough for either girl to fit through. Without speaking, both turned and walked back to the slightly brighter end of the cavern. They didn't need words to understand there was no way out.

Shallie sat on the floor with her back against a wall of cool stone. Tlik'chik joined her. Shallie passed the envelope to the alien girl. "This was for you, anyway," she said. "You might as well have it."

Although it was obviously a struggle, Tlik'chik forced a smile as she accepted the envelope. Then she dug into a pocket in her tunic and pulled out a long, narrow box. She handed it to Shallie, gesturing for her to open it. Inside lay what looked like a handful of chopsticks tied into a bundle with a silky red cord.

"*Itri*," Tlik'chik said. "*Wol-ken*. Shallie."

Shallie accepted the sticks and examined them. Although they were polished smooth like chopsticks, they varied in lengths and had different colors painted on each end. They were very pretty, but she had no idea what they were for. She smiled at Tlik'chik anyway. "Thank you! I love them."

Tlik'chik set her envelope down on the dusty floor of

the cavern and motioned for Shallie to put the sticks down on it. When Shallie did, the alien girl untied the cord and proceeded to lay out the sticks in a complicated pattern, chattering to herself a little as she did so. Shallie didn't understand a word, but she concentrated on the lilting sound of the girl's voice anyway. It was better than worrying about the howl of the wind far above them outside.

Although she knew the alien girl couldn't understand the instructions for playing itri-sticks, Tlik'chik kept talking to distract herself from their predicament. And once the sticks were laid out, it wasn't too difficult to explain the game through gestures and examples. Shallie seemed to catch on quickly, apparently intrigued by the intricacies of color-matching and strategic placement that made itri-sticks both complex and fun.

As they played, they taught each other the names of the colors. *Do-ta* was *red*, *chok* was *yellow*, *bek-ta* was *blue*. Tlik'chik knew there was no way she would remember all the alien words, but she was determined to learn them at least as well as the other girl learned the names unfamiliar to her. Tlik'chik won the first three games, but clapped her hands in surprise and delight when Shallie won the fourth.

Shallie smiled and gathered the sticks together, binding them carefully with the cord. "Thang-gue," she said, but Tlik'chik didn't know the word. Hoping it would be all right, she smiled back and nodded. She picked up the packet Shallie had given her earlier and looked at the alien girl with a question. Perhaps she'd show Tlik'chik what was inside now. As Shallie nodded and took back the packet, Tlik'chik couldn't stop herself from glancing up toward the opening high above them. Dust still drifted in, dancing and whirling madly as it rode the air currents down into the cavern that had become their prison.

Shallie showed the alien girl the opening in one end of the

envelope and Tlik'chik slid the papers out. Even in the dim light, bright colors lit up the pages. Tlik'chik's smile spread as she examined Shallie's drawings.

"Here's a dog," Shallie said, pointing. "We keep them as pets, sometimes. Cats, too, like this one. *Cat*," she said, tapping the picture.

"Cat," Tlik'chik repeated.

"House," Shallie went on. "It's where we live. We go inside," she told the alien girl, pointing to some people she'd drawn and walking her fingers over to the house.

"Inside!" Tlik'chik agreed with obvious delight.

Shallie handed her one of the drawing sticks she'd included in the envelope. "You draw one," she urged.

Tlik'chik frowned, then took the drawing stick and turned one of the sheets of paper to the blank back. With quick, sure strokes, she sketched an odd-looking tree with a round sort of hut nestled in its branches. On the ground she drew what might have been herself. She tapped the figure and then the hut. "Inside! *Tou'lach*."

"Tou'lach," Shallie said, wondering if it was the word for "inside" or "house." Mentally she shook her head. It didn't matter. As long as she and Tlik'chik could distract themselves with the pictures, the way they'd done with the stick game, at least they weren't panicking.

But she couldn't help thinking the bellow of the wind above their heads sounded even louder. She strained to hear her parents' voices calling for her, but they just weren't there.

They went back to the pictures. "Present," Shallie said, tapping a wrapped gift she'd drawn with a birthday cake. She tapped the envelope and the papers, and then Tlik'chik's arm. "Present. For Tlik'chik."

The alien girl's face lit up. "Present," she repeated. "*Wol-ken*. For Shallie!" She pointed to the sticks they'd played with, and then tapped Shallie's arm. They really did seem to be making progress.

Shallie smiled back at her, but as Tlik'chik bent over the next page, she saw the alien girl dart a quick, concerned look up. Listening for her own parents' calls, Shallie wondered? Far overhead, the wind continued to howl like an angry beast.

Tlik'chik was worried. Even though she was enjoying this little game of language with Shallie, the sounds of the storm far above them continued to rage. The scouring wind would have erased their tracks almost instantly, and the swirling dust would make it impossible to see. Had anyone even noticed which way they'd gone?

By the time they'd looked at all the pictures and Tlik'chik had drawn more for Shallie, they'd both learned a few new words. But what would they do next? Go back to itri-sticks? Tlik'chik felt her stomach grumble, and she remembered the foodpod in her pocket, left over from breakfast. Glad of the distraction, she pulled it out and opened it, then offered it to Shallie.

The alien girl looked uncertain. Tlik'chik squirted some of the smooth paste into her own mouth, then held it out to Shallie again. Hesitantly, Shallie took it and dabbed a tiny amount onto one finger, then tasted it. Her eyes watered and she blinked, passing the foodpod back to Tlik'chik. Shallie smiled slightly and held up three fingers, shaking them *no*.

Despite her hunger, Tlik'chik slipped the foodpod back into her pocket. If Shallie couldn't eat, she didn't want to, either. At least not yet. But now she felt the chill that had descended on the cavern without her noticing, and she realized food was not the most urgent of their problems. Beside her, Shallie shivered. And the light from above had dimmed even further. It was almost gone. Tlik'chik imagined the planet's short day drawing to a close, the bright orange sun fading. The cavern would soon be dark, and cold. Maybe very cold. They needed to think about the coming night.

Taking up one of the drawing sticks, Tlik'chik sketched a fire on the back of one of the pages. Surely Shallie would recognize it?

Shallie nodded at the drawing and glanced around the cavern. She crawled forward from where they'd been sitting, and came back with one of the dead tree parts littering the floor. Tlik'chik nodded, and together they scoured the cavern for things that might burn. This time they didn't separate but by unspoken agreement stayed close to one another.

The pile they assembled was woefully small. Tlik'chik squeezed one of the branches between her fingers and thought it felt damp. Would it even burn? And if it did, what they'd gathered would be consumed quickly. It might provide a bit of heat and light, but not much.

Shallie must have been thinking the same thing. Above the pile, she held two stones she'd picked up and struck them quickly together. No spark. Tlik'chik could barely make out the alien girl's face in the smudge of light left to them. She looked grim but determined.

The next attempt brought a spark, but the twigs didn't ignite. A second spark landed on the twigs and a tendril of smoke wisped up for an instant, but disappeared as the spark went out.

Tlik'chik looked around again, although they'd been over every bit of the cavern. Then she saw the envelope. It, and the papers inside it, would burn—but how could she suggest sacrificing the other girl's gift? If Shallie was angry at the idea, it could cause a rift between their people before they'd even started to get to know each other.

Of course, it would only become a problem if they were ever found.

Shallie blinked back tears of frustration. They needed to get this fire going, to give them some warmth and light. She was almost afraid to hope, but it sounded like the storm on the planet's surface might be quieting down. Maybe their parents and the others would be able to begin searching for them, even though she knew the day must be almost over.

She saw Tlik'chik's eyes land on the envelope of papers and knew immediately what the other girl must be thinking. They would burn. But could she suggest burning them? Shallie caught her eyes and nodded. "It's okay," she said, holding up a finger and flicking it the way Tlik'chik had done to mean *yes*. "I'll draw you some more."

Kneeling, Tlik'chik slowly pulled the drawings from the envelope and crumpled them up almost reverently, as if performing a ritual. She placed the crumpled balls of paper under and around the twigs. It still looked like it would make only a brief, sad, fire.

The itri sticks bumped in Shallie's pocket as she leaned forward to strike the rocks again. *Wood*. They were wood, too! Shallie's hand moved toward her pocket but stopped. They were so beautiful, and such an elegant gift! Could she possibly suggest burning them?

But Tlik'chik seemed to have realized Shallie's thoughts, as well. She nodded. "O-kay," she said carefully, and pointed to the pile of paper and twigs. "Okay, Shallie."

Shallie passed Tlik'chik the itri-sticks, and again, with careful precision, the alien girl added the sticks to the pile. She met Shallie's eyes and nodded. Shallie struck the rocks together. Nothing. Again. Spark. Again. *Spark*.

Tlik'chik leaned over and gently blew on the sparks. One went out, but one flared and caught the paper it had landed on. The edges curled and blackened as a growing flame licked across Tlik'chik's picture of a fire. Smoke curled up from the end of an itri-stick as flames flickered around it.

Shallie set down the rocks she'd used to make the sparks, and scooted around the fire, close to Tlik'chik. As more and more of their tinder caught and smoke rose toward the hole far above them, Shallie felt the alien girl put an arm around her shoulders.

"Okay," Tlik'chik said.

Shallie nodded as the fire pushed back the cavern's chill.

"Okay," she agreed. "We'll be okay."

She hoped they were right.

Tlik'chik dreamed she heard her father calling her name.

He seemed to be far away, and as so often happens in dreams, she couldn't open her mouth to answer him. Other voices joined her father's, some strange and speaking a language she didn't understand. But she did recognize one word. Shallie.

She jolted awake just as Shallie did the same. They'd fallen asleep with their backs against the cavern wall, arms around each other to preserve the warmth their fire had lent them. It had burned down to embers now, but tendrils of smoke still wafted up toward the sky, escaping into the sunlight. The cavern had lightened again, and the dust had stopped falling; the opening high above them was a bright hole in the darkness. The roar of the storm was gone. There were only the voices.

Beside her, Shallie jumped to her feet, shouting up to the hole. Tlik'chik joined her.

"Here! We're down here!" she called. Tlik'chik knew Shallie was yelling the same thing in her own language.

Shadows appeared at the opening.

"Tlik'chik! Are you all right?"

"Yes! We're fine!"

"Shallie!"

"We're here!"

"We're lowering a rope for you!"

A rope snaked down from above. Shallie turned to Tlik'chik with bright eyes. "Okay!" she said, pointing to the smoke rising from the embers. "We did it!"

Tlik'chik nodded. The searchers must have seen the smoke rising from the hole and knew where to find them, even though the massive storm would have erased all traces of their footprints. She saw Shallie glance down at the remains of the fire, and their gifts to each other. She looked up and caught Tlik'chik's eye, smiling sadly.

"Itri-sticks," she said. "I liked."

Tlik'chik nodded. "Draw-ings," she said. "Shallie make more?"

Shallie agreed with a smile and threw her arms around Tlik'chik in a tight hug. Tlik'chik hugged her back and smiled. The real gift was still right there.

Addicted to Love

The first time Frank Garret sat down in the blue leather chair on the opposite side of my desk, I didn't know he was dead. My cousin Oliver didn't seem to pick up on it either, when he showed Frank in from reception. My new client wasn't looking great, mind you; he was obviously a man who'd been through some stuff. But he seemed as solid and well, alive as any other client I'd ever had.

Hell, more alive than some. And I didn't notice anything strange when we shook hands, except that his grip was cool and firm.

Oliver left us reluctantly, as usual—he hadn't quite grasped the concept of "assistant" as opposed to "partner" yet—and the client didn't waste any time.

"I need you to find my wife," he said, leaning forward with his elbows on his knees, hands twisting a battered Jays ball cap nervously.

I thought, another divorce case, here we come, but I didn't say it. Before I could say anything, in fact, he held up a hand.

"I know what you're thinking, Miss Sheridan, but it's not like that. She doesn't even know I'm looking for her. And I promise you that she hasn't run away from me." He paused and glanced out the window, although there was not much to see on the other side but a dingy back alley. "Not deliberately, anyway."

The guy wasn't making a whole lot of sense, but I

decided to hear him out. I didn't have much on the go, and these days I could track down a "missing" person in twenty-four hours or less if they'd used a credit card or checked into social media.

"Would you like a cup of coffee, Mr. Garret? Tea? Oliver will be happy to bring it." Oliver would fume to me afterwards that he wasn't the maid, but the clients don't need to know that.

He shook his head. "Call me Frank. I'd love one, but it's not possible. And I don't have much time."

"All right, we'll get to business, then. And please, call me Acacia." I pulled my notebook out of the drawer and wrote his name at the top of a blank page. "Your wife's name?"

"Ellie Garret. E.P. Wyse-Garret," he added. "The writer."

I felt my eyebrows lift slightly in surprise. E.P. Wyse-Garret was the acclaimed author of the Frankie and Ellie mysteries, featuring a wise-cracking and lovable pair of middle-aged sleuths based loosely on herself and her husband. Something tickled the back of my brain. She'd been in the news a few weeks ago, but I couldn't remember why. I'd been in the middle of the Medstrom case without a lot of attention to spare for local celebrity news.

"How long has she been missing?" Funny there'd been nothing on the newsfeeds about her disappearance.

"A month now," he said, misery twisting his features as he continued to mash the hat. "But look, you gotta understand, no-one else thinks she's missing. It's only me who can't find her."

I squinted. "So, she's on vacation? Or a writer's retreat or something?" I cudgeled my brain. What had that news item been?

He shook his head. "I don't know. She's not home, hasn't been there since just after—well, about a month. I don't have any way to contact her, but I need to. She needs me to. She just doesn't know it. And I don't have much time!"

His voice rose to a despairing wail and I stared at him,

trying to get that news story back from my recalcitrant memory. And then the right mental file drawer opened. Weeks ago, Ellie Garret's husband Frank, inspiration for the beloved sleuth Frankie Pasquale, had been killed in a car accident.

He must have seen the penny drop behind my eyes, because his shoulders slumped even further. He seemed to...shimmer...a little, and for a second the chair back wavered into view behind him. "Yeah," he said, "I'm dead. And the Frankie and Ellie series will be dead, too, if I can't find Ellie. And you're my only hope."

I don't take on many ghosts for clients. Most of them are too caught up in the whole clanking chains and walking through walls schtick, even the ones who'd like you to find out who murdered them or whatever. It gets tiresome, and my job should never be tiresome. Olympia Investigations offers somewhat niche services to non-humans, along with our more mundane clients. I'd named my detective agency after my (100% mortal, as far as I knew) maternal grandmother, since the family quirk was generally acknowledged to have started with her. Whatever the provenance, my mother and her siblings, and now their children, are able to see, communicate, and interact with all manner of beings, many of whom slide under or past the radar of most humans. Ghosts, vampires, werewolves, demons, fae...these make up a lot of my clientele.

Which is why my cousin Oliver was a decent choice when I decided I needed an assistant. He's arrogant, bossy, and wants to be a full partner even though he doesn't even have a PI license, but he has the requisite sense—sixth, seventh, who knows?— to deal with any client without freaking out.

But ghosts are rare, and ghosts who can appear normal enough to fool me into thinking they aren't dead are really rare. I was intrigued. First things first, though.

"All right, Frank, I do have to get this out of the way first. If you're a ghost, how do you propose to pay me?"

He nodded. "Thought about that. I feel certain Ellie will take care of it, but if she doesn't, I can direct you to a couple of places where you'll find items of sufficient value to cover the fees."

I frowned. "Items?"

"I lost a gold ring at the back of our garden once, digging flower beds for Ellie. Never could find the thing, and was Ellie upset—she'd given it to me. Now—I can see it plain as day. You could retrieve that and sell it." He shrugged diffidently. "There are a few things like that."

The possibilities of ghosts as lost item finders had never come up before. Interesting, but I shelved it for now. "All right, we can work with that. Tell me about your wife's disappearance."

He closed his eyes and wavered for a moment. "After— the funeral, she announced that she wouldn't write any more Frankie and Ellie books. I thought that was a terrible shame—and worse, those books are her livelihood! If she keeps writing them, I'm sure she can live comfortably off the royalties for the rest of her life. I could go in peace if I knew she'd be okay."

I nodded to encourage him.

Frank drew a deep breath. Or appeared to. Maybe it was just a habit. "I wanted to tell her not to be so foolish, to go on writing them. At first I didn't know why any part of me was still hanging around. Why I couldn't just go on to whatever's next. Then I thought it must be to give her that message. And—I couldn't bear to leave her. When I stayed close to her, I felt better. Stronger. Like maybe if I stayed close enough, long enough, I'd be able to, well, manifest. Talk to her." He got up from the blue leather chair and paced my small office. Looking closely, I could tell that his feet didn't really touch the worn brown carpet, but hovered an inch above it.

He stopped behind the chair and put his hands on the back, one still clutching the Jays cap. "It was like...like a physical hit, when I was near her. Like I was addicted to my wife." Frank chuckled nervously. "Sounds weird, I know."

I shook my head and smiled. "Not weird. Sweet. So did

you do it? Appear to her?"

His face sagged. "I did, finally. A couple weeks after the funeral I felt like I was strong enough. I didn't want to be some see-through horror and frighten her. I wanted this." He gestured to his surprisingly solid-looking body. "I waited until she was alone, and I put all my effort into manifesting."

I could guess what was coming next. "It didn't go well?"

He shook his head. "She thought she was hallucinating, going crazy—I don't know what. I tried to calm her down, tell her why I was there, but she wouldn't listen. Ran out of the house crying, and drove off somewhere. I didn't have the strength to follow her, didn't know where she'd gone." He circled to the front of the chair and sat down again. "Then three days later, she came back with her sister. Ellie packed some stuff, they left, and I haven't felt strong enough to go hunting for her." Tears seemed to glisten in his eyes, and I wondered what would happen if they spilled over. Would they leave little ectoplasmic droplets on the carpet?

Frank sighed. "All my energy went into that meeting, and when it went south, it drained me. I've been hanging around our house, getting as close as I can to her things since then, building up the energy to appear to someone else. It takes a lot longer when she's not there physically. The energy for me to...er, feed on, is weaker. I didn't go to her sister, or her agent, or her editor, because I'm afraid it'll go down the same and I won't be able to come back from it again. If I could even build up enough energy to do all that. I need someone who can do it for me." He looked at me very steadily from blue eyes that, at the moment, didn't look ghostly at all. Just sad. "Will you do it for me? Will you find my Ellie?"

The dust in my office must have been particularly bad that morning. I had to blink my own eyes a couple of times to clear them. "Frank," I said sincerely, "I'll give it a try."

"Just let me come along. I can help! I haven't been out in the field in weeks!"

Oliver stood blocking my exit from the office, arms crossed over his chest and a delicate frown darkening his brow. Frank had...left, not by the front door but by unceremoniously dissipating to—somewhere. I'd told Oliver that I was going out to check out the house where Frank and Ellie had lived, and that's when he'd leapt elegantly in front of the door and made his demands.

I protested automatically. Oliver and I have always had a prickly relationship, even when we were kids, and it's followed us into adulthood. My mother says we're too much alike, at which observation I usually roll my eyes and abandon the conversation. "Who's going to watch the office, answer the phone, if we both leave? I hate to break it to you, but that's sort of your job, you know?"

Oliver closed his eyes momentarily, as if to ask some higher power for strength. "You said I'd have a chance to learn the job from an investigator's point of view," he reminded me. "That it wouldn't be all office work. We're supposed to be a team. And we can forward the office phone to my cell."

I sighed. "Oh, all right." I suppose I had said the team thing when I hired him. And a second pair of eyes might come in handy at the house.

Oliver grabbed his windbreaker from the hook behind the door and slipped it on with a grin. "Excellent. I'll even spring for coffee on the way."

Frank had told me where I could find the spare key to the house he and Ellie had shared, and on the way I filled Oliver in on the parameters of the case. The neighborhood was middle-class tidy, with well-groomed yards fronting homes that ranged from new to fifty or sixty years old, but well-maintained. I parked on the street a few houses away from the address Frank had given me, and Oliver and I walked casually up the drive and around to the back of the two-story saltbox, sipping our takeout coffees and chatting as we walked. I found the key just where Frankie had said, taped inside one of the hollow tubes of a set of wind chimes by the back door. We slipped in, and I felt pretty sure no-one had taken particular notice of us.

The porch featured windows covered with rattan blinds, lush greenery, a couple of wicker chairs, and a small closet. It led into a kitchen with clean, white-painted cupboard doors and red brick accents; homey, cozy, and cared-for, but chill now with the extended absence of its inhabitants. Ellie and her sister must have tidied up before she'd left—it didn't have the air of a hasty exit. I opened the fridge and found it empty of pretty much anything but long-lasting condiments. Oliver stood in the middle of the room, sipping coffee and observing. A wall phone hung nearby, but the notepad on the counter beneath it was blank. I pulled a pencil from my bag and rubbed the side of the lead lightly over the surface of the top page, revealing a jumble of marks from notes written on previous sheets. Nothing was particularly legible or seemed important. I hit the phone's redial button, but the number that appeared on the screen matched the one Frank had given me for Ellie's sister.

In the dining room, the light from the large windows tinted slightly green as it passed through the plants lining the windowsill and suspended from plant hangars. They looked healthy enough, so someone must be watering them. The sister? In the living room, a book lay on the sofa. A paper protruded slightly from near the back cover, so I crossed the room and picked it up. The book was a mystery by another well-known author. The paper turned out to be a brochure from a local real estate agent. I raised an eyebrow and showed it to Oliver.

"You think she wants to sell?"

I shrugged. "Could be. Maybe too many memories here." I pocketed the paper and returned the book to the sofa. Dust lay thick on the coffee table, another testament to the house's deserted state.

As I turned to leave, a shimmer distorted the air near the doorway, and Frank appeared between me and Oliver. A little less solid-looking than he'd been in my office, but he smiled thinly.

"You found your way in."

I returned the smile. "No problems. I hope you don't mind that I brought Oliver along to help me out."

"Not at all." Frank gave Oliver a nod and a smile.

"Nice house," Oliver said.

Frank nodded and the smile faded. "Sure is," he agreed. "I miss it already, and I'm still here, sort of."

"Well, I haven't found much yet," I told him, hoping to distract him from that line of thought. "There was a real estate brochure in a book in the living room. Think Ellie's planning to move?"

Frank shook his head. "We were looking at cottage properties before..."

"Ah, okay." So that was a dead end, so to speak. "I'm just heading down the hall."

"I'll walk with you," he said. "Just along here is Ellie's office."

I stood for a moment, studying the room. This one might warrant a more careful search. It was a bright, cheery space, with plants crowding the windowsills and a hand-hooked rug covering most of the laminate floor. Two of the walls held floor-to-ceiling bookshelves. Oliver ran his finger along the spines on one shelf, while I inspected her desk. A stack of colorful sticky notes contained jottings and scribbles that I assumed related to story ideas—at any rate, nothing looked like travel plans.

"Can I check the computer?" I asked Frank.

He shrugged. "Sure, I guess."

I sat down in the padded leather desk chair and booted up the machine, looking the question at Frank when the screen paused, asking for a password.

"FridayNightCoffee," he said with a sad smile. "It was a little joke between us. We never went to bed early on weekends, so we could drink coffee as late as we wanted on Friday nights."

I typed in the phrase and the machine completed its startup routine. By the time it finished, Oliver had come to look over my shoulder. I clicked open the files list and groaned. It would take a month to look though this many files, hoping to stumble upon something useful. I glanced over some recent documents, but they seemed to also pertain to her writing, or research she'd been doing for the current book. Nothing helpfully labelled "travel plans" or "itinerary," so that was a dead end. A laptop desk leaned against the wall, but I didn't see a laptop—presumably she'd taken it with her, wherever she was. Eventually I shook my head.

"Nothing I can see here."

"Were you upstairs yet?" Frank didn't sound too hopeful, but he looked a little more solid now. Maybe talking about Ellie, and being in her space, helped him, too.

I shook my head and shut the computer down. We climbed the stairs to the second floor, Oliver trailing behind us, unusually quiet.

Frank led me into the master bedroom. On one side of the bed, a pile of books had been haphazardly stacked in a basket that was too small for the task it had been set. I checked the closet and drawers. All of Frank's clothes still seemed to be in the closet. Ellie must not have had the heart to deal with them yet.

The second bedroom had been used for storage. I popped the lid on a large storage container marked "summer clothes" and found it full to the top with women's wear.

"I guess it's safe to assume she hasn't taken off for warmer climates to the south," I said, snapping the lid closed again.

"That doesn't narrow things down much," Frank observed in a glum tone.

"No, but it's something."

I glanced around the bathroom, but nothing seemed out of the ordinary or appeared to be a clue.

"That's it for the house, with the exception of the basement," he said, leaning against the bathroom door jamb and crossing his arms over his chest. "You want to go down there?"

"Think there's any use?"

He shook his head. "I doubt it. Ellie never really liked to go down there anyway."

"Okay then. Best to make our escape before any nosy

neighbors come to investigate." We went back down the stairs, the silence of the house pressing around us. In the back porch I turned to him. "You want to come with me?" I don't know why I asked, but it seemed like the polite thing to do.

Frank shook his head. "I'm feeling pretty...thin," he said. He looked it, too. "Think I'll hang around here, try to build up a little more energy."

"All right. Check in with me when you can."

Five minutes later Oliver and I were back in my car and driving out of the neighbourhood. I drummed my fingers on the steering wheel as I pondered my next move. I was going to have to look further to find out where Ellie had gone to ground.

"Well, that was depressing," Oliver observed, looking out the side window.

"I know."

"I hate that Frank's dead. It doesn't seem fair."

I sighed but didn't argue the point. "I'm going to try Ellie's sister next," I said. "I'll drop you back at the office. I want you to try and get appointments for me with Ellie's agent, and her editor."

"You think they'll see you? What will I say it's about?"

I pondered. "Just tell them I'm trying to locate her in relation to a case I'm working on," I said finally. "That's all you know. If they'll see me, I'll figure out what to tell them."

"All right." Oliver tipped his coffee cup up to catch the last dregs, although they'd be cold and unpleasant by now. "I'll actually be glad to get back to the office."

A little shiver prickled goosebumps down my arms, thinking of the lonely house and its sole ghostly occupant. "I hear you," I said. "Let's get back to the land of the living for a while."

Ellie's sister, Charlotte MacLaren, lived in a small white bungalow perched in a yard given over almost entirely to flower beds. One narrow walkway led from the sidewalk to the front porch, edged by lush borders of delphiniums and lavender. Three shallow steps led up to the porch, which had been invitingly decorated with wicker chairs and a comfortable-looking swing seat suspended from the sloping roof overhead. I climbed up, resisting the urge to try out the swing, and knocked politely on the cheery yellow door.

I heard footsteps inside. Then came a pause during which I was probably surveyed through the peephole, and then the door opened. A diminutive woman with grey-streaked hair and a clutch of laugh lines bracketing her brown eyes regarded me with a slightly puzzled air. She was perhaps in her fifties and wore trendy jeans and a flower-print t-shirt.

"Can I help you?"

I showed her my PI's license, giving her a chance to get a good look. "I'm looking for Ellie," I said, and quickly put up a hand to forestall any protest as a frown began to shadow her face. "I know, it's a terrible time for her, but I'm not looking to intrude. I have a very important message that I'm trying to get to her, that's all."

The frown softened a little. "I can give her any message you have."

"So you do know where she is?"

She ran a hand down the side of her jeans and quirked a half-smile at me. "I'm her sister, of course I know where she is. That doesn't mean I'm going to tell you."

I smiled as engagingly as I could. "No matter how important I tell you it is? I really have to deliver it in person."

Charlotte shook her head a little and sighed. "She doesn't want to see anyone—not even me, truth be told. I have to respect that." She motioned me to take a seat in the swing and came out onto the porch, closing the door behind her. She didn't sit, but leaned back against the porch railing, crossing her arms. "Can you tell me what it's about?"

I sat on the swing and it swayed under my weight. It would have been lovely to curl up on the cushions and let the breeze push it into gentle motion. I wondered how many times Ellie and Frank had sat here when visiting.

I pulled a deep breath. "The message is from Frank, Charlotte."

Her face pinked and the frown came back. "Frank's dead. He left something before he died?"

"I can't really go into the details," I said carefully. "But please believe me, Ellie would want to get this message. I wouldn't be involved in anything I thought would make things worse for her."

She shook her head. "Things can't get any worse. But it's not like Frank knew he was...knew that anything was going to happen. How could he leave a message?"

"I'm sure Ellie will explain it to you after I've talked to her," I said.

Charlotte looked past me. I wasn't sure if she was trying to see inside the window of her house or just didn't want to meet my eyes while she thought it over. Finally she shook her head again.

"I can't tell you." She held up a hand just as I'd done to her, to stop my protest. "But I'll ask Ellie if I can tell you," she said. "That's the best I can do."

I could tell from the hint of steel in her voice that I wasn't going to get any further with her. Charlotte reminded me a little of a teacher I'd had once, and with her, no amount of wheedling would budge a decision. I stood up and offered her one of my cards, then held out my hand. "I appreciate that," I said, "and Ellie will, too. Please speak to her as soon as you can, all right? There's a certain amount of urgency."

She took my hand, and her clasp was firm and warm. "I'll talk to her. That's all I can promise you."

Back at the office, Oliver reported that the editor had agreed to see me, but not until next week. He hadn't caught up with the agent yet. Next week might be too late to do Frankie any good, but maybe Charlotte would come through for me before that.

Frankie showed up briefly at my office before I headed home for the day. He wasn't looking so good. I mean, yes, he was dead, but aside from that. This time, there was no way I would have been fooled into thinking he was a normal human.

"You're not drawing as much energy from the house anymore," I guessed, eyeing him speculatively.

He shook his semi-transparent head. "Ellie's been away too long. Her power is fading," he said. "I'm worried. I don't know what will happen to me if I just evaporate without getting to talk to her. It feels so important."

"Well," I said, "I talked to Charlotte today, and she's going to talk to Ellie. So things are looking up!" Frank looked so dejected I had to stay positive.

He stood from the blue leather chair and walked to the window, peering out. Could anyone outside see the ghostly apparition in my window? Not likely.

"I just don't know if I can last much longer," he said. "I might only have one more chance, and what if she reacts the same way she did before? What if I just scare her?"

I drew a deep breath and sighed. "I'll try my best to prepare her," I said. *Mrs. Garret—Ellie. Your husband's a ghost, but he has an important last message for you.* She'd probably just think I was crazy, and insensitive into the bargain.

He turned from the window and looked at me with soft, ghostly eyes. There was only the barest hint of the blue they'd been in life. "I appreciate everything you're doing. You should go and get that ring from the garden soon, in case this doesn't work out and I disappear. You've earned it. And if Ellie comes back to the house it'll make that more difficult for you."

I waved a hand. "The job's not finished yet. Let me worry about that end of it, all right? And you're still going to be here a while. I'm sure of it."

The ghost of a smile lifted the corners of his mouth. "Don't wait too long, Acacia. See you soon—I hope."

And with a touch of one transparent hand to the brim of his hat, he was gone.

I spent a fretful night, worrying that I wouldn't hear from Charlotte soon enough, or that I would hear from her and the news would be bad. In the morning, I was just unlocking my office door, balancing takeout coffees in a tray for myself and Oliver, when my office phone started to ring. I answered it breathlessly. It was Charlotte.

"Miss Sheridan?" she asked. "I've spoken with Ellie, but I'm afraid it's no go. She simply doesn't want to be disturbed, and she doesn't see how you could possibly have a message from Frank for her."

I dropped into my chair, feeling leaden. "Did you try to persuade her?"

Charlotte was quiet for a moment. "I told her that you seemed very sincere to me, but I didn't push her, no. This is a terrible time for my sister. I want to be very careful with her. Surely you understand that?"

"I do," I said with a sigh. "But this message would certainly bring her more peace...maybe some closure. Would you ask her again?"

"I'm sorry," she said firmly. "I took you at your word, and I did what I promised, but without knowing more, I'm not willing to push Ellie on this."

I floundered wildly for an idea. I couldn't tell her about Frank—she'd write me off as a nutcase. But I needed to prove to her that I was serious, that I really had something. "Could I drop by again later today, then?" I asked her, desperate. "I'll tell you more about what's going on."

There was a longer hesitation this time. I might have piqued her curiosity.

"I'll be home after three o'clock," she said finally. "But I'm not making any promises beyond that."

"Thank you. You won't regret it. See you at three."

I hung up and wondered what I was going to come up with, in the next six hours, to make Charlotte believe me.

After pacing my office for an hour and hashing the problem over with Oliver, we'd thought of only one possibility.

I drove out to Frank and Ellie's house again and let myself in at the back door. After carefully closing and locking it behind me, I called, "Frank! Frank, are you here?"

I moved into the kitchen and Frank came into the room from the other side, gliding silently. He looked about the same as he had yesterday.

"You look better!" I told him, but he only gave me a skeptical half-smile.

"Any news?"

"Let's sit down," I said, pulling out one of the kitchen chairs. Frank sat in it, and I pulled out another for myself. "So far, no luck," I told him. "Charlotte talked to Ellie, but she wouldn't agree to see me."

The ghost hung his head. "That's it, then," he murmured. "It's over."

I put out a hand to pat his arm, but of course it went right through. I pulled my hand back, feeling awkward. "Look, don't give up yet," I told him. "I have an idea."

He raised his head, a faint glimmer of hope in his eyes.

"I know you don't have the strength to manifest anywhere but here," I said. "But what if I could take something to Charlotte that would convince her that I've seen you, talked to you, and this is important. I might be able to convince her to tell me where Ellie is."

He shrugged his shoulders. "Sure, it might work. But how are you going to prove anything to Charlotte?"

I dug in my bag and pulled out my notebook. "What if you wrote her a note? Would she recognize your handwriting?"

Frank seemed to sag in on himself a little more, although he looked at me kindly. "Sure," he said, "But Acacia, how am I going to hold a pen? I'm not as substantial as I was the day we met. I've—thinned out a lot since then."

I bit my lip. "I know, but it's the only thing I can come up with. What if we go to the part of the house where Ellie's energy is strongest, and see what you can do?"

"I've been spending most of my time in our bedroom," Frank said. "I figure, we spent the most time together in that one spot, a third of our lives sleeping, right? But it's just not working anymore."

I thought for a moment. "That's one way to think about it," I said slowly, "but you're looking for Ellie's energy. Wouldn't it make more sense to look in the place where she probably expended more than anywhere else?"

Frank perked up. "Her office! Why didn't I think of that?"

I nodded. "Worth a try. You know, I noticed when we were here before that you perked up a bit in there."

When I followed Frank into Ellie's office, he went straight over and sat in the chair at her computer. He closed his eyes and I waited. Then he opened them and nodded. "I think I feel a difference. Let me hang out here for a while and we'll see what happens."

"Great!" Now to work on the other part of my plan. "I was thinking about what you said. Can you tell me where that ring is? I might as well try to find it while I'm waiting."

Frank nodded, his eyes sad again. He must think I didn't believe our plan was going to work, but all he said was, "Good thinking," and then proceeded to tell me precisely where to dig in the garden at the bottom of the hedge-rimmed yard. "There's a trowel in a basket in the back porch," he told me. "You shouldn't need anything else."

I'm not one for yard work, but fifteen minutes later I was back in the house, rinsing the ring under warm water at the kitchen sink. In the cupboard underneath I found some cleaning supplies and an old toothbrush, and in no time the ring gleamed gold in the noonday light, apparently no worse for the years it had lain in the earth. The cleaning revealed an inscription: My two addictions – words and you.

Frankie turned brighter eyes to me when I entered the office. The chair he sat on was barely visible through him, just the hint of an outline, and the colours in his clothes and skin were intensified. "It's working!" I exclaimed. "And I found it!" I held the ring out for his inspection.

He smiled and put out a hand, and I held my breath as I gently placed the ring on his palm. If it fell right through, it would be devastating for both of us.

But it sat, steadily aloft, on his palm, winking in a shaft of light from the window.

"If I can hold this," Frank said on an intake of breath, "let's try that pen."

It took a painstaking half-hour as Frank figured out what he wanted to say, and he laboriously wrote it in my notebook. By the end, though, he held the pen with ease and seemed as solid as when I first met him.

"You should probably come with me now," I said as I tucked the notebook back into my bag. "You're back to full strength, and if Charlotte tells me where Ellie is, we could go there right away."

Frank's brow furrowed under his Jays' cap. "But if I move away from here, I'll start to fade. What if I can't come back again?"

"I think we have to take a chance." My eyes lit on the shelf beside Ellie's desk, where copies of her books proudly lined a shelf. "Okay, wait. I have an idea. Stay put for half an hour, and I'll be back, okay?"

He looked puzzled, but nodded. I patted him on the shoulder—successfully, this time—and hurried out to my car. I called Oliver and said, "I have a mission for you."

"Thank the gods. I'm sitting here bored out of my mind. Did Frank write the note?"

"Yes, but he needs a boost. Close the office for half an hour. Here's what I need you to do."

It actually took me forty-five minutes to run my own part of the errand and meet up briefly with Oliver before returning for Frank.

I pulled up in front of Frank and Ellie's house this time and simply called into the air, "Frank? Can you hear me? Can you come out to the car?"

He materialized in the front seat beside me. "What are you—hey," he said, turning to me in surprise. "I still—feel it. Ellie's energy. How can that be?"

I nodded toward the back seat, and Frank turned to look. Bookstore bags filled the seat, each of them holding copies of Ellie's books. Oliver and I had hit every store in the city between us. Frank turned to look at me again, understanding dawning on his face.

I nodded. "Ellie's energy. It's all there, in her books. And now it's portable." I shifted the car into gear and checked the rear view mirror. "Let's go talk to Charlotte."

Back at Charlotte's house, I parked on the street and walked through the profusion of flowers again to the front porch. The door opened as I put my foot on the first step, and she came outside. I climbed the steps and smiled.

"Thanks for agreeing to talk to me again."

She sighed. "It's foolish of me, really. I guess I just wish you really did have a message from Frank, and that it might help Ellie a little."

"Let's sit on the swing," I told her, and settled into the cushion at one end. Charlotte took the space beside me. I reached into my bag and pulled out the notebook in which Frank had written his note.

"I know you went to Ellie's house with her and helped her pack for this trip," I said gently. "Did Ellie tell you anything about why she wanted to get out of the house just then?"

Charlotte glanced at me, then away. She shrugged. "It makes sense. The house is full of...reminders. She and Frank lived there together for thirty years. I don't think it's all that odd—"

"But did she say anything...happened? In particular? Anything that frightened her or made her even more upset?"

This time when Charlotte looked at me, she held my gaze. Finally she sighed. "She thought she saw...something. She was afraid she was losing her mind from the grief. She didn't know how else to handle it."

"She thought she saw Frank," I said firmly. "She thought she saw his ghost."

Charlotte went pale. "How could you—? You couldn't know that."

I opened the page to Frank's note and held it out to her. "I know it, because it's what happened."

Hesitantly, she let her eyes fall to the page and run over the words. I heard her sharply indrawn breath, but she kept her eyes on the page, apparently reading it again.

Dear Lottie,
I know Ellie and I were the only ones who ever called you that, so I hope between that and the handwriting you'll believe this is from me. Please help Ellie understand that I need to see her—I need to tell her some things before I...move on. I frightened her before, and that is killing me; well, you know, it would be killing me if...anyway. Please tell Miss Sheridan where Ellie is; she'll get me to her. And tell Ellie not to be afraid. This is real, and it's important. This is the last favor I'll ever ask of you, Lottie. Promise.
Your loving brother-in-law,
Frank

Charlotte finally looked up at me with eyes glistening with tears, and I knew she would help.

Frank still sat in the car, looking as solid as he had when I'd left him.

"Come on," I told him, holding the door. I suppose it wasn't technically necessary, but it seemed like the right thing to do.

"Don't tell me Charlotte's still not on board? I have to show myself to her? I can't leave the books!"

"We won't need the books. Charlotte just told me what I'd already suspected," I told him. "Ellie's here."

He stared at me. "I thought Charlotte said she didn't know where Ellie was?"

I shrugged. "She lied. She was protecting her sister, and I'm sure it seemed like the right thing to do at the time. But your note convinced her. She's gone inside to try and convince Ellie. But that will be a lot easier if you're standing there too, don't you think? Just give me five minutes first to help Charlotte prepare her."

He smiled. "I'll see you inside," he said, and

disappeared.

I shut the car door, hoped no-one had seen me talking to an empty car, and hurried back up the walk. I knocked once on the front door and let myself in.

"We're here," came Charlotte's voice. I followed it.

Ellie Garret stood in a bright sitting room, near wide windows facing out into Charlotte's considerable garden, arms crossed over her chest and a defiant look on her face. Charlotte stood next to her, one hand on Ellie's arm. Charlotte turned to me.

"She's not buying my story, or yours," she said with a smile that bordered on tears.

"This is nonsense. I don't know what your game is, but it's a horrid thing to do—" she broke off, as close to tears as Charlotte was. She wasn't going to be easily convinced, and I had to make her more receptive to the notion before Frank actually joined us. I reached into my bag and pulled out the ring.

I stepped toward her, holding it in my open palm. The sunlight caught it and the ring gleamed. "You don't have to believe me, Mrs. Garrett," I said. "I'll admit it's a crazy story. But maybe you'll believe this. Frank told me where to find it."

She looked at the ring with puzzlement.

"It's Frank's," I told her. "The one you gave him, that he lost in the garden. Read the inscription."

She reached out slowly and took the ring. She turned it and peered inside, letting the light illuminate the tiny, flowing letters.

My two addictions – words and you.

Ellie's hand trembled and she almost dropped the ring, then clutched her fingers around it. She looked up at me, eyes wet. "Frank's really here?"

"I am," Frank said from the doorway behind me, and it was a lucky thing there was a well-stuffed wing chair right behind Ellie. She sank into it, eyes fixed on the apparition of Frank. I turned to look. He was as solid as I'd ever seen him, if a bit shaky. He crossed to Ellie, though, and sat in a matching wing chair opposite her. Leaning forward, elbows on knees, he pulled off his Blue

Jays cap and twisted it in his hands just like he'd done in my office.

"Ellie," he said in a hushed voice, almost as if he were afraid to frighten her away again, "I might not have long. Can we talk?"

She swallowed hard and nodded. Charlotte and I tiptoed out and she closed the door behind us. We went to the kitchen, where Charlotte made us tea.

Later, the door to the living room was still closed when I left, but I thought I heard laughter behind it when I passed.

A week later I got a lovely card and an even lovelier cheque in the mail from Ellie Garrett. No, of course I didn't keep the ring—I didn't even tell her Frank said I could take it as payment. Even if they'd replaced the lost one years ago, there was no way I was taking it back. But the cheque more than covered the time I'd spent on the case. She told me in her card that there's a new Frankie and Ellie novel in the works, and I'll have my very own autographed copy when it comes out, so Frank got his message across.

But I knew that already. Frank made one last visit to the office, the day after he and Ellie spoke.

He materialized without warning, standing beside the blue leather chair. Oliver was sitting in the chair as we went over some case notes, and he almost fell out of it when Frank appeared. Frank grinned rakishly and tipped his Jays cap to us when we both jumped.

"You're feeling better," I observed.

He heaved a deep sigh. "I came to thank you," he said. "Both of you. I don't know what's next. I'm feeling strong as a horse after spending time with Ellie. She's like a tonic. I always joked that I couldn't live without her," he added with a smile.

"Love is the drug, as they say," Oliver observed with a grin.

"But I don't know how long that will last, so I came by to give you this." Frank reached forward and placed a folded piece of paper on my desk.

I raised my eyebrows. "What's this?"

Frank tucked his hands into his pockets. "Remember I told you I knew where to find a few...items that you might recover as payment?"

"Like the ring. Yes, you did say that."

"Well, I know you didn't take the ring back from Ellie," he said. "And she's going to send you payment in full for what you did. But that," he nodded to the paper, "is a little something extra from me. You can do what you want with it—nothing at all, or, comes a time when you need a little help...let's just say something there might come in handy."

I took the paper and opened it up. There were five items listed in Frank's distinctive handwriting, each with a brief description of where each could be found. "Seriously? Some of these things—"

He shrugged and put a hand up. "It's up to you. They've all been lost so long, no-one else is going to find them or claim them. Just think of it as a little bit of...insurance," he said with a wink. "And thanks again."

And then he was gone, as quickly and without ceremony as he'd appeared.

"What's on the list?" Oliver asked, leaning forward with wide eyes.

Slowly I smiled, opened my desk drawer, dropped the slip of paper inside, and closed and locked it. "I'll tell you later," I said, "maybe. Let's just say that a little insurance is never a bad thing."

"You're not serious," Oliver said, collapsing back into the chair with a groan. "You are the Worst. Boss. Ever."

"Why don't you get us both some coffee, and we'll finish up these notes," I suggested sweetly. Maybe my mother's right, and we are too much alike.

Oh, I'll share it with him eventually. After all, we're a team.

Through Others' Eyes

Jack stepped out of the lift just as the incoming message alarm sounded on his personal comm.

"Damn!" he muttered, and broke into a run, footsteps echoing in the empty corridor. Shiftchange had been ten minutes ago. The evening crew would be gone from the station bridge, heading gratefully for their bunks as soon as Oléus arrived to take his place at the communications console. They wouldn't wait for Jack, even though he was officially the Watch Leader. Jack was usually late.

Until Jack arrived, though, Oléus couldn't do much beyond accepting the message and reading it. So Jack ran—or tried to. His injured arm jostled in its sling with every step, sending bright waves of pain along the length of the plasma burn. Jack gritted his teeth and slowed his pace. Oléus would just have to wait as long as it took him to get there at a fast walk.

Oléus had already dimmed the bridge's day lights and brought up a pale azure cast to the room by the time Jack arrived. He and Jack had decided the color suited their long nighttime shifts. Jack liked it because it calmed him, helped him forget the fiery moment of agony when the plasma had seared the flesh on his left arm and stuck him here on the station until the wound healed. The alien liked it because—well, who knew why Oléus liked anything? He was as inscrutable as any Vilisian. Except when the neural Link was up.

Jack shivered at the thought.

Oléus already had his face positioned in the message viewer, the pliant neoprene hugging his wrinkled flesh securely. Only the alien's low, slightly upswept ears remained in view, and his neat plait of glossy black hair hung over one shoulder.

"I'm here!" Jack slid carefully into the well-patched watch chair across from Oléus, holding his arm high in its sling to avoid the armrest. His heart thudded in time with the steady cadence of the air recyclers, and the pulse reverberated painfully deep in the injured arm. The message was probably just a check-in, but there was always the chance that the Chron had launched a new attack.

Oléus reported from the viewer. "Recon Flight Able-Ten reports possible Chron movement in the Beta Comae Berenices system," he said. "Requesting we relay this report to the next station and all ships in range. Watch leader, please confirm."

"Go ahead and relay it, Oléus," Jack said quickly. He glanced at the Link helmet resting on his console, the blue light twinkling on its iridescent surface, but made no move to pick it up. "The Jertenda colonies are in Beta Comae. Millions of people."

"Jack, you must confirm. Do you need help with the helmet?" Oléus hadn't taken his head out of the viewer, but obviously Jack hadn't had time for a proper confirmation.

Jack sighed. "No, I can manage it." *I just don't want to.* Favoring his left arm, Jack fumbled the waiting helmet off the console and awkwardly slipped it on. It enveloped his head and face, and he fought the familiar gasp of claustrophobia as the world shifted from pale blue to black. Tiny neural jumpers nudged painlessly into place all over his shaved scalp. He tried to ignore the pervasive aroma of sweat as he groped for the touchpad on the outside of the helmet and pressed it to activate the Link.

The world of the station bridge sprang back to life again on the inside of his visor, bizzarely altered. Colors he could not name added depth and complexity to the familiar consoles and screens, and heat signatures danced dizzyingly over everything. Most importantly, the words of the message hung suspended before his eyes. Or rather, before Oléus' eyes, because that was the Link's function. To let Jack see the world through Oléus' eyes.

Let's get this over with. The message was brief and Jack scanned the words quickly. The Link technology worked, but not perfectly. Sure, Jack's own eyes couldn't see the message, but he could read it through Oléus' as long as they were Linked. The downside was that eerie echoes of whatever else Oléus was thinking about slid along the edges of Jack's consciousness, like ghosts wandering around in his brain. This time it was the girl again. He tried not to notice her, as if she might go away if he ignored her. The Vilisians claimed not to mind this mental privacy leak. Jack hated it.

They also claimed that it didn't work both ways, but who really knew? Maybe they were just very good at keeping secrets. Jack had only one important secret himself, and he wanted to keep it his own.

It had been a critical military breakthrough to discover that the humans' new allies, the Vilisians, were not only attuned to higher frequencies of sound than humans, but also adapted for a breadth of vision that humans did not possess—and neither did their common enemy, the Chron. The ability to communicate with allies in a way that enemies cannot possibly intercept is an advantage in any military endeavor. Especially if those enemies have the ability, however limited, to make brief slips along the timeline, and are currently kicking the crap out of your entire race and your few allies.

"Message confirmed, Comm. Relay at once." Jack pressed the touchpad again to break the Link and gratefully eased the helmet off his head as soon as the jumpers disengaged. The recycled air of the bridge felt dry and cool against his face, but his arm protested violently at all this unaccustomed movement. Jack's eyes watered.

Of course it would have been better, easier, if the machines could have done all the translation, but hell, it was the middle of a war, R&D time was limited, and they were lucky to come up with something that worked at all to translate vision between the races. Humans had never been the most trusting species, and although no one would come right out and say it, they weren't willing to give the Vilisians full control over communications, allies or not. By the time they could have worked out all the details of developing new technology together, the two races would have been wiped out.

The foundation for the tech—the Link helmet—was, ironically, a form of Vilisian entertainment. The military put the best minds on adapting it, and the trust issue was solved—not perfectly, but quickly, which was more important at this point. So humans and Vilisians worked in pairs for all communications, neurally linked, all messages viewed and confirmed by both races before they were relayed. It was cumbersome, but it worked and kept both sides happy. If the Vilisians were insulted by this obvious lack of faith, they never mentioned it.

Oléus' long amber fingers danced over the keypad for a minute or two, relaying the message, then he eased his face free and settled back from the viewer, blinking dark, oval eyes. "Good evening, Jack. That was the only new message since I arrived."

Every night, Jack thought he would have become accustomed to the slight delay between Oléus' lips moving and the digitized voice issuing from the speaker around the alien's neck, and every night he discovered he was wrong. It was so brief, such a tiny asynchronization, that it shouldn't matter, but it always made Jack twitch with the urge to adjust something, to fix it. There was no fixing it, however. Vilisian voices were pitched too high for human ears to hear, and although the computer translation worked fine, it simply didn't function as quickly as the organic brain. Human or Vilisian.

"Okay, good." Jack automatically ran a systems check, a station-wide anomaly sweep, and a defense tracking analysis, using only his right hand to key in the sequences. He wasn't expecting to find anything amiss, and he didn't.

"Would you like to see the message log for the last

shift?" Oléus asked the same question every night, and every night Jack shook his head. If there was something important, Oléus would tell him. For non-vital messages, Jack didn't care to undergo the Link necessary to view them.

"No thanks. Anything interesting happen?"

"You could make that assessment for yourself if you cared to view the log," Oléus chided him. Again the slight delay made Jack feel like he was watching a vid with its video and audio segments out of sync. "It is your prerogative as Watch Leader."

Jack chuckled. "I'd just as soon sit here nice and still and have you tell me about it."

"Your arm again?"

"Yeah, it's giving me hell." Jack's grin faded. "Shouldn't have tried to run in here."

"The only messages were checkpoint affirmations and automated cruiser scan reports. No enemy sightings. Until that last."

"Well, let's hope Able-Ten was wrong and we're in for a quiet night," Jack said. Tiny servos whirred inside the watch chair, adjusting for his weight as he leaned back, resting his injured arm gingerly on his chest.

Oléus nodded toward Jack's arm. "Will you let me take a look at it tonight?"

Every night before Jack had waved off the suggestion, but tonight the pain was bad. "Were you really a doctor before the war?"

Oléus smiled, the wrinkles in his skin thinning and flattening. "Certainly. I still am. And I have learned a few things about human physiology as well. Shall I prove it?"

Jack let go of his hesitation and nodded. Oléus crossed to Jack's chair with the fluidity of motion that seemed so out-of-place among the humans and dog-footed Lobors on the station. Vilisians appeared almost to float when they moved, and the soft robes they favored only enhanced the effect.

The touch of the alien's hands was equally light. Jack scarcely felt the sling sliding off, and knew that Oléus had begun to remove the bandages only when they stuck to the wounds on his arm. He drew a sharp breath to keep from groaning, and caught one of the aromas that seemed to drift from the skin of all Vilisians. Some humans theorized that the scents were part of the Vilisian language, but it didn't seem like anyone was willing to ask the question.

An odd clatter, like a mother's tongue-click of disapproval, came from Oléus' speaker. "How long since these were changed?"

"I guess I should have gone down to the medbay yesterday," Jack admitted.

"Or the day before that," Oléus suggested. "One moment." He glided back to the comm and drew a palm-sized, lustrous box from beneath it. At the touch of Oléus' long fingers, its pearly panels unfolded to reveal an amazingly large storage space packed with healers' implements.

Jack smiled. "Is that your 'little black bag'?"

The alien's thin lips twitched into a smile. "I do know the reference. It is accurate to a point, although personally I think this is far superior." He selected a tiny vial and applied a few oily drops to the gummy bandages. They lifted away from the skin like flower petals opening to the sun, and Jack caught a whiff of something like peppermint.

"It is certainly an ugly wound," Oléus commented as he inspected it.

"Plasma cannons aren't meant to inflict scratches," Jack said with a careful shrug. "I guess I'm lucky it didn't take the arm right off."

"You are even luckier you made it back to a station. Chron prefer not to leave survivors." Oléus used a thin transparent rod to smear ochre paste over the wound. Peppermint gave way to the odor of burning rubber.

Jack didn't answer, feeling his gut tighten at Oléus' words. He sighed as the injury cooled instantly, the pain receding and disappearing like a tide going out. "What is that stuff?"

"Your doctors would probably call it a 'home remedy,'" Oléus said with a smile.

"Well, I don't care what you call it, it works. I should have let you look at it days ago."

"Which, I believe, I suggested." Oléus closed his medical case and returned to the comm. "We'll leave it open to the air for half an hour or so, and then I'll re-bandage it."

With the pain gone and the doctoring finished, Jack's mind immediately crept back to the neural Link. Jack would have preferred to think about almost anything else, but the ghostly thoughts transferred during a Link were not easily banished.

The young Vilisian girl who had crossed the Link again wore vibrantly alien flowers in her dark hair. She danced along the side of a stream with aimless joy, stooping now and again to toss a pebble into the current. Her garments were pink and...some color Jack couldn't name. His own eyes had never seen it, and he'd guess no human eyes could. But Oléus' had, and now it existed in Jack's experience as well.

The same girl was frequently in Oléus' thoughts during the Link. Jack had never asked Oléus about her. Human-Vilisian relationships were rarely close, since the aliens tended to stay aloof. Many long night shifts together had made Jack realize that it was more a natural reserve in the aliens' nature, which he actually appreciated. Oléus was possibly Jack's best friend on the station, but they didn't talk about things like the memories. Personal things. Jack didn't want to stray into dangerous territory.

"It must have been terribly painful," Oléus said.

Startled, Jack said, "What?" A hot flush stung his face, as if he'd been caught rummaging through Oléus' quarters.

"Your injury. I'm sorry, it must have been very difficult for you to continue piloting your craft afterward."

"It was rough, all right. I barely had the strength after I finished off the Chron to make it to the jump point. Sometimes I guess you just do what you have to do." It was his standard answer whenever the subject of his Chron encounter came up. Jack had given it so many times now it almost sounded like the truth, even to him.

He never made eye contact when he talked about it, though. He didn't think he was that good a liar.

Oléus was silent for a moment. "Do you think we can win this war?" he asked abruptly.

"Of course we can. We will." The response was automatic, although it sounded hollow even to Jack.

Oléus made an odd movement of his head and shoulders, the Vilisian equivalent of a shrug. "I hope you are right, but sometimes that hope gives way to fear. To fight an enemy who has never even attempted communications, whose proper name we do not even know..."

"And who can timeslip," Jack added slowly. "Even if they can't do it all the time or very well..."

Oléus sighed and reverted to typical Vilisian understatement. "It is worrisome."

Jack shifted uncomfortably in the worn Watch Leader's seat, listening to the servos struggle to adjust beneath his weight. They'd never talked about the outcome of the war before; he was always careful to keep the conversation from becoming too personal or serious. It was too dangerous to talk about personal things once you'd shared the Link. How did you keep from blurting out something embarrassing, something that you shouldn't even know? Everyone said the Vilisians didn't mind, but Jack didn't want to test the theory.

The comm alarm buzzed again and Oléus turned immediately to the viewer, ending the discussion. Jack grimaced, relief at the end of an awkward moment mixing with dread at what was to come. He had no doubt another neural Link was in the offing, and the prospect seemed worse than ever in light of the current conversation.

"Chron incursion into Beta Comae Berenices system has been confirmed by three other flights," Oléus reported, his voice clipped but steady. "Command is rerouting all available cruisers and warships to the area. Relays to all in-range craft are requested."

Jack had already reached for the Link helmet. It wasn't a night when he was going to get away from it. He read the hovering words and confirmed the relay. That took a while, because they had to search the region for in-range craft and confirm the message with each one individually.

Jack could sense that Oléus was trying to keep his attention on the task at hand, but random thoughts broke through at intervals anyway. Perhaps they'd been loosened by the conversation. The little girl again, this time at a party. Other Vilisian children, gathered around Oléus as he read to them from a beautifully illustrated scroll. The interior of a large building, quiet and serene as meditating Vilisians sat on ornate pillows and the floor beneath them pulsed with muted light. A brief flash of something that might be Vilisian sex. And a shadowy memory of pain, a wound that Jack could not identify. His arm throbbed in empathy for the space of a few heartbeats. It was the first negative memory that he'd ever picked up from Oléus. Jack had the impression that the Vilisian pulled his mind from that memory as quickly as he could. As deliberately as Jack tried not to think about his...accident.

When the relays were finally finished, Jack tugged off the Link helmet with a sigh of relief. Oléus seemed equally glad to extract his face from the viewer, wiping sweat from the furrows in his brow with a cloth from his medical bag.

"I must apologize," he said to Jack. "I found it difficult to concentrate on the task at hand tonight. I am sure there was some memory crossover."

"That's okay," Jack said, not meeting the alien's eyes. "I hardly noticed."

The attack came without warning at the midpoint of the shift. The Chron hadn't been timeslipping as often lately, prompting hopeful speculation about dwindling resources. They'd obviously decided to use some on a timeslip tonight, however, crossing from Beta Comae Berenices to the relay station in only seconds. Jack was staring out the scratched viewscreen at the star-dotted darkness when three Chron ships materialized. He had just enough time to hit the alarm with a yell before the first pink-veined plasma bursts erupted from the ships. Lightning-like flashes spiderwebbed across the viewscreen as the station shields absorbed the initial hit.

Jack sprinted for the bridge gunstation, the pain in his arm barely registering. Adrenaline took over—adrenaline and fear and a sickening nausea.

They've found us. Is it my fault?

He threw himself into the red gunner's chair and punched numbers into the targeting computer, forcing the thought away. The soft foam of the seat molded itself to his body, hugging him against the padding and holding him steady. Plasma bursts blossomed silently in the spacedark and Jack let his pilot's reflexes take over, returning the barrage. The Chron ships were fast, but with any luck, the station's targeting computers would be faster.

"Jack!" Oléus' voice came to him over the wail of the alarm. "What can I do?"

"Send a distress code on all frequencies! To anything close enough to get it!" A Chron ship burst apart in a bright swirl of debris. Pale streaks of plasma blazed from all guns on the station now and Jack felt slightly less alone.

"But you'll need to verify—"

"Forget it! I can't leave the gun! Just send the message!"

"But—"

"Just do it!" Jack roared. "I trust you!"

The station shook with the force of a Chron blast and a sharp crash sounded from the access corridor outside the bridge. Jack swore silently. The shields, at least in some areas, must have failed.

Jack's fingers flew over the targeting computer and the gun whirled on its mount, sending blast after blast at the remaining Chron.

"It's done!" Oléus shouted. "Help is coming!"

Another hit shook the station, almost hurling Jack from the gunner's chair despite the clinging foam. He steadied himself with both hands, pain sending fiery fingers up his injured arm from the strain. He felt barely-healed skin separate. Behind him, the bridge reverberated with a series of shattering thuds, and he thought he heard Oléus call his name. The alarm's banshee wail stuttered, then doubled in intensity. Somewhere, the station hull had been breached.

But there was only one Chron ship left. Jack blinked sweat and dust from his eyes and set the targeting computer again. The plasma bursts from the other gun stations had slowed, and Jack wondered how many of them had been taken out altogether. The last Chron darted into view and Jack's gun responded. Fiery light blazed on the port side of the enemy ship.

And then it disappeared. Jack swore. It hadn't exploded, just winked out. It must have had enough power left for one last slip.

Just like before. The thought rose in Jack's mind and he pushed it down, along with the pain in his arm, extricating himself from the gunner's chair and striding toward the bridge. The lights flickered, but held. The air recyclers thudded steadily. Maybe it wasn't so bad...

"Oléus, did you get—" The words froze in his throat as he took in the chaos on the bridge. Half the infrastructure had collapsed, leaving Oléus buried under debris. Jack could just see one amber-colored hand, part of a dusty sleeve. He shoved rubble aside in a frenzy, uncovering his friend bit by bit like some weird archaeological find.

The gravity of Oléus' injuries was horribly obvious. Coppery stains seeped through the fabric of his robes, and one arm twisted back at an unnatural angle. The characteristic spicy Vilisian odor clotted in the air. Jack struggled to get him into the Comm chair.

Oléus coughed, and his eyes flickered open. "Jack," he gasped, his voice harsh but intelligible through the speaker. "You must summon one of the other Comms. I cannot—"

Jack glanced toward the access corridor, blocked solid by fallen debris. He shook his head. "Nobody's getting in here for a while, I'm afraid. You've got to hold on. We have to catch any messages coming through or no one will know where the Chron are."

Oléus shook his head weakly. "My injuries—I know how severe they are. I'm a doctor, remember? Get my... my 'little black bag.'" He tried to smile, but it dissolved into another bout of coughing.

Jack scrambled through the wreckage, rummaging under the comm until he found Oléus' kit. He brought it over and pressed where he had seen Oléus touch it earlier. It opened silently.

"Good." Oléus gestured to the kit. "There's a round gadget in there. Clear face. Circuitry inside."

After a moment of searching Jack held up a disc. Oléus nodded. "Same section—some vials of yellowish liquid, and an injector."

Jack wordlessly found the other items, holding them up for Oléus to confirm.

"Attach the disc behind my left ear."

Jack did as instructed. The skin behind Oléus' ear felt cold and leathery. "Is this for pain?"

Oléus began to shake his head, winced, and went still again. "You must put me in the viewer. Give me an injection, one of those vials every hour. Here, at the base of my neck. Put the Link helmet on and keep it on, because I won't be able to tell you when there's a message."

Jack recoiled. Put the helmet on and keep it on? No way. Especially not with Oléus in this state. "Why can't you tell me when there's a message? No one else can get to the bridge. We'll have our hands full here. I'll have to try and clear some of this mess—"

Oléus grimaced. "Because, for all intents and purposes, I will be dead."

"What?"

"That neuronal booster will keep my brain active enough for you to use my eyes. The emergency nanodes in the injection will stabilize my brain chemistry, breathe for me, and keep my visual systems functioning. The Link will function. But that is all."

Jack stared at the alien while the meaning of the words sank in, then swore. "Isn't there—there must be something else in your kit. I can't just let you die!"

"There is no other option. And little time. You must do this before my brain stops functioning." Oléus coughed raggedly again. "And that will not be long."

Jack punched up the station comm, trying to steady his voice. "Can anyone get to the bridge? I need a Vilisian doctor and a Comm, right now!"

Faint replies came in from various parts of the station, but all the replies were the same—no one was in a position to help him. The station was stable, but severely disabled.

"Jack? You must do it now."

Jack turned back to Oléus, fighting the urge to scream. It wasn't the Link; the Link be damned. He was about to lose the only friend he had on the station. And he had to be inside Oléus' brain while it died.

He met his friend's dark eyes, and for once they were not difficult to read. Pain. And determination.

Slowly he helped Oléus get as comfortable as he could. As he was about to lower Oléus' face into the soft embrace of the message viewer, the Vilisian put a long-fingered hand on his arm.

"Jack. I know. I know what haunts you—that you didn't make certain the Chron who wounded you was dead before you jumped back."

Jack stared at him, uncomprehending. Oléus nodded.

"The Link...the leakage does go both ways. But you humans are so fiercely individual. How many of you would Link if you knew the truth? We Vilisians...we keep our secrets. And yours."

Something rose in Jack and then drained away as quickly as it had come—anger, shame, hurt? He hardly knew, and didn't care.

"What if this is my fault?" he whispered. "What if they followed my jump?"

Oléus shook his head. "In your heart, you know that isn't true. He couldn't have traced your jump. You engaged the scramblers."

Slowly Jack nodded. "I did. I know that. But still—"

"No. You aren't responsible. And you're not a coward. It isn't cowardly to save one's own life."

"It is if it's at the expense of others."

"But it wasn't. You've just said that." Oléus' voice was faint and breathy now, but he continued to speak. "I can help you. I know you haven't been able to make yourself accept what happened."

Jack said nothing.

Oléus nodded and fetched a deep, rasping breath. "Once you've established the Link, open your mind to mine. Vilisians have the ability to change our memories. Adjust them to what we want to remember. The old memories are still there, but we keep them...submerged. You humans do it to some extent, but it's mostly subconscious. You don't have the same control."

"I still don't understand."

"You saw the young girl in my memories?"

Jack flushed. Oléus had known.

"It's nothing. I knew you were getting her. That's my daughter...or rather my daughter as I would like her to have been. She was killed at the beginning of the war. She was only an infant. Those memories are ones I would like to have of her. But they are constructs only."

"But...they seem so real!"

"They do." Oléus smiled crookedly. "They have been a great source of comfort to me."

"But they're not true. They're just a story you tell yourself," Jack said slowly.

Oléus tried to shrug, and winced. "What is real, Jack? Isn't reality brutal enough that sometimes we deserve something better? Something that lets us hold onto life instead of give ourselves over to death? Once we're Linked, search my mind for your memory of what happened with the Chron. It's there. It came through clearly many times. In my brain, you can alter it whatever way you like, and it will go back with you to your mind. You'll know how. Within an hour it will be more real to you than what actually happened. And you can get on with your life." He smiled thinly. "Think of it as a gift, my friend."

Oléus' body trembled in Jack's arms. "You must hurry," the alien urged. "Position me in the viewer. Attach the booster." His breath came in short gasps, the harsh sound horribly amplified by the speaker around his neck.

Jack moved to follow his friend's instructions, his limbs heavy, his head thick. Gently placing Oléus' head in the neoprene mask. Affixing the neuronal booster where the alien had directed. Making the first injection of nanodes to keep the brain working after circulation and natural respiration had stopped. Then he stood with his hand on Oléus' back as the moments ticked by. The Vilisian robes were as soft and fragile as rose petals under his fingers. He didn't move until Oléus' breathing became shallow and precise, controlled by the nanodes.

He picked his way through the debris of the silent bridge and dimmed the lights before sitting in the watch chair. Gingerly he took up the iridescent Link helmet and slipped it on, feeling the neural jumpers slip into place. The world swam, then refocused through Oléus' eyes. There were no messages, just the now-familiar, completely alien view of the bridge, clouded and indistinct but there. Jack gasped as images from Oléus' brain flooded across the Link. The nanodes kept it active, but without Oléus to concentrate on stemming the tide, the memories flowed as freely as a river in springtime.

After a time Jack did as Oléus had told him, and let his own consciousness move inside the alien's brain. It was surprisingly easy to wander there, among memories familiar and strange, real and invented, until he found his own memory of the Chron encounter. He pulled a sharp breath at its vividness. It had lost nothing in crossing the link to his friend's consciousness. The pain of the pink-veined plasma burn still raged here, the smell of his fear made his stomach clench, the taste of his shame soured his mouth as he watched himself make his jump toward safety.

Still, Oléus had been right. Jack had fought as long as he could. He'd engaged the scramblers before he jumped.

As Oléus had told him, he knew how to manipulate the

memory. He dampened the burn of the plasma wound and manufactured his defeat of the Chron, the enemy ship blossoming in silent fiery convulsions under his own plasma bursts, a rain of debris shooting past his ship. Only then did he turn his ship to the jump point and make the jump, only after he was sure it was safe.

It was a great memory.

For a moment he admired it, savoured it, clung to it like a lifeline. The way things could have been. Should have been.

Had not been. After a time he pulled away, left the altered memory in Oléus' dying brain, grateful for a gift he couldn't fully accept. His own memory, the real one, would have to suffice. He pulled his mind back to the devastated station bridge, to his dead friend, to his duty. He watched for messages through Oléus' eyes, relayed them, and waited for help to arrive. It took a long time. Oléus' life flowed across the Link in spurts and trickles all the while, and Jack received it stoically, no longer afraid of the ghostly impressions that took up residence now in his own mind. Somehow there was room, always would be room for every memory. For his friend.

When help finally arrived, he disengaged the Link helmet and pulled it from his head almost hesitantly. It seemed lighter, smaller in his hands. His face reflected back from the iridescent surface, distorted and oddly-colored, the way things looked to him through the Link. *The way Oléus had seen him.* Jack looked at it for a long time before setting it gently on the console. He would not be afraid to wear it again.

Upload

They've made me comfortable, or tried
arthritis-pocked bones protest every surface now
muscles fatigued beyond resting
Death beckons a bony invitation—
I decline.
I choose the upload.

A week now, neurojacked into the console
threadlike filaments tracing
the secret convolutions of my brain
compiling the message that is me
Eighty-nine year-old ET
phoning myself home.
Today.

I write this poem because
I have ciphered my life in poetry
the only immortality
to which I dared aspire
So many words, so many years
and now reduced to words—
is it such a poor reduction in the end?

Is this the last poem I will write?

Will my uploaded self
still think in the cadences
of line and stanza
emotion and image?
Or will I compile/compute/calculate/respond
in precisely packeted bits of data;

filtered through thought loop and memory engram code
of this particular elderly female poet
but emerging as something other.
This poem will be
uploaded like all the rest
will I read it later and wonder who I was
to write such a thing?

Who will I be?
Decoded/recoded/encoded/uploaded into my new APC
Ambulatory Personality Console
intuitive interface, self-directed motion
best they can do right now,
but in ten years, they say, we'll have RPR's
Robotic Personality Repositories

arms, legs, face
Save a picture
it can even look like me.

The preparations pause
one last chance to reconsider:
death or discontinuity?
My daughter is here
truest poetry I ever wrote
She holds my hand, smiles through tears
Will she recognize me

talk to me still in keyboard stutter
fingers skittering over the keys of my APC
if she finds it too unnerving to speak to a machine
while I blink-flash my responses
upon the screen of my face

answer in synthesized mother tones
Will she still read love in my pixellated, digitized eyes?

I nod.
The neurojack tugs at my scalp.

Somewhere, someone taps a key.
Eighty-nine years of
thought and word and memory and me
stream out of my brain
like atmosphere pushed rudely aside by vacuum
like blood welling up in a vial
I still feel my daughter's hand...

<Darkness. With a silicon flavor.>
Sensory inputs blink into being
I see the room <too sharp, adjust filter>
And there is my <beautiful> daughter
She hesitates, torn between the husk on the bed
and the ergonomic contours of my new APC
"Mom?" she asks.

"I'm fine."
<synthesized mother voice operating
within normal parameters>
<soothing>
I offer the pre-programmed equivalent of a smile.
More tears. But I think she understands.
Her mother is still here.

I take stock.
<no pain>
<no fatigue>
No blood, no heart, no hand, no breast, no brain
but still the words, thank God;
I am reduced to words
but the words are enough.

Back in the Game

ChipSets & WireHeads Magazine
Vol. 3, Iss. 10, October 2019
Interview with Kevin "w00t" Cho
Lead Programmer, Gods of Sundered Heaven II
by Squall Games, Inc.

CSWH: Kevin, can you start out by telling us when you knew there were serious problems with the Gods of Sundered Heaven II game interface?

KC: Well, I wasn't really worried until a god died and the next thing I knew we were in trouble. Mike warned me a year ago not to do it, but I was already half way through writing the patch and I thought we—the programming team—could fix the problems. We had over 16 million players at that time, and I just couldn't stand the thought of shutting down and disappointing all those dedicated GOSH II fans.

CSWH: And "Mike" would be Michael "Infinite Loop" Allen, the original Lead Programmer on the project?

KC: Yeah, that was right before his...you know...difficulties...just before I got promoted to Lead. He's doing great now; I talked to him on the phone last week—he's still in the hospital, of course—but he told me the hallucinations have almost cleared up. And he can see a computer again without blacking out. He's made real progress.

CSWH: Great to hear. So you say you didn't really start to worry until the god died? Weren't you already concerned that your MMORPG (Massively Multiplayer Online Role-Playing Game, for the uninitiated) had apparently resurrected actual gods from Earth's history and empowered them in the virtual environment of the game?

KC: Concerned? Man, we were stoked! You've gotta admit it takes mad programming skills to resurrect gods. It's what made GOSH II so popular! I mean, GOSH I did pretty well, but when the actual gods came online in the second version, registrations went berserk.

CSWH: I've heard that the whole resurrecting gods thing was actually an accident.

KC: (coughs) Yeah, well, sure it was. I mean, who would think that was actually possible? Mike wrote the original algorithms so that the gods in the game would be as much like their historical counterparts as possible. Sometimes I think it was all that research that drove him bonkers—I mean, caused his temporary break with reality—and not what happened later. But when it became obvious that the gods had evolved beyond their programming—

CSWH: Is there any explanation even now for how that happened?

KC: (Interviewer's note: Mr. Cho looked extremely uncomfortable at this point) I don't...Mike can explain it better than I can...when he's coherent...but I'll try. Seems like the algorithms were so perfect that when avatars in the game started worshipping the gods, you know, making alliances, tithing game credits to the temples...it was like the gods actually had human worshippers again. Turned out that's what gods need, in order to wield power —followers. It's actually pretty simple when you think about it. (laughs nervously)

CSWH: Perhaps a bit too simple, don't you think?

KC: (pause) Yeah, you could be right. Mike says it's partly because GOSH players identify so intensely with their avatars—their characters in the game. I mean, look, you've got players who have GOSH running in the background while they work, while they eat, even while they sleep.

CSWH: While they sleep?

KC: One thing we learned from other MMORPG's that came before GOSH was that many players hated to lose game time to mundane things like sleeping. So we introduced the concept of double avatars, so that a player could actually go and sleep or be AFK—

CSWH: AFK?

KC: Yeah, away from the keyboard...and program their avatar with instructions to play a different, secondary avatar during that time. They can keep racking up experience, running spells to make materials, that sort of thing. They can be in the game, actually playing, 24/7.

CSWH: So you're saying that characters in the game can also play their own characters? Wow. Whose idea was that?

KC: (looks away and mumbles)

CSWH: Sorry, I didn't catch that.

KC: It was Coyote's idea.

CSWH: Coyote. You mean 'Coyote' as in the native North American trickster god?

KC: Er, yeah. He was one of the first gods to...evolve, in the game.

CSWH: So by creating these double avatars, that would effectively double the number of worshippers for the various gods?

KC: That turned out to be the case, yeah. We didn't really...I mean it wasn't...yeah.

CSWH: Can you tell us when the gods began communicating with you personally?

KC: (lights a cigarette) For me, it was right around the time Mike was having his...difficulties. He mentioned a few times that he thought the gods in the game had...you know...become fully realized and autonomous...and that they were talking to him.

CSWH: What did his co-workers think of these claims?

KC: (laughs) I thought he was crazy. Then one day I'm sitting at my workstation, working up a new quest line, and I hear this voice from the speakers. I thought someone was joking around.

CSWH: What did the voice say to you?

KC: It said..."This quest line will upset the game balance. You must reduce the experience and remove 16% of treasure drops, and increase mandatory tithing to 11%."

CSWH: And it turned out to be not a joke?

KC: No, it wasn't a joke. It was Baldr.

CSWH: Baldr?

KC: Yeah, Norse god of justice. He's pretty picky when it comes to game balance, same as Samash and Honos...there's a few of them. Look, can we talk about something else? My hands start to shake when I talk about...Them...too much.

CSWH: Just a few more questions, please. Can you tell me how many gods were programmed into GOSH II?

KC: Jeez. Only about twenty to start with. Mike put in the big-name ones, you know...Thor, Ra, Zeus, Shiva...the ones we thought players would recognize.

CSWH: And now?

KC: (pause) A few thousand.

CSWH: A few thousand?

KC: Well, I haven't personally counted them, but yeah, there's a lot.

CSWH: Can we go back to the god who died? How did that incident change the course of what's happened?

KC: Well, He wasn't one of the original twenty. We'd come to grips with the fact that the gods had self-realized inside the game, but we wrote a new patch, thought we had it under control. Then some new gods appeared. We thought the servers had been hacked, or maybe someone on the programming team had gone rogue, or maybe had a breakdown like Mike, but it wasn't that. Turned out the originals started bringing in some of Their old friends.

CSWH: They could do that?

KC: Yeah. Obviously. They're gods, man. *Gods.*

CSWH: Right. So then?

KC: Well, the game was really getting screwed up with all these new gods, for a while we were losing players pretty fast...the gods were fighting for players' allegiance, messing with the quest lines, that kind of thing. We couldn't patch fast enough to keep it under control. Game balance was completely out of control, and players started to get angry. That's what happened to the god who died. He was just gaining strength with some new worshippers and then they all left the game out of frustration...and He couldn't hang on.

CSWH: What god was that?

KC: (looks uncomfortable) I'd rather not say. Anyway, the other gods saw what happened and realized that They couldn't do things completely without us, the programmers. Mike...left...okay, they carried him out in a straightjacket, screaming...and I started working on a patch to incorporate the new gods. 'Round the clock, man, like, we lived at the office for six months. Once that was ready, we could handle any number that might come online. Mike thought we should shut down, but...it just wasn't feasible. And honestly...I don't know if They would have let us.

CSWH: So, let's talk about the current situation.

KC: Do we really have to?

CSWH: I think our readers would be very interested to hear your thoughts on it. The gods from GOSH II have certainly grown beyond Their original programming now. Does your company have any thoughts on that?

KC: Well, we certainly never thought They'd expand outside the game servers and onto the rest of the Internet! (laughs, a trifle hysterically)

CSWH: That caused some chaos at first. It's had some

serious repercussions.

KC: I actually thought it was pretty funny the way They kept editing each other's Wikipedia entries for a while...

CSWH: Yes, although once They really understood how powerful control of the Internet made Them—

KC: Yeah, yeah, I know where you're going. It's gone way beyond that, I'll admit.

CSWH: Your company, Squall Games, has been trying to put a positive spin on these developments, pointing out that the gods will keep the Internet powered indefinitely now, regardless of what happens to energy supplies anywhere in the world, since Their continued existence depends on it.

KC: Yeah, I think that's definitely a good thing. And if They do grow beyond the Internet—

CSWH: What do you mean? Is that possible?

KC: (whispers, apparently to himself) What? Oh, sorry, I...no, no, I won't. No. I won't.

CSWH: Kevin?

KC: Uh, yeah, sorry. No, I was just joking about that. Haha! They could never get outside the Internet. We're really sure about that, we wrote a new patch for that and everything. It's all good. Look, are we done here? I've gotta get back to a new game we have in development...GOSH: The Reawakening. You wouldn't believe what we're going to do with that one.

CSWH: I'm sure it'll be interesting, to say the least. Thanks for your time, Kevin. And good luck.

Waiting to Fly

The bright, bejeweled electronic bird circled and spun one last time above my head, then dropped like a stone. With a flourish of my right hand, I reached up and pretended to pluck it out of the air. With my left, I furtively tugged open the concealed pocket in the rear of my coat and let the gadget fall inside, drawn to the beacon nestled inside the pocket.

With all eyes in the concourse crowd transfixed on my clasped right hand, I opened it slowly, revealing that the bird had disappeared. The gathered children, who had initially looked greenish and lethargic after their recent space travel, now erupted in squeals and laughter while even the tired adults smiled and clapped. I bowed theatrically, sweeping off my tall black top hat. I deposited it with practised carelessness, open end up, on the metal decking at my feet. Then I began tidying my props, feigning indifference but listening hard for the telltale chatter of plastic credit chips landing inside. I smiled with relief as the impromptu audience showed their appreciation.

One man stepped up and proffered a hand, a girl of about six with wild black curls at his side. "Great show. Thanks," he said. He glanced down at the girl. "We definitely needed something fun just now."

I shook his hand, then knelt in front of the child, sneaking the bird out of my concealed pocket and

146

cradling it in my palm. "Would you like to touch it?"

Her brown eyes went wide and she stretched out a cautious finger, stroking the iridescent head. Surreptitiously I brushed the remote, making the bird tremble a little under her touch. I hoped the glue wasn't too noticeable, where I'd affixed the new eyes. That would ruin the illusion.

"What's your name? I'm Lucy."

"Stella," she said absently, eyes fixed on the bird. "How did you make it come back?"

I smiled. "Magic, of course!"

"Okay, Stella, let's go." The man gave her hand a gentle tug, and dropped another plastic credit into my hat. She went reluctantly, turning back to wave once as they crossed the station concourse toward the lift. The girl looked very tiny, passing underneath the clear domed ceiling, an unimaginable vastness of star-dotted black sweeping above. The family must have taken station berths while they waited for the next colony ship. I glanced into my hat, feeling a twinge of guilt. Berths were pricey; colonists mostly poor, having spent what they could muster on the costs of passage. I shrugged and tipped the credits into my other pocket, then slipped the hat into the prop case. Don't feel guilty. It's a good show and folks pay what they want.

"Got your papers for the week, Lucy Daz?" a gravelly voice rumbled behind me. The voice should belong to a hulk of a man, but the concourse officer stood as tall and reedy as if born on a low-gravity planet. His blue security uniform sagged, as if it had been made for the man who would fit the voice. Thin hair, the nondescript colour of a rocky moon, clung close to his head, and narrow eyes the same shade peered at me.

"All in order, Haxton." I pulled the security pouch from inside my shirt and fished out my performer's license. He swept a spindly finger over the flexible plastic square, activating the contents, and ran a cursory eye over the text, most interested in the date stamp at the bottom of the page.

He tapped the e-sheet. "No more than six

performances a day." Just like always.

I grinned. "The magic runs out after five anyway, then I gotta recharge." Just like always.

It wasn't the magic that ran out, it was the birds' battery charge. I liked to think of this exchange as our little joke, although Haxton never laughed or smiled at it.

He handed the license back wordlessly. I'd already procured a single credit from my pocket, and slipped it into his hand as I accepted the document. Haxton and I had an understanding. My license was in order, but concourse security could always find "issues" if they wanted. Haxton required a small stipend to keep the "issues" at bay, and I went along with the program. What I fed him wouldn't delay me getting my own spot on a colony ship more than a few months, and that was still a long way off. He pocketed the credit with a nod and a not-quite-smile.

Since this had been my fifth performance of the day, I wouldn't risk the birds' batteries on a sixth. As I picked up my case, an man unfamiliar to me unfolded a table on the other side of the concourse and began setting out rows of tiny bottles. I knew most of the regular buskers and hawkers, but not this guy. He wore a cloth cap in grey plaid, and a worn, many-pocketed vest that strained against the buttons clasping it over his rotund midsection. His face was round, too, and cheerful. He spotted me heading in his direction, case under my arm, and grinned.

"Heading spaceward soon, miss? Try a bottle of Doktor Dohlman's Patented Space-Sickness Particulate! Mix it into any drink for quick relief of all your space sickness symptoms! Even wormhole travel is easy with Doktor Dohlman." He swept a hand across the array of bottles. Each bore the same label and held a spoonful of white and pink crystals.

I held up a hand and shook my head. "No spacefaring in my immediate future, unfortunately." I picked up a bottle and examined it. The price was an outrageous number of credits and I set it back down carefully. "I didn't know there was any cure for wormhole sickness."

The man nodded his head eagerly. "It's a recent breakthrough! Look at some of these testimonials!" He whipped out an e-sheet and tapped it. A long string of quotes resolved on the surface.

Space-sickness is no longer traumatic, thanks to Doktor Dohlman!

Doktor Dohlman takes the pain out of space travel!

I travel the universe in comfort. Thank you, Doktor Dohlman!

I glanced at them and smiled. "Are you Doktor Dohlman, then?"

He laughed, belly shaking with mirth. "Oh no! I'm no doctor! Merely a traveling merchant, spreading the word of Doktor Dohlman's wonderful discovery to these poor souls who need it. Wormhole travel is the wave of the future, but we need to make it palatable for everyone who aspires to be a colonist." He gestured to the station concourse, which was actually sort of deserted just now.

"Well, good luck," I said, although secretly I didn't mean it. If many colonists spent their credits on his medicine, they'd have even less to spare for appreciation of my little magic show. I pointed across the concourse. "I'm over there most days, so I'll see you around."

He stuck out a hand. "Mert Piler, at your service."

I took the hand. His grip was firm. "Lucy Daz," I told him. "Of Dazzling Aviatronics." I held my prop case up so he could see the script and colourful birds painted on the side.

"I'll have to take in a show," he said, and let go of my hand. His gaze darted over my shoulder, seeking another potential customer.

"Sure," I said. "See you around." I made my way to the metal stairwell at the far end of the concourse. As usual, I'd drop in and see Versey on my way home.

Or what passed for home, here on Damyadi Station.

Versey sat alone in the engineering bay when I looked in, bent over an e-sheet—a book, or the news, or a manual. Wisps of hair the same steel-grey as the concourse's metal decking had escaped her ponytail and trailed around her pale, motherly face. Her bulk, encased in a grease-stained blue overall, pressed against the arms of her chair.

"Hey, Versey," I said, settling my prop case inside the doorway.

"Lucy!" She dropped her e-sheet and left her chair with an agility that always startled me, gliding across the bay. "How was it up there today?"

I shrugged and took a stool at the worktable. "The usual. Where's Rel?" I cleared a small space of tools, screws, metal bits, electronics chips and shards of iridescent Brekman crystal lattice. Then I emptied my accumulated credit chips into the space to count them.

Versey retrieved my prop case. Peripherally, I saw her carefully lift out my six mechanical birds and array them on the charging strip in the center of the worktable. "Got home from school, did his homework, and headed up to the star lounge to watch for liners coming in to dock." Versey's son was seven years old and obsessed with all forms of space vehicles. In the absence of siblings of my own, Rel was like a little brother to me.

"As usual," I observed.

She smiled and nodded. The birds' crystal shards glittered under the high-powered lights, creating the illusion that the mechanical creatures twitched and fluttered with life. Versey added the beacons and controllers to the strip, then picked up the first bird to inspect it. She tsk-tsked.

"What?"

"This piece is loose." With a pair of tweezers she gingerly wiggled a shard of crystal on the bird's wing. It fell, shattering on the table's hard surface.

"Versey!"

She shook her head. "Don't fret. I'll replace it. Always lots of leftovers." The crystals played some mysterious but vital part in the workings of the station's energy system. Deftly she sorted through the lattice discards scattered around the table until she found a piece the right size and shape. Or close enough.

"Anything interesting happen down here today?" I asked, as she nipped and trimmed the edges with sharp cutters.

She uncapped a glue bottle and shrugged. "One of the air recyclers browned out for an hour or so. Skip came down to 'oversee'—which meant he stood around for half an hour with his arms folded, scowling while I sent a repair bot into the ducting. Looked like a stasher must have piled some stuff against it and the duct partially collapsed."

I carefully didn't comment on the stasher. "Sixty-nine," I said, after I'd re-counted the credits. "Here's your thirty percent." I pushed a stack across the table toward her and re-pocketed the rest. Versey and I had a good partnership. She provided the bits and scraps I used to build my birds, and a place to do the work, and we split the take. We were both saving up for colony passage. I didn't know what I'd do without Versey.

She ignored the credits, intent on affixing the glittering bit of crystal to the bird.

"Hey, there's a new guy up on the concourse. Get this —he's selling some kind of medicine to prevent space-sickness. Says it even works for wormholes. Pricey as hell. Is that even possible?"

One eyebrow rose, but her eyes didn't leave the bird. "Not that I've ever heard, but I guess it could be. They'd get more colonists if they could treat that problem."

I rested a hand on my chin. "You think it stops that many? I'm going as soon as I can afford it, regardless."

At that she did look over at me with one eye. "You ever been space-sick?"

"Not that I remember." I might have said it a little defensively. I was only five when my parents brought me to Damyadi Station, so I didn't remember much about the trip. "But you're willing to face it, too."

Versey turned her attention back to the bird. "True. It's hellish if you're one of the unlucky ones and get it really bad, but I'd still rather be planetside."

It wasn't that Versey didn't like being an engineer, I knew. She freaking loved it. Not everyone would enjoy being closeted down here with machines for company, but it suited her just fine. She claimed to like machines better than she liked people. Present company excepted, she always added. But she'd told me once that her first love was vehicles. Trucks, tractors, cars, rovers—the things you only saw planetside. That's why she wanted off the station. At least, that's what she claimed. Her partner had gone out on a wormhole exploration run six years ago and never come back, leaving her and Rel on their own. I figured the station also held memories she'd like to escape someday. Same as it did for me.

Versey's colony passage would cost more than mine, because of her weight, and because of Rel. Which was why I'd put twenty-five credits in her stack and kept forty-four myself, even though I called it thirty percent. She'd kick up a fuss if she noticed, but she rarely counted them.

I stood. "Gonna go get something to eat. I'll stop by later for the birds, okay?"

She nodded absently, intent on inspecting the next bird.

"You want anything?"

"No, thanks. I hope you did the math right on those credits, Lucy."

I hid a grin. "Pretty sure I did, Vers. See you later."

And I hurried out of engineering.

I didn't think I could have been the cause of the air recycler problem, but I dropped in to check my stashout before I hit the concourse market. Versey and I never discussed exactly where I lived, although she had to know I was a stasher—someone without "official" living space on the station, who made a home somewhere in the recesses of the station's structure. We were technically illegal but not persecuted by security—most stashers contributed to the station economy while they saved up enough for colony passage, and didn't make trouble. When my parents had died in a shuttle crash, no-one really knew what to do with me, but Versey had helped as much as she could. For the rest, I figured it out myself. By the time I was orphaned I'd had the run of Damyadi for five years, and I knew the station as well as any child knows his or her home neighborhood. My stashout, behind one of the hangar bays, was pretty sweet. Ducting and cables for the bay ran along the "ceiling" of a four-foot-wide, five-foot-high utility shaft. I easily slipped in and out through the rarely-used access door. Turn right, scuttle twenty feet along the shaft, and you'd find my space; a bedroll, a metal footlocker that had belonged to my father (locked, and chain-locked to a metal strut), a battery-run lamp that I charged periodically in engineering, and best of all, a small hidden panel behind the cabling. It held an electrical box and also made a perfect hiding place for my tightly-wrapped bundle of credit savings. My spot was warm, dry, and only noisy on nights when a repair crew worked overtime in the hangar. Just this year I'd had to start ducking my head to fit, but I didn't mind. I figured the low ceiling discouraged intruders.

As I expected, all my stuff was well clear of the ducting. Everything looked just as I'd left it. Stashers had a code—if you found someone else's spot, you left it alone. I wasn't trusting enough not to hide the credits, though. There's trust, and then there's stupid.

The concourse market was busy when I emerged from the stairwell, bustling with a load of new colonists waiting for the next big liner. Faces still looked greenish from their recent travels, so the food vendor lines were short—I walked right up to a kiosk and bought a pita sandwich. If I ate it quick and retrieved the birds, they might have enough charge for one performance for this fresh audience.

A large crowd had gathered at the other side of the concourse, and I wandered over, munching my sandwich, to see what the attraction was. I shouldn't have been surprised to see Mert Piler at the center, hawking Doktor Dohlman's Patented Space-Sickness Particulate energetically. Pale, sickly-looking colony hopefuls were buying it up like crazy. I smothered a grimace. Maybe I wouldn't bother with the birds. These folks were primed to spend their spare cash on medicine right now, not entertainment. Mert caught my eye through the crowd and tipped me a broad wink.

I wasn't sure what it meant, and I didn't like it much, but I saluted him with my half-eaten sandwich and walked away. Maybe the crowd would be more in the mood for magic and colorful birds tomorrow.

A weight hit my back and I almost dropped the pita, but managed to hang on to it as I twisted around and looked down into the laughing blue eyes of Rel. He hugged my waist briefly and said, almost breathless, "Lucy! You should have seen the ship that docked a little while ago! It's called the *S.W. Celestial Princess* and so many people came over in shuttles! You could probably fit everyone on Damyadi Station on it and it would only be half full!"

"Cool. I saw a lot of those people on the concourse."

"Someday I want to be the captain of a ship like that." He walked beside me, chattering happily about the star liner, and I pulled half of my remaining sandwich free and offered it to him.

He took it, and in the brief moment while his mouth was full, I said, "What about going to a colony planet with your mom?"

Rel swallowed and smiled at me pityingly. "That's only until I'm old enough to be a pilot, Lucy. I'm not going to be stuck on a planet my whole life. Who'd want that? I like to be where I can see the stars, and the ships. Are you coming down to get your birds?"

I nodded, wishing just a little that I could see my own life unfolding so clearly.

Mert Piler stood at the back of the small crowd for my first performance the next day. He watched with apparent fascination while the birds went through their aerial acrobatics, to the squeals of delight and applause of my audience. The birds soared, wings glittering, up close to the dome, silhouetted against the star-dotted canvas of space, then darted and dove over the heads of the crowd. I'd been smart to wait until this morning. The crowd looked better for a night's sleep, ready to experience the excitement of being in a strange and—for them—exotic place. I didn't pay much attention to Piler, focusing instead on the kids in the crowd and the parents who'd pay if those kids were well entertained.

Piler returned for the third performance of the day, and again for the fifth. In between, he hawked Doktor Dohlman at his table across the concourse. He lingered after my fifth performance while I chatted with some of the spectators and packed up my birds and equipment.

When the others had wandered away, he came up to me, chuckling. "I have to hand it to you, young lady, you're good."

"Well, thanks," I said, genuinely pleased. It was nice to be recognized by a fellow busker, even one with different talents.

"I can't figure out your angle," he said, shaking his head. "That's impressive."

I hitched the bird case under my arm and paused, puzzled. "My angle? I'm not sure what you mean."

He treated me to another broad wink. "Your game. Your con. You know. I thought you must have a dipper, but if you do, they're good. Even I couldn't spot them."

Reflexively, I took a step back from him. I shook my head. "I don't have a con, or a—a dipper. I just do a magic show."

His face stayed jovial, but the look didn't reach his eyes. They were hard little steel rivets as he shrugged. "Hey, you don't want to tell me, that's fine. I just thought we could chat about the business."

I didn't move, unwilling to head in any particular direction in case he followed me. A hot, angry burning seared my chest and my fingers twitched as if they'd like to grab something, but I willed myself not to do or say anything else. Station admin wouldn't continue to benevolently ignore me if I started a fight on the concourse.

Mert Piler seemed oblivious to my reaction. He touched

a knuckle to the brim of his hat mockingly. "See you around, then, Lucy Daz." He turned and ambled over to his table.

I stood still till he reached it and began setting out the rows of tiny bottles. Then I fled to engineering.

"I don't trust him," I told Versey as I settled the birds on the charging strip. I'd related my conversation with Mert Piler. "When he said chat about the business he didn't mean just selling stuff on the station."

She shook her head. "Sounds like a real con artist to me."

"He must be running a scam with that so-called medicine of his," I said, trying to keep my voice steady. "And what's a dipper, anyway? He said he thought I had one, but he couldn't spot them."

Versey absently tucked a loose strand of steel-grey hair behind one ear while she examined the birds. "A dipper is a pickpocket. Piler thought you were running a pull and grab. You pull the audience's attention with your magic show, and the dipper grabs whatever he can from pockets and bags."

"That's rotten," I sputtered. "I'd never do that. These people have staked everything they have on colony passage. Half the time I feel guilty about the credits they pay me!"

Versey stroked the back of one of the crystal-glittering birds, as if by calming it, she could calm me, too. "Don't worry about it, Lucy. Who cares what he thinks?"

I drummed my fingers on the scarred metal surface of the worktable. "I don't care what he thinks," I said finally. "But I can't stand a liar. And what if he's selling fake medicine to all those people? He'll get away with it, if he is. They won't know it doesn't work until they're gone on the colony ship, and by the time they get planetside, they'll be busy getting settled. Who's going to reach back to the station to file a complaint?"

"True," she said. "But we don't even know for sure that's what he's doing. You'll do best just staying out of his way. People like that can be dangerous."

Versey's words were casual, but something heavy hung in the air between us, squeezing around me as if the engineering bay had been over-pressurized. I knew what it was. The shuttle accident that had killed my parents five years ago, when I was only ten. Caused by counterfeit, flawed drive cells, substituted so that someone could make a few extra credits. They'd basically been killed by a con man.

"I know." I stared at one of my birds, my thoughts in a jumble. What could I do? "But I'm going to keep an eye on him, just the same."

The next morning, little Stella and her dad were back for my performance. She hung on his sleeve, cajoling him to stay around until the show finished finished, I could tell. Sure enough, when the act was over, she ran over and hugged my legs.

"Can I touch one of the birds again?" she asked, lisping a little in breathless anticipation.

"Of course," I said, laughing. I knelt down. "Hold your two hands out like a cup," I told her, and sat one of the birds on her palms. Her eyes and smile both widened.

Her father slipped a credit into my hat, then watched Stella for a moment, smiling, before he glanced over his shoulder. "Okay, Stella, we should go now."

"We're going on a big ship tomorrow!" Stella told me excitedly, reluctant to relinquish the bird. Then her smile faded. "But I'll be sad, because I won't see you any more!"

I stood and patted her head. "Well, I'm going on a big ship someday, too. Maybe I'll catch up to you."

Her father looked across the concourse again, and I realized he was glancing over at the Doktor Dohlman table. My stomach tightened.

"Thank Miss Daz and let's go, Stella."

The little girl handed the bird back to me with a sigh. "They're so beautiful," she said wistfully. Her father took her hand and half-turned.

"Sir?" I blurted.

He turned back.

"If you're thinking of buying some of that...medicine," I said in a rush. "I'm not sure it's really...I mean, I think that man might be—" A burning flush prickled at the back of my neck and spread around to my cheeks. Should I even voice my suspicions? I had no proof. But I hated, hated, *hated* the thought of Mert Piler scamming sweet little Stella and her father. A few others who had been in my audience lingered as well, eavesdropping shamelessly.

Stella's father raised an eyebrow, then glanced down at his daughter. "Might be taking advantage?"

I nodded. "I'm not sure, but—"

"That's okay. Thanks for the warning." He stroked Stella's unruly curls. "I half-figured it was too good to be true, but I thought maybe it was worth a try."

"I don't have any evidence," I said. "If it might help with the space sickness—"

He smiled. "I'll discuss it with my wife before we decide. It's pricey. And we'll take your suspicions into account."

He reached out a hand, and I took it. His clasp was firm and warm. "Thanks for looking out for us," he said with a nod to Stella. "And maybe we'll see you colony-side, some day." He dropped another credit in my hat as he and Stella walked away, in the direction of the food kiosks, not the table lined with shiny bottles of Doktor Dohlman's Patented Space-Sickness Particulate. The others dispersed as well, some holding muttered conversations and glancing over at Mert Piler's table.

I stooped to retrieve my hat and stood to find Piler's eyes narrowed on me from across the concourse. Even at this distance I felt the liquid heat of an angry glare in those previously cold steel rivets. He couldn't have overheard my conversation with Stella's father, but obviously he thought he'd read its meaning.

Now he very deliberately raised his hand and 'shot' me with an imaginary gun.

I pretended not to notice, gathered my case, and tried not to run as I left the concourse.

"So now he hates me," I summed up. I'd told Versey the story over mugs of hot cocoa in engineering. She'd taken one look at my face and lit the little burner she kept down here. Rel came in when we were halfway through, and by silent agreement we talked about something else until he'd collected his own mug and settled in the corner with a book. When we took up the conversation, we kept our voices low.

"I wish I knew for sure," I fretted. "What if his medicine really works, and now Stella's going to be horribly sick without it? I probably shouldn't have said anything at all."

"What if you're right, and you just saved her parents a lot of credits? What if it's actually dangerous?" Versey said reasonably. "We need to find out for sure."

I nodded, fingers clenched around the mug so tightly my knuckles were white. "If it's fake, I'll report him. I don't care if he's mad. Maybe I could buy some, and get it tested somehow." My heart fluttered at the thought of dipping into my hard-earned savings. But I'd do it if I had to.

Versey shook her head, tapping her fingers on the side of her mug. "He'll be suspicious now. Probably wouldn't sell it to you. Or to anyone who isn't a colonist. Any idea where he's staying?"

I shrugged. "Probably took a berth. He doesn't strike me as a stasher."

"He might be too tight with his money to take a berth," Versey mused, staring into her cocoa. "More of a fly-by-night operator. Arrive at a station, make what he can fast, take off again. Don't leave a trail that's easily followed, and hope you don't run into any of your victims down the road."

"He'd have to use his name and ID to get a berth. But if he had a stashout," I said slowly, "and a person could find it..."

"Another stasher would know the station pretty well," she said, still apparently mesmerized by the contents of her mug. "And if they had access to the station schematics, too..."

We sat in silence for a little while. As I'd suspected, Versey knew I was a stasher—but obviously, she didn't mind. And she was willing to help me out with this. Just like she helped me with everything. Rel laughed at something in his book and I felt a momentary chill of worry that Versey could get into trouble for helping me with this. But I knew the thought of kids—kids like Rel— suffering because of Mert Piler's con, bothered her, too. The chill receded under the warm rush of friendship I felt for her and Rel and this space, the closest thing I had to family. For a minute, hands wrapped around the steaming mug, I felt happy and content.

Until I remembered we were talking about tracking down Mert Piler's stashout and stealing from him. The image of him shooting me with his finger rose in my mind with horrible clarity, and brought the chill back with it.

I ran my usual performances the rest of the day, because I didn't want Mert Piler suspecting anything. I studiously ignored his table, and he didn't come near mine. I could almost convince myself I'd imagined that angry gesture, but when I felt his eyes on me I knew the anger still simmered behind them.

At the end of the day I hurried to my stashout and exchanged my "work" clothes for a station-issue coverall. Station policy entitles everyone to a free one, and lots of folks use them to save wear and tear on their few good clothes. A good-natured concourse tailor had helped me create a long-tailed coat for my performances, and Versey and I had spent hours sewing on shards of Brekman crystals to make it sparkle. It was one-of-a-kind, on Damyadi Station at least, so it stood out too much for skulking around incognito. I pulled my hair into a knot on top of my head and covered it with a nondescript hangar crew cap. It wasn't exactly a disguise, but I did look different from Lucy Daz of Dazzling Aviatronics.

I took the long way back to the food kiosks so I didn't

have to cross the concourse, and emerged behind the noodle-maker's. With a bowl of spicy noodles in hand, I slid into a seat half-turned away from the concourse. Mert Piler edged into my peripheral vision if I turned my head slightly. Colonists crowded around his table and my stomach twisted, but I forced myself to eat the noodles like nothing was wrong.

"Hey, Daz, you don't look like yourself. You in disguise or something?" said a gravelly voice, and I looked up to see Haxton standing next to my table. He balanced a plastic tray holding three bowls of noodles, two steaming mugs of spicy chai, and a bulb of water. He'd exchanged his security uniform for a coverall just like mine, and I was surprised to see that off-duty, he looked younger.

I gulped and almost choked on a noodle. Did he know what I was doing? But one corner of his mouth twitched up in a half-smile and I knew he was teasing.

"Just seeing how the other half lives," I said, forcing a grin.

"Keep it up and you'll look like a real colonist," he said, and moved to sit at a nearby table. A thin, friendly-looking woman with blunt-cut dark hair and a little girl who looked about ten waited for him. The girl smiled up from under long straight bangs and showed him something she'd drawn on a sheet of e-paper. She had a bright smile and I recognized her as a station kid who sometimes came to my performances. She always put a credit in the hat.

Haxton had a family? Shocking, but it made sense. Some people could afford passage only as far as a station, then took work there to save up the colony fare, like Versey. But colony fare for three people? That would take some time. I thought about where she got credits to put in my hat and begrudged Haxton his extra weekly payment a little less.

By the time my noodles were gone and I'd bought and eaten a bowl of honeyed yogurt, Piler was packing up his wares for the night. I felt a pang of worry that he'd come to the kiosks for something to eat, but he didn't. Instead he headed right, presumably toward the stairs. He'd go down, probably, to the berths levels. The stairs up led to the station's administrative levels, and I couldn't imagine he'd have business there.

I followed him as casually as I could manage, pausing at the corner of Starview, the only actual restaurant on the station, where I'd never eaten. I could, I suppose, spend some of the credits from my savings, but food seemed too fleeting a thing to waste them on. Warm, garlicky scents wafted out, rumbling my stomach even though I'd just eaten. Peering around, I saw the top of Mert Piler's hat as he clattered down the metal stairs.

I took a deep breath and strolled to the stairs myself, starting down them with my hands stuck in the pockets of my coverall to still their trembling. Even if Mert Piler glanced up, I didn't think he'd recognize me; all he'd see was the bottoms of my shoes and a figure in a generic station coverall, but I felt ridiculously conspicuous. He descended another level, to M4, which was all berths and storage lockers for colonists and station residents—crew, business owners, and people like me, on indeterminate stopovers. I tried to hurry but not clatter on the stairs, so I wouldn't lose Piler in the circular corridors.

The curving hallway allowed me to keep him in sight while staying mostly concealed if he looked back. If he stopped at one of the berths, he'd take a minute or two to unlock it; I could note which one it was, then sneak up and get the number on the door after he'd gone inside. He didn't stop at a berth, though; when I heard his footsteps go silent and peeked around the curve, he stood fiddling with the latch on a service duct.

I grinned. So he was a stasher, just like me. That was good. If I could find his stashout, I wouldn't have to pick a lock, like I would on a berth.

My grin didn't last long, though. It would be risky following him into the service tunnels, and even more likely that he'd catch me—with no-one else around. I didn't like that prospect.

Palms sweating and heart racing, I stood with my back against the wall. I pulled out the flexible e-sheet Versey had given me and activated it, scrolling quickly through the schematics until I got to M4 and navigated to this section. I found the service duct easily enough; it ran between two berths and curved along the outer wall of the station for fifty feet or so before descending to the level below, M5, and running out to one of the docking bays. It shouldn't be too hard to find Piler's spot.

A soft rattle sounded down the hall and I risked a look —Mert had emerged from the duct and was in the process of replacing the cover. I ducked down the hallway leading to the inner ring of berths and listened as his footsteps approached, then echoed off the metal stairs as he ascended. My heart fluttered and dove like one of my birds and I pulled in deep breaths and blew them slowly out. This would be the perfect time to look for the stashout. He was probably gone up to the main concourse for something to eat, or maybe to spend the rest of the evening in Sandro's Bar.

Before I could talk myself out of it, I scurried back to the main hallway and down to the service duct cover. The three latches took longer than they should have to open, because my hands were shaking again. Once inside the tunnel, with the cover propped in place, I relaxed. The tunnels felt more like home than any other place on the station, with the exception of engineering. And that was mostly Versey.

The tunnel was lower than mine, so I had to duck my head. It must not be very comfortable for Mert Piler, taller and bigger around than I was, so I took that as an indication that he didn't intend to stay on Damyadi Station very long.

The first stashout I found was tucked into an alcove, under a control panel for the ventilation system. It wasn't Mert's—a pair of women's pants and a ruffled blouse, showing only slight signs of wear, hung next to the panel door. I moved on. Another alcove revealed a coiled pile of cables, covered by a blanket. A metal footlocker, similar to mine but older and dirtier, stood nearby. There were no clues to the owner, but I didn't think this was Mert's, either. No supplies case or table, and nowhere to hide them.

When I reached the narrow metal stairs leading down to the lower level, I figured I'd found it. Under the stairs, where I thought Mert could probably just fit if he wriggled a bit, was a little enclosed closet. Every inch of space on a station is utilized, so the closet probably held more control panels, or extra storage space for the crew who worked in the nearby docking bay. Even without checking Versey's schematics, it looked big enough for a pretty nice stashout.

When I wriggled close to the door I noticed the shiny new silver padlock rammed through one of the latches. The station admin quietly overlooked most illegal stashouts, but it was forbidden to interfere with access to any part of the station. You could hide things, but you couldn't lock out station staff. Mert Piler was either taking a chance, or he'd bribed someone to look the other way.

I thought of Haxton and the credit he easily accepted from me each week. It probably wasn't that hard to bribe someone. Reporting the lock wouldn't do much good.

With a sigh, I slid back out to the staircase. I wasn't going to find out anything more about Mert Piler's stashout tonight.

It's lucky my performances are second nature to me now. I was so distracted the next day, constantly checking the crowds at Mert Piler's table and worrying over what to do about him, that I probably would have crashed several birds if they'd needed my full attention. As it was, they swooped and spiralled overhead, crystals sparkling like the stars beyond the concourse dome, twirled and danced in the air like live things unconcerned with my intervention. Piler chose to completely ignore me, but his animosity reached cold fingers across the concourse.

Around midday, a wave of new arrivals flowed from shuttles into the concourse, and I tried to force Mert Piler from my thoughts. I put on my most engaging manner, hoping to draw a travel-weary audience who would enjoy the birds and open their pockets. Although many were still drawn to his table, I had good crowds for two performances and was rewarded with a gratifying number of both smiles and credit chips.

I was taking a break and enjoying a cool bulb of water from one of the kiosks when I heard a male voice bellow, "You!" I looked up to see a tall traveller stalking across the concourse toward Mert Piler's table. He was accompanied by one of the rarely-glimpsed Lobor aliens. The dog-like Lobor kept pace with the man, its lightly bouncing gait setting loose pants fluttering around its legs, but it seemed to be remonstrating, trying to hold the man back from approaching Piler. The man ignored the Lobor, extending a shaking finger toward Piler. Mert had gone a little pale, his forehead glistening with sweat under the concourse lights.

The man reached the table. "You sold me garbage!" he shouted, his accusing finger trembling just under Mert's nose. "Miracle cure for space sickness, indeed! I almost died coming from Mars!"

Mert Piler held up both palms, trying to placate the enraged customer. "Sir, I'm sorry, there must be some mistake—"

"No mistake," the man spat, snatching up one of the little vials and shaking it at Mert. "You sold me this phony medicine six months ago. Probably thought you'd never see me again, did you? But I know you, sir! I'd recognize your lying face anywhere!"

Mert Piler looked like he might be about to argue, but suddenly changed his attitude. "My apologies, sir, I didn't recognize you at first. It's true, in the odd instance, an individual might not experience the full positive effects of Doktor Dohlman's Powder. Other medications could interact, or perhaps the individual's unique physiology might make them so susceptible to space sickness that even this miraculous cure is not enough—"

"Save it," the man barked. "I'm not interested in any more of your—"

"BUT," Mert raised his voice, drowning out the cantankerous customer, "in a case such as this, I'm happy to offer a full refund on the cost of the medication.

Never let it be said that Mert Piler doesn't stand behind his product."

I glimpsed a young woman in one of the new Nearspace Protectorate uniforms heading toward the table to investigate the commotion, and I wondered if she'd sparked Mert's sudden turnaround. As he spoke, Piler dug in his credit pouch and hastily counted out chips, then with a flourish offered a handful to the man. "Here you are, sir, a complete reimbursement on your purchase, and my sincere apologies for your discomfort."

The man's Lobor companion, a look of what certainly seemed like embarrassment stretched over its dog-like muzzle, seemed to be urging him in a low voice to take the offered credits. With a final glare, the man snatched them out of Mert's hand and stalked off, with a grumbled warning, "Buyers, beware!" to the assembled, gape-mouthed crowd. As Mert began to prattle to the crowd about how rare such a failure was, I went back to my side of the concourse, thoughtful. The Protectorate officer paused and seemed to lose interest, now that the altercation was over.

But I felt excited. Here was more evidence that Mert Piler really was cheating people. He might claim it was a rare occurrence, but he hadn't been shocked to be confronted—just concerned that the confrontation wouldn't spook other customers. He probably tried very hard never to run into any of his victims once they'd been sucked in by his claims. More certain than ever that he couldn't be trusted, I had to find out for sure what was in those vials. I just couldn't see how. I could try to find the angry man—but the alien with him made me nervous. By all accounts the Lobor were peaceful beings, but I'd only glimpsed a few before this, and I didn't think I was ready to come into close contact with one.

During the last show of the day, a little pale-haired boy with the luminous eyes and thin limbs of someone born on the lunar colony waved to a bird dipping and twirling above him. "Hey, bird! Hello, bird! Look at me! Down here!"

Smiling, his mother patted his head. "I don't think the

bird can see, you, sweetie. She's too busy flying." She winked at me.

I smiled back. And froze for a second. What if—

I snapped out of it and threw a hand out just in time to catch the bird plummeting toward the concourse floor, presenting it with a flourish to be petted. "Now she can see you," I said, but my mind whirled. I couldn't get into Mert Piler's stashout, but maybe something else could. I couldn't wait to pack everything up and get down to engineering to tell Versey my idea.

When I got there and breathlessly sputtered it out to her, she looked skeptical. "I've never made one to run silent," she protested. "That's going to be complicated."

"But you don't have to make one at all," I said with a grin, and went to the cabinet where Versey stored the repair bots. I pulled out one of the smallest ones, spiderlike and compact enough to sit comfortably in the palm of my hand, with room to spare. "All you have to do is modify one of these, sync it to my remote, and I'll do the rest. With luck I won't even have to move it when he's there."

Versey's face had crinkled into a broad grin. "And if we set the feed to record—"

"Then we'll have proof of whatever he's doing," I finished. "If there's anything, of course."

We sat in pleased silence for a moment, and then Versey said, "You'll have to get pretty close, to control the bot with your remote. It's not like sending one into a duct, because those routes are preprogrammed into the bot's memory. It might not be safe."

I shrugged. "I'll find a spot. Don't worry. You'll help me with this, won't you? If he's cheating people, we have to stop him."

Versey heaved a deep sigh. "Yeah, I guess we do. Let's see that bot."

The next evening, I waited until a crowd had gathered around Mert Piler's table, and then hurried off to his stashout. I knew I should be safe for a few minutes, but my heart pounded out a staccato rhythm as I nudged the tiny bot under the door and used my remote to make it crawl up the wall inside. Versey had fitted a small camera receiver to a headset, so I watched the feed from the bot with one eye while I maneuvered it around inside the stashout, and prayed that Mert didn't come looking for more supplies.

If I'd hoped for something obviously incriminating inside his stashout, I was disappointed—no bags or boxes labelled "Fake Medicine." The bot's camera lens showed me a worn-looking bedroll, a leather document bag, a metal trunk twice the size of my footlocker, and some clothing strewn around.

I swallowed my disappointment. I'd hoped to see enough before Mert came back, but it looked like I was going to have to stay a little longer. Time for Plan B.

I sent the bot up onto the ceiling of Mert's stashout. We'd padded the magnetic feet to muffle the click-click of its spidery legs against the metal it climbed, and Versey had made the joint hydraulics quieter. I guided it into a dark corner, keeping its camera pointed down into the living area. With luck, Mert would come in, do something bad, and I would catch it all on the bot's recorder.

My headset would store the video, so if I couldn't retrieve the bot right away, it wouldn't be a big deal. As long as Mert didn't notice it. If he found it, he'd surely connect it to me.

Once the bot was in position, I hurried down the stairs, emerging into the docking bay I'd seen on Versey's schematic. The echoing space lay submerged in shadow, quiet and empty. One small runabout, used to ferry passengers and cargo to ships too big to dock at the station, crouched on the starwise side of the bay, its windows and running lights dark. I set my back against the wall and slid down to sit, wincing at the chill metal. I hoped the wait wouldn't be long.

After twenty minutes, I was fidgeting. Then the light in the camera feed changed; Mert must have opened the closet door. I clasped my hands tightly, nails biting into my palms. A shadow moved into the closet and snapped on a little press-lamp attached to the ceiling. As I watched, Mert set his folding table against one wall, then knelt and opened his supplies case. His inventory had been depleted by about half, and I clenched my hands tighter. Had all those people been ripped off?

Mert opened the metal trunk and counted out several handfuls of empty glass vials, standing them in rows in the half-empty case. I grinned. I'd positioned the camera in the perfect spot and had a clear view of exactly what Mert was doing.

Until he shifted, apparently searching for a more comfortable position on the hard metal decking. I swore under my breath and bit my lip. Now Mert's body blocked the camera's view.

Slowly I pulled the remote from my pocket. I had to move the spider-bot, but with no microphone, I couldn't monitor how much noise it made. As delicately as if I were guiding one of my soaring, air-dancing birds, I nudged the bot to the left. One of the waiting vials came into view. Mert didn't look around, so I guessed the bot hadn't made a discernible sound. I nudged again, picturing one of my birds twisting silently in mid-air. More vials now, along with a corner of the metal trunk.

A millimeter at a time, I guided and nudged the bot until Mert's hands were in view again. Now he meticulously dipped out pink crystals from an unmarked metal tub with a tiny spoon, guiding the crystals into the vials through an equally tiny funnel. I squinted at the camera feed, but no further details resolved. I wanted to punch the metal floor. The pink crystals could be actual medicine. He set the tub down, revealing the beginning of a printed label. HIMA—.

Four letters told me nothing. Mert pulled a large paper sack from the trunk and began adding a teaspoon of white crystals from it to each vial. This label was clear — SUGAR.

My palms felt suddenly sweaty, slick with excitement. Settle down. Sure, the sugar could be a filler, or it could have a legitimate purpose, like masking a bad taste if the pink crystals really were medicine.

I had to know more. I wiped my palms down the legs of my coverall and ran a thumb over the remote. If I could send the bot to a slightly different angle, maybe I could—

The camera feed filled with a sudden blur and then jolted sharply to black. I leaped to my feet, tapping a finger against the headset. The picture returned, blurry at first, then sharpening to focus on a pair of shoes. I knew instantly what had happened—the bot had lost its grip on the ceiling and tumbled to the floor behind Mert Piler. He'd certainly heard that.

Now the camera feed swam and wavered as he picked up the bot. The image wobbled sickeningly as he raised it, and I had a fearsome view of his angry face. Then he dashed it to the floor and a second later the feed went black again and stayed that way.

I heard the door of Mert Piler's stashout closet burst open and clang against the wall.

I stood frozen inside the docking bay, my back still against the wall. Footsteps sounded on the metal stairs— going up or coming down? If Mert came down, he'd find me—I'd had to stay close enough for the remote to work. I almost bolted for the door across the docking bay but... hesitated.

Mert must have left the door of his stashout open, as he charged off looking for the bot's owner. There hadn't been time for him to close and lock it.

If he'd gone up the stairs, I could get in.

I pressed myself tightly to the wall, shut my eyes, and listened hard. The footsteps seemed to be growing more distant. I edged to the bay doorway and risked a quick peek.

No-one there. Mert had gone up. But I wouldn't have much time.

I flew up the stairs as quietly as my birds. As I'd suspected, Mert had rushed out and up, leaving the door ajar. I ducked inside. The spider bot lay irretrievably smashed to bits. I ignored it and snatched up the tub of pink crystals to read the label.

HIMALAYAN PINK SALT

I glanced inside the trunk. No other "ingredients" that might go into Doktor Dohlman's Patented Space-Sickness Particulate. Sugar and salt. That's all it was. Mert Piler was exactly the fraud I'd suspected.

And his footsteps were coming back down the stairs.

Fast.

I darted out of the closet, clutching the container of salt. Without video from the spider bot, I had no proof of Mert Piler's lies unless I took the evidence with me.

I didn't have to look up to know how close he was, so I didn't hesitate as I dashed back down the stairwell.

"Hey!" His shout erupted too close behind me, his footfalls echoing like drumbeats on the metal risers. His breathing was laboured and raspy and very loud.

I flew down the steps again, swinging around the corner at the bottom into the docking bay. I made for the door at the other side, Mert Piler hard on my heels. I passed the runabout regretfully—if I'd been a little further ahead of him I might have been able to hide inside it.

"I know...it's you...Lucy Daz!" he shouted, panting between the words. "You're...dead...if I—"

I reached the docking bay door and flung it open, emerging into a hallway that looked like every other hallway on the station. For a heartbeat I froze, disoriented.

A strong hand grabbed my arm from behind and swung me around. Mert Piler's hard, hot, rivet-eyes stared into mine as he panted. "You little—"

He was stronger and bigger, but I was angrier. A reasonable part of my mind knew that he wasn't the man responsible for my parents' deaths—but it had been someone just like him. The reasonable part of my mind melted away under a wash of white-hot rage.

Putting all that anger behind it, I smashed the metal container into Mert Piler's nose and felt the crunch of breaking bone. Pink crystals sprayed into the air and blood gushed in a horrible bright river over Mert's mouth. I jerked my other arm out of his grip as he fell back, clutching his face and spluttering blood.

I ran. I still wasn't sure where I was, but eventually I'd reach another stairwell—the station was circular, after all. I risked a glance into the salt container—still half-full.

A berth door opened ahead and a man stepped out. I dodged around him.

"Stop...her!" Piler screamed from behind me, his voice thin with pain and outrage. "Stop, thief!"

Instinctively, the man reached out for me and caught my sleeve, but I jerked away and sped on. I might be a thief, but Piler was worse, and I had to get to someone who'd listen. I hoped the second man wouldn't get involved. Piler's injury might slow him down, but the new man was fresh.

I reached the stairwell alcove and started up, taking the stairs two at a time. If I could keep ahead for two levels, I'd be on the main concourse, surrounded by people. I wanted to head for engineering, but that was clear on the other side of the station. Pain burned my thighs as I vaulted up the stairs, wishing for wings like my birds. A tight band squeezed my chest as my lungs fought to supply my body with enough oxygen to keep going at this pace.

A cacophony of steps on the stairs behind me told me that the new man had indeed joined the chase. My palms were sweat-slicked and the tub of salt almost slipped out of my hand. I hugged it against my chest. Just a few more steps—

I burst out of the stairwell onto the main concourse and risked a glance behind me. Miraculously, they weren't in sight yet. But in the second I wasn't looking, I ran smack into a thin man in a blue security uniform, who'd just stepped away from one of the food kiosks with a steaming bowl of noodles.

We both staggered back from the impact. Noodles and pink salt flew into the air like two of my birds, and came down much less gracefully. I sat down hard on the metal decking. The guard stumbled, couldn't regain his balance, and went down, too.

Haxton—because of course, it was Haxton—regarded

me with angry grey eyes and growled, "What do you think —"

Mert Piler, looking like he'd escaped from a slasher holo, staggered up and cut him off. "Arrest her! She broke into my stashout! And look what she did to my nose!" He turned to smirk horribly at me, lips and teeth dripping like a vampire. I knew what he was thinking. He'd probably paid Haxton to look the other way about the lock, so he figured he had the guard in his pocket.

I scooped up a handful of pink grains. "He's defrauding colonists with fake medicine! And," I added with a meaningful stare at Haxton, "you can't 'break into' anyone's stashout, since no-one's allowed to put locks on anything. Right, Officer Haxton?" I tried to send him a message with my eyes as well as my words. If Piler accused Haxton of accepting a bribe about the lock, I'd say there hadn't been any lock there.

A small crowd had gathered, and the words *fake medicine* triggered a low muttering. The salt container lay nearby, and I grabbed that, turning the label and the handful of salt toward them. "See that? Look familiar? Anybody here been taken in by him?"

"Officer," Mert said, ignoring the crowd as he tried to wipe the blood from his face with his sleeve, "I assure you that this girl is imagining things. I'm sure you'll see her and her lies properly dealt with." He winced as his hand brushed his quickly-swelling nose.

It didn't take a genius to read the meaning in his words. There'd be a credit bonus coming Haxton's way if he could make this little incident go away. And Haxton knew I didn't have the resources to make the same kind of offer.

But—I looked at Haxton. Our relationship had always been strictly business—and under-the-table business, at that—but I felt like we had a connection. He was a colonist-in-waiting, just like me. With a little girl with long, straight bangs and a bright smile.

"I just want to tell station admin what I found," I said. "You can't let him scam colonists with fake medicine. It's not fair. He's hurting little kids."

Haxton's eyes narrowed. I could almost read his mind. On the one hand, a big payout from Mert Piler would get Haxton and his family that much closer to a colony ship berth. On the other, he knew how hard it was to scrabble that fare together, and how much it would hurt to find out you'd wasted precious credits on a swindle. And been made a liar when you told your kid they wouldn't be space-sick.

He stood slowly, brushing salt from his uniform and picking off stray noodles. "Scoop up as much of that as you can," he instructed me. Then he spoke into a communicator. "Officer Palmer, put a guard on the storage closet on level M4, section 3, above the docking bay. Stay until I get there."

Mert Piler started to bluster again, but Haxton held up a hand. "Save it. We're all going to station admin. Let them sort it out." He grimaced at Piler. "Grab some napkins and clean off your face."

He waved the seething Piler ahead and nodded to me. A nod that I thought—hoped—said, *us against him, right, Daz?*

I nodded back.

With my evidence and an examination of the contents of Mert Piler's sealed vials—nothing but sugar and salt, as I predicted—the station admin lost little time in putting him, under guard, on a ship going far away from Damyadi Station. No station had the resources to deal with courts and trials and jails, so they'd log an incident report against Piler and get rid of him. Let him be somebody else's problem. Not a great system, but they did what they could. I took the time to find that Nearspace Protectorate officer I'd seen on the concourse, and tell her what had happened. She might or might not follow up, but it felt like the right thing to do.

A week later, I was in engineering with Versey, charging and repairing birds. Versey had a new one under construction, complete with tiny lights for its faceted eyes. Rel sat at one end of the worktable, building a starship model of out bits and pieces. At least he said that's what it was. I wasn't too sure, but he was having fun with it.

"I was thinking, maybe we could put a camera in one," she said, "and let kids watch the video through a headset. It'd be like they were flying. They'd love it!"

Rel looked up at that. "That would be stellar! Can I be first?"

She smiled at him. "If I get it working, you sure can."

A knock sounded at the door, which was unusual—no-one ever knocked at engineering.

"Come on in," Versey called.

The door opened and Haxton stuck his head in. "Security check," he said.

"Very funny," Versey said. "Come on in, Doug."

"Doug? You guys know each other?" I looked from one to the other.

Versey shrugged. "You stay here long enough, you get to know everyone, Lucy."

Haxton crossed to the worktable and set down a cloth bag. He tousled Rel's hair as he passed. "Admin ordered Mert Piler's stashout cleaned up and everything in it confiscated," he said, looking at me with his pale grey eyes. "This isn't official, but this," he poked the bag, "is a little reward for helping keep the station safe."

The bag clinked as credits slid against each other.

I sucked in a breath. The bag surely held more than I'd make in a month from performances.

But it hadn't been just me. "You deserve part of the reward," I said. "You believed me."

Haxton winked at me. "Don't worry," he said. "Who do you think was in charge of the confiscating?"

He left with a smile and a wave for Versey. I stared at the bag for a minute and then pulled it over.

"Well," I said, dumping out the credits and starting to count them, "you deserve your cut of this, since you modified the repair bot."

"Just make sure you do that math right, Lucy Daz. Thirty percent, no more," she instructed me, fiddling to fit a piece of crystal onto the bird's wing.

"Don't worry," I said, counting extra into her pile when she wasn't looking. "I'll do it exactly right."

Between us on the table the birds glittered and gathered energy, waiting for their chance to fly.

The Price of Roses

Dorothy deftly slid the thorn strippers down the stem of the last "Crimson Glory," wincing as the arthritis cramped her fingers. She added the rose to the others in the vase, then massaged the ache out of her hand, lips pursed against the pain.

The phone shrilled, and she had to move the heavy vase aside to reach it, grimacing again. "Hello, and thank you for calling *Rose Among the Thorns*. How may I help you?"

"Hi, Mum, it's just me." Stephanie's voice sounded tired, although it was only mid-morning. "You sound stressed. Arthritis again?"

Dorothy stifled a sigh. "Oh, maybe a little, honey, but I'm fine. You're the one with a 5 o'clock voice when it's only ten-thirty. What's wrong?"

"Nothing, just busy. Listen, I might have someone interested in the shop."

Dorothy didn't answer, and Stephanie breezed on.

"I was just talking to Mike in sales the other day about it, and he said he had a niece with some capital who was looking for something to sink it into. He talked to her and she'd like to have a look at the place. She might drop by

177

today."

Dorothy made herself count to ten before she answered.

"Mum? Are you still there?"

"I told you, Steph," Dorothy said as evenly as she could, "That I haven't made any definite plans to sell the shop."

"I know, but we've been through this, Mum. It's just getting too hard for you. You deserve a rest, you know. We'll work out the money questions—"

"It's not the money, and I don't want a rest." Dorothy glanced around the shop, at the brimming buckets of multi-hued petals. "What could be more restful than this?"

Stephanie huffed, an exasperated sound that Dorothy knew only too well. "There's the arthritis, too. You can't just keep ignoring that."

"Honey, I have a customer," Dorothy lied. "I'll call you back later. Bye." She didn't wait to hear anything else, just gently but firmly placed the receiver back in its cradle, closed her eyes and took a few deep breaths.

When she opened her eyes the first thing she saw was the arrangement she'd been working on, and she let her mind settle back on that, regarding it with a practiced eye. It needed another "Summer Sunshine," she thought, for balance. She reached for the flower and the strippers, breathing deeply to try and calm the tension her daughter's call had triggered. The shop was mid-morning quiet, and in a few minutes she'd go and brew her usual green tea restorative, sort through the mail, and then tackle the afternoon's orders with Melissa.

The vase of roses was striking, and a little smile of satisfaction lifted the corners of Dorothy's mouth. It was an indulgence, certainly, keeping a bouquet of this size in the shop simply for her personal enjoyment, but wasn't enjoyment the principal reason for growing roses in the first place? And if a customer or two were impressed enough to order something similar instead of the usual unimaginative half-dozen reds, well, that wasn't a bad thing.

Dorothy always chose some of the best specimens in the shop for her own arrangements, selecting unerringly for form and substance; graceful shapes and crisp, thick, velvety petals. Today she'd created a "flame dance," as she liked to call it, a lush mix of hybrid teas in red, yellow, orange and white, the colors so vividly hot they seemed to glow with an inner energy. A spray of white gypsophila floated behind the roses like a cloud of smoke, and studded among the blooms stood stems bearing only rose leaves, emerald greens so dark they might have been charred by the heat of the flowers around them.

The door behind Dorothy opened then and Melissa came in from the greenhouse with a grin and an armload of blooms.

"We'd better get busy soon, Mrs. B.," she said, distributing the flowers among the buckets that lined the walls of the shop. "I've got a fistful of orders for this afternoon."

"I know," Dorothy said. "I'm almost through here." She stepped back, considering her bouquet from different angles. "I think it's just about perfect."

Melissa came to stand beside her, and Dorothy caught the earthy scent of loam that clung to the younger woman's gloves. "As usual," she said. "No-one can put them together like you can, Mrs. B."

"Well, I've taught you just about everything I know," Dorothy said, "And a good thing, too. If Steph has her way I won't be here much longer."

Melissa frowned. "She's not still on about you retiring, is she?"

"More than ever. Now she's telling people I'm looking for a buyer."

"What? Would she really make you sell the shop?" Melissa's eyes mirrored her own concern.

Dorothy shrugged. "Well, she can't exactly *make* me sell it; I'm not senile yet. But she can put pressure on me, and you know how good Stephanie is with pressure."

The younger woman smiled. "She is that. Too bad you couldn't have convinced her to work here instead of up in that office tower. She'd be a lot less stressed and a lot happier."

"I don't know. She always said it was too boring when she worked here as a teenager," Dorothy said wistfully. She did wish she could have instilled her love of the flowers in her daughter, but they were different personalities.

"Boring? Geez, you've got it all here," Melissa said, ticking off her points on her gloved fingers. "Births, deaths, weddings, breakups, make-ups, sickness and recovery—people send flowers for everything that happens in life. It's like a regular soap opera, the things people will tell you when they call or come in."

Dorothy grinned. "I know. But Steph never seemed to get that." She sighed suddenly, glancing down at her hands. "But maybe she's right about this. It *is* getting harder, I can't deny that."

"Oh, forget about Stephanie. You'll be running this place for a long time yet, Mrs. B., mark my words. Now I'm going to go and put the kettle on for you, and once you're ready just ring the buzzer and I'll come and help you with the orders." She put an arm around Dorothy's shoulders and squeezed, careful not to smudge Dorothy's blouse with her gloves.

"Whatever you say," Dorothy said, forcing a smile. Melissa was a dear, and if Stephanie did convince her to sell the shop, she'd make it a condition that Melissa had a job here for as long as she wanted it.

Just as the door to the greenhouse closed behind Melissa, the bell above the front door chimed, and Dorothy looked up to greet the customer. A youngish man entered the shop hesitantly, stopping just a few steps inside. He glanced around at the rainbow array of open buckets brimming with roses, but his gaze came to rest almost immediately on Dorothy's flame dance on the counter. Even across the room Dorothy heard his sharp intake of breath.

He strode over to the counter, his eyes on the roses, not on Dorothy. "Are these—I mean, good morning," he stammered.

Dorothy smiled. "Good morning. They're beautiful,

aren't they?"

He nodded, staring at the roses with an odd intensity. "Are they for sale?"

"Not this particular arrangement, but I can do one like it for you. It wouldn't be ready until late this afternoon. Would that be all right?"

The man shook his head, his eyes flickering toward Dorothy only briefly before he looked back to the roses. "No, I need something I can take with me now. I don't have much time." He seemed to shake himself out of his reverie then, and turned to Dorothy. "Er...you don't have any blue roses, do you?"

Dorothy chuckled and shook her head. "Not yet. Probably never will, either. Roses don't come in blue, I'm afraid. Of course, tell people they can't have something and someone has to prove you wrong. I'm sure there are scientists somewhere working on blue roses right now, with all their gene-splicing and what-not."

"Yes, I'm sure there are," the man said absently, glancing down at the pile of mail waiting to be sorted. On top of the stack was a brochure for computer maintenance and backup services. He gestured to it. "I guess you're not too worried about all this in your line of business."

Dorothy laughed. "Computer bugs aren't the kind that bother roses," she said. "Aphids, now, or thrips or spider mites, maybe. Not the electronic kind. I get by in here with just a cash register, without ruffling too many petals." She pushed the mail and the big rose arrangement to opposite sides of the counter. "So what can I show you in a bouquet?"

The man took a deep sigh and let it out, relaxing visibly. He ran a hand through his tawny hair, leaving bits of it sticking up wildly. "Well, I'd like something like that," he said, nodding to the flame dance, "Even if you can't do something that fancy while I wait, it's okay. I'd just like a lot of different kinds of roses mixed together."

"Were you thinking of this particular color combination, or something else?" Dorothy made a note on her pad.

"Not really—I mean, it doesn't matter," he said, shoving his hands deep into his pockets. "Just a nice mixture. Different kinds...different species, if you have them."

Dorothy frowned a little. "We generally stay with one particular kind of rose in an arrangement. But it doesn't have to be hybrid teas. I have antique roses, climbers..."

The man licked his lips. "But I might, I mean, I might not leave them all together. I might, say, put them in different vases or something, a few here and there, you know? So I'd like a variety. You don't have to arrange them or anything. Just wrap up a bundle."

"Well, all right," Dorothy said hesitantly. "How many?"

"How much do they cost?"

"Fifty-two fifty for a dozen. Did you want that many? I can sell them by the half-dozen or individually."

He pulled a smooth leather wallet from the pocket of his trousers. "I'll take three dozen," he said with a wide grin. "As many different kinds as you have."

"That's going to be one big bouquet," Dorothy said. "I hope she appreciates it, whoever she is. All right, just let me write it up here." She pulled out an invoice slip and wrote in the date. "Your name?"

"Oh, it's...um...Hunter, Max Hunter."

"Address?"

"I don't—I mean, you don't have to fill that all in. I won't be using the receipt for anything."

Dorothy glanced up, surprised by a tightness that seemed to tug at the man's voice, like a taut wire thrumming.

"I'm sorry," he said haltingly. "I'm just...short on time."

Dorothy shrugged. "Okay, Mr. Hunter." She rang up the sale on the ancient cash register, pressing the stiff keys gingerly with her tender fingers. "With tax, that will be one hundred and eighty-one dollars and twelve cents, please."

Carefully the man counted out nine crisp twenty-dollar bills, dug in his pocket and added a bright two-dollar coin to the stack, and handed Dorothy the money, smiling.

As she took it, however, something about the toonie

arrested her movement. It was...different, wrong somehow. It took her a moment to focus in on the burnished coppery core of the coin...where a man's face stared back at her. Not the Queen—her son, Charles. And bold enough now that Dorothy stopped to look, the impossible numerals curving in the silvery ring over the King's head. *Next* year.

Dorothy's heart pounded once, heavily. The coin must be counterfeit. And if the coin, then what of the suspiciously crisp bills? Suddenly everything about this young man felt false.

"Is something wrong?" Max Hunter's voice betrayed the slightest tremble.

She couldn't make herself look up. "No, no," she said, trying to force a lightness she didn't feel into her voice. "This must be...one of the new toonies, is it? I guess they've minted them early."

She could feel his eyes on the coin. The money weighed heavily on her palm, pressing down against the aching bones inside. He looked at the coin for a long moment while Dorothy looked at him.

"Dammit," he finally whispered. "They gave me the wrong one."

Dorothy moved then, backing as far away from the counter as she could, holding the money out from her body as if it were a snake. "Look, mister, I don't want any trouble. Here, you just keep this and I'll get you the roses, too. It doesn't matter."

"No!" Max Hunter's voice was anguished. "No, no, the money's perfectly good! It's just—it's just...early."

"Early?" Dorothy didn't move. The man wasn't making any sense. "That's what I said, they must have minted them early." Maybe it was true. Maybe she was a foolish old woman. He wasn't acting like a criminal.

"But you can't spend—you'll get into trouble—Oh, damn, I've really blown it," he said suddenly. He turned and crossed to the shop door in one swift movement, and Dorothy felt a swell of relief. It ebbed quickly when he flipped the "open" sign to read "closed" from outside, and slid the deadbolt home. Dorothy glanced under the counter. Where were her shears? There was nothing else in the shop she could use as a weapon, if it came to that. Could she press the button to buzz the greenhouse without him noticing? But that might only put Melissa in danger, too.

When he turned back to her he held up both hands as if to halt her thoughts. "Don't be frightened. I just have to explain some things to you, that's all, and I can't have anyone else coming in here or I'll be in even more trouble."

Willing her hand to be steady, Dorothy carefully set the money down on the counter and folded her arms over her chest. "I'm listening."

He didn't come back to the counter, just stayed where he was, near the door. "I only need the roses. I have to collect as much varied rose DNA as I can. This seemed like a good place."

"Mmm—hmmm." Dorothy said.

"Remember when I asked you about blue roses?"

Dorothy nodded.

"Well, where I come from, we have the opposite problem to yours. The only roses we have are blue ones. The others have all been lost."

Despite her fear, Dorothy felt one eyebrow lift skeptically. "Lost? And where would you come from, then?"

The man fetched a deep breath and blew it out in a long, slow sigh. "From the future."

Oh—kay, Dorothy thought, *he's not a criminal, he's a wacko*. She said nothing.

"This is my first assignment," he continued. "I shouldn't be telling you any of this." He ran a hand through his hair again, nervously. He looked wilder than ever, but his voice was strong and confident. "I had to make sure I was far enough back, before they started to get close with the research. That's not for a few more years, so I'm safe that way. But either the techs messed up on the money, or the time-targeting was off. That coin will be perfectly good—next year. But I don't want you to spend it too early and get in trouble."

"I won't be spending it at all," Dorothy said with more asperity than she would have thought possible, "Because I'm not keeping it."

"No, please, you must keep it," he implored. "If I don't go back with the roses I'll get kicked back down to a tech job again, and if I just take them without paying I'll get tagged by the ethics filter, which would be worse. Please, please let me buy the flowers. You have to believe me."

Dorothy snorted. "I don't have to do anything, young man." She meant to stop there, but his words had made her curious. "But explain this to me. Say I buy your story. What happened to the roses? Why do you—how can you—have only blue ones?"

He took a step closer, but stopped when Dorothy frowned. "Okay. They found out pretty early that you can't just take a blue gene out of a petunia and put it into a white rose. It's not that easy. The blue pigment is delphinidin, and it doesn't work unless it's in an alkaline environment. Rose petals are acidic. Then they found an enzyme that would convert amino acids in a particular bacteria to indigo."

Dorothy's look must have said *get on with it* because he said hurriedly, "Right, you don't need all the details. The upshot of it all was that after a while they found the right combination of genes and enzymes and bacteria and who knows what else, and they got blue roses. Only problem was, they eventually got some kind of blue super-genes, always dominant in breeding crosses, and they got out of control."

He looked at the flame dance arrangement on the counter. "Then—some other things happened, and a lot of information, including genetic information on a lot of plant and animal species, was lost." He met her eyes again. "I'm not going to tell you about that. I can't. I won't. And a really, really long time later, we're able to come back and try to fix things. And that's why I want—why I need—the roses."

"It's a good story, I'll give you that." Dorothy looked around the shop slowly, at the riot of reds and yellows and oranges and pinks that surrounded them. What if it

185

were true? What if all this were lost, and the mythical blue rose all that was left? It was a lesson in 'be careful what you wish for,' that was certain. But humans always did seem to have trouble learning that lesson.

"A really, really long time, you said. What else have the scientists come up with, then, besides blue roses? Anything worthwhile?" Dorothy asked suddenly. Of course she didn't believe him, but the story was interesting.

He flushed. "We live longer," he said. "I'm eighty-two."

"Really." He looked fifty years less than that. "What about diseases? Cancer? Diabetes?" She held up a knotted hand. "Arthritis?"

"We're...still working on those," he admitted. "We've made some progress."

Dorothy felt a sudden rush of anger. If he was going to make up a stupid fairy tale, he might as well make it a happy one. "And yet they're sending you back in time for *roses*?" She snatched up the money from the counter and crossed to him, her face hot. "Here. Go on back where you came from. You're not getting any of these roses just so a bunch of idiots can fix a stupid mistake. It's not even an important mistake! You still haven't got the big things right and now you want your roses back? Well, you can't have them. Not from me."

Max Hunter flinched back, and the hand he held out to accept the money was cold and trembling. His throat clenched as he swallowed.

"I'm sorry—I thought you'd understand. I thought—" He looked over at the flame dance arrangement where it blazed on the counter. "I thought you'd understand why they're important."

The door to the greenhouse opened and Melissa poked her head in. "Ready for tea, Mrs. B.?" she asked, then added, "Oh, sorry, I didn't know we had a customer."

"That's all right, Melissa," Dorothy said, turning to force a smile at her. The man stood unmoving.

"Just had another walk-in order out back," Melissa said happily. "A hospital order. New baby. I'll get that started and you can come on back when you're finished here." She let the door close behind her.

Dorothy turned back to face Mr. Hunter. His last words were still echoing in her ears as her anger drained away. *I thought you'd understand why they're important.*

The words pricked Dorothy like thorns. She thought suddenly of the thousands of roses she'd grown and bought and sold over the years—roses for love, for birth, for death, for everything in between. The rich language of their colors, the sweet heady fragrance, the silken, leathery caress of their petals. What would her life have been like without them?

Wordlessly she turned and walked slowly and deliberately around the shop, thinking, pausing in front of this container and then that. When she came back to him, she held five roses in her gnarled hand. She pointed to them, one by one. "A pink climber, 'Dorothy Perkins'; a red hybrid tea, 'Mr. Lincoln'; a yellow shrub rose, 'The Pilgrim'; an orange grandiflora, 'Solitude'; and a white antique rose, 'Jeanne d'Arc'. Remember their names, Mr. Hunter." She slipped one of the twenties out of his unresisting fingers, and the coin as well, and pressed the five roses into his other hand.

"I'm giving you a deal. Take better care this time," was all she said.

He nodded solemnly. "Thank you. We'll try. I'll tell them—I'll tell them what you said." Then he turned, unbolted the door, and left without saying anything more.

Dorothy stood unmoving in the silent shop for a long moment, surrounded by the myriad shades of the roses, so breathtaking, so eloquent, so short-lived. Crazy or not, Mr. Hunter had been right about one thing. They were important to her. She wouldn't be giving any of this up anytime soon, no matter what Stephanie said.

"Blue roses!" Dorothy muttered, shaking her head. She straightened her shoulders, rang the twenty dollars carefully into the cash register, and dropped the impossible coin into her pocket. She massaged her aching fingers for a moment. Then, smiling, she went to help Melissa with the day's orders.

Why Little Green Men Don't Dance

There must be lots of other places they can go, out of all them bright stars up there behind the clouds.
-"Out of All Them Bright Stars," Nancy Kress

"D'ja ever notice," says my friend Dave, staring at the slowly-receding head of foam on his fifth beer, "that Greenies don't dance?"

We're having our usual after-shift drinks in Chalkie Jack's Bar & Eats. Me and Dave, we're there for the bar more than the eats, but there's lots of other folks having supper and even some couples shuffling on the tiny dance floor.

And I should tell you right now that I don't like the way Mayor Dave Gorman's been telling this whole story. Which is why I'm putting it all down myself, just the way it happened.

So anyway, there's three Greenies in Chalkie Jack's bar that night when Dave has his epiphany, just sitting quiet and eating some kind of alien-looking salads, and no, they sure aren't dancing even though the music isn't half bad. Next thing I know, some country king starts caterwauling from the jukebox and Dave gets up and walks over to them. I hear him say to the little fem, "You like to dance to this one?"

She looks up at him, round green head swivelling on her pencil-thin neck, and smiles that real polite smile full of perfect white teeth they all have. She says, "No, thank you anyway," and the three of them stand up and push in their chairs and leave. Just like that. No fuss, no hurry, they just go. They must have paid their bill already 'cause neither one of the waitresses goes running after them.

Dave shrugs and comes back to his beer. "See?"

Now, Dave's one of those guys you can't always tell what he's thinking about. Deep, I always thought. Deep as a well, and full of things you can't see, only the bits you can dip out a little at a time. I used to think that made him smart, smarter than me. I'm just the funny guy.

So I say, "Well, she wouldn't dance with you for sure," and then I shut up, 'cause I don't know where Dave's going with this and I sure don't want to look stupid.

Dave says, "Okay, but why?"

"Maybe she didn't like your ugly gob," I say, but really I've got no answer, 'cause before now I never thought about it. I can see that Dave has, though, so I put the wheels in motion, too.

And if you're thinking that Mr. High-and-Mighty-Mayor-who-wants-to-be-your-Congressman Mr. David Gorman wouldn't've called them "Greenies," well you know, and I know, and Dave knew, that it wasn't considered exactly polite. But we all know that's what most folks called them anyway. Back then he was just Dave Gorman, stevedore same as me, and since I'm writing this to let folks know what really happened, that's how I'm telling it, whether you like it or not. Whether Dave likes it or not. So just shut your trap and keep reading.

Two nights later we're back at the bar again and Dave's

had a few and I've had a few. I've been thinking about what he said the other night, so I says to him, "You know what, Dave?"

And damn me if he doesn't say, not even looking up at me, "They don't run, either, do they? Greenies don't ever run."

I just stare at him. That's what I was going to say. It didn't take me long to realize it once I started thinking. They never ran, mostly just walked around slow and careful. I always put it down to Earth's gravity or them looking so frail. You kinda expect weird things from aliens. At any rate, they didn't run, they didn't dance, and they never really moved fast at all. That's what me and Dave both noticed. Dave first, and then me, no matter what Dave says now.

There aren't any Greenies in the bar tonight, so we keep on drinking and when my gut's starting to feel beer-warm and easy I says to Dave, "Why'd they come here, you think, Davey-boy?" We never really talked about it, before. Not even when my Beth was so sick. Especially not then.

"Governments seem to like them okay," says Dave.

"Well, I know that. Why wouldn't they? They don't need jobs, just sell information to whatever country they want for good money and then spend it right back. They even bring half their food down from the big ship and pay fair money for the rest, and I never heard about them bothering nobody." I finish another beer, the last of it lukewarm going down. "Governments love the green bastards."

I know, I know, but their skin was green, for God's sake, and not saying it don't make it any different. They were green, and they were short, and they looked exactly like they'd stepped out of one of them old comic books or pulps. How could we help calling them "little green men" right from the start? I mean, it wouldn't have been natural otherwise. And Dave thought the same way, no matter what he says now.

So then Dave says to me, all thoughtful, "Seems to me we got a lot of questions about them Greenies, don't we?"

"I guess so, Dave," I says.

"That make you wonder anything, Lenny?"

I shrug, 'cause I still ain't sure what's churning around in that brain of his, but Dave's ready with his own answer anyway, just like always.

"Why ain't anyone else asking questions?"

For once I get a word in. I say it real quick before Dave can jump in again. "Maybe the governments already asked all those things, and got answers, and they just never bothered to tell everyone else in the world."

Dave looks at me like he can't believe I thought of that all by myself, and then he looks back at his beer, last one of the night it's got to be or his Ellen and my Beth will both hit the roof. "Yeah, but what if they never asked the right questions, Lenny? Or what if they only heard what they wanted to hear?"

I feel a queer twist in my stomach that's got nothing to do with the beer. Kinda scary, the thought that maybe the Greenies had pulled one over on all them governments despite how we'd accepted them.

So there we are, full of beer and just about ready to go home, and maybe nothing else would've ever happened if one of us hadn't said, "Maybe we ought to get ourselves some answers."

Dave's trying to say now that it was me who said it, but I know it was him. He started it all, and he's the one got me spooked. Anyroad, by the time we've walked halfway home, we've decided that the next day after work we'll set out to start testing Greenies.

We want to do it right, which means looking for a lot of Greenies. I mean, just 'cause one won't dance with you don't mean none of them will. We spend most of the next week, when we ain't at work, drivin' around to every bar in town so Dave can ask Greenie fems to dance. I ask a couple, too. None of 'em will, but I say that don't prove nothing. Tell the truth, I'm getting tired of the whole thing by the third night and ready to think we're acting, well, stupid.

I don't say that to Dave, of course, but I can tell he picks up on it. So next night Dave says he's got lots of bright ideas and tonight we're going to try something different. First off, Dave tells me to go and borrow my mother-in-law's dog, Chickpea. Funny name for a dog, you're thinking, kinda cute. Only he's the meanest cuss in town, bit two people already and would've been put down long ago except he belongs to the second-meanest cuss in town and no-one wants to butt heads with Her. Me and Chickie and a length of copper pipe came to an understanding a long time ago and he never even barks at me now. Not like Her. We ain't come to our understanding yet, but lately we get along okay for Beth's sake.

So me and Dave and Chickpea sit in Dave's truck in the dark end of the parking lot at Chalkie Jack's for a while, and Dave's teasing Chickie with a scrap of meaty steakbone to get him riled up. I'm thinking that's kinda mean and Chickpea don't usually need no help getting riled up anyhow, but I don't say nothing to Dave.

Finally two Greenies come out of Chalkie Jack's and Dave opens his door and lets Chickpea out. Of course Chickie has to take a quick leak on Dave's front tire first and I'm laughing and Dave's swearing and then Chickie smells the Greenies and he's off like buckshot, letting loose a howl that would scare a cross-eyed coyote.

Well, the Greenies jump when they hear that howl and for a weird second they don't look quite right, like someone flashed a spotlight on them, real quick, then off again. Chickpea's barrelling down on them like a demon and I gotta say, I'm still laughing 'cause I expect them to turn tail and run like little green devils.

They just stand there, waiting.

I stop laughing.

Chickpea gets to them and dives at one, knocking him down like a ten-pin on an easy split, and I'm outta the truck running. Dave's right behind me. Oh, Sweet God, I'm thinking, 'cause Chickpea could tear that Greenie's head off his spindly neck with one good bite, and I gotta get to him fast.

"Down, boy!" I'm yelling, like it would do any good with that muscle-headed mutt. "Get off that, Chickie, come here! Chickpea!"

I can hear him snarling now and I'm thinking how easy it's gonna be for him to kill that stupid Greenie and how much crap Dave and I are gonna catch, when the second Greenie, the one still standing, just reaches down cool as icewater and touches Chickpea's shoulder with a little silver rod. Don't ask me where he got it 'cause I wasn't watching. Maybe outta that queer little belt they all wear.

Chickpea falls over, stiff as if he's already been gutted and stuffed over at Denny's Taxidermy.

We run up and the other Greenie's getting to his feet and brushing himself off. I drop down by Chickpea first thing, 'cause if that damn dog is dead my marriage is over and maybe my life in this town, too, but he's already coming out of it and shaking his head like a puppy who's just skidded into the kitchen wall again. Dave hasn't said a word so I stand up, keeping a hand on Chickie's collar, and start apologizing, making out how the dog slipped out of the truck by accident, but the Greenie waves a bony hand at me.

"Do not alarm yourself. I was uninjured in the attack."

I don't really like the way he says, "in the attack," like he knows it was on purpose, but Greenies all talk real proper and it's hard to know what they mean sometimes. They seem okay, not mad or nothin', just turn and walk away, so I start dragging Chickpea back to the truck. I'm madder than a scalded cat about the whole thing and wondering how Dave talked me into it. That's just like Dave, though. He's a real talker.

Once we get settled Dave starts up the truck and says, "Well, they didn't run, but they sure looked weird for a second there. Did you see that? Mark it down, Lenny. Wonder if we can find some more tonight?"

I got my lips pressed together tight while Dave's talkin', and then I just say, real quiet, "No more for us, Dave. I gotta make sure Chickpea's okay. Just drop us off." I ain't marking anything down but I'll let Dave notice that by himself if he wants. I'm not usually one to back down but I don't want to fight with Dave. He's supposed to be my buddy after all even if I'm starting to think he's going wrong about these Greenies.

He don't say nothing else about it, just drops us off, and Chickie looks okay by the time I'm shutting him in his doghouse. I walk home alone from there, watching that big dark sky full of stars and cussin' Dave for making me think about all these things. I done enough hard thinking in the last year to last me a lifetime.

For two weeks or so after that I only see Dave at work. He's busy after every shift and he doesn't show at Chalkie Jack's for a beer. I get the feeling like he's still mad about the night with Chickpea, but he's jokey and large at work like nothing's wrong, so I can't say nothing about it.

Then Saturday night after our shift gets out late he says, "Come over to the house for a beer, Lenny," so I guess we're friends again and I go.

Ellen's over at her mother's, Dave tells me, and the house is quiet. We've had one beer and just talked about work and football when Dave says, "Lenny, I've got something to show you." He pulls out this ratty notebook and starts flipping pages.

Even though I realize I've been half expecting it, I'm still blown away by what he's showing me. Almost every night for the past two weeks Dave's spent driving from here to Grandville to Sand Point and who knows where else, stopping in bars asking Greenie fems to dance, almost running Greenies down with his truck, making them jump by leaping out of unexpected places and God knows what else, and writing it all down in this book.

I think he's out of his mind.

"I was kinda pissed after that night with Chickpea," he says, letting the *I'm sorry* into his voice but not saying it. "But now I had to show somebody. Look at it, Lenny. Read it." He shoves the notebook into my hands and goes to the kitchen for more beer.

I'm looking, all right. No Greenies dancing, no Greenies running, none jumping. He's got a lot of notes like "a

194

flash of light," "looked shimmery," and "glowed" any time he did startle one of them or get them to move a little bit fast. He has that written down next to the first entry, the one with Chickpea, too, so I know what he means.

Dave comes back with two cold ones and a bowl of mostly smashed-up potato chips. "What do you think?"

"Dave," I say honestly, "I don't know what to think." I take a handful of chips. They're half stale, but eating them gives me something to do while Dave keeps talking and I don't have to answer for a few minutes.

"There's something up with those green bastards, that's for sure. Look." He points to all the notes that mention the light. "What the hell is this light, anyway? You saw it that night with Chickpea, didn't you?"

I nod, mouth full of tasteless chips. When Dave starts talking again I wash them down with cold beer. I can tell he's excited, the way he's jabbering.

"When they gotta move fast, they make this light, and I think they don't like that, so they don't move fast if they can help it. They got secrets, I know it. They ain't who or what they say they are, and they worked a dodge on the government by selling them fancy information. Maybe half of it ain't even true! I can't believe no-one's ever noticed this before!"

I have to speak up then, but I keep it real quiet and easy. "But what if they did, Dave? What if the government knows all about them lights and why Greenies don't dance and all of it? What if they just decided not to tell us?"

"Yeah, well, it's gotta be something bad, then, for them to keep it that secret."

"What if it's not bad? Or what if it is, but they decided it's worth it?"

Dave looks at me again like he did in the bar that night, like he's surprised I thought of that. Like he's surprised I thought of anything at all. I'm starting to wonder if he looks at me like that a lot when I don't know about it, and I don't like it.

He puts on his deep-thinking voice and talks proper as any Greenie. You've all heard him do that when he was speechifyin' for the mayor's job. "What could be worth it, Lenny? What could be worth being lied to, and maybe put in danger, and just betrayed?"

I swill the last of my beer, 'cause I'm mad again and this time I know I got to say something. "Oh, I don't know, Dave. How about curing cancer? That's only since they got here. Could that be worth it? Or that grain that'll grow just fine with hardly no water so people don't starve? Think that was worth anything, Dave? Or how to burn gas that don't screw up the air so much? You think those things aren't worth it? You think we paid too much for those?"

"How long have Greenies been here, Lenny? Seven years. Seven years that silver mothership has been hanging over us. God only knows what they've been doing to us all that time."

I can't believe I'm hearing this. All along I thought Dave was okay about the aliens, like most people after the first shock wore off. Even the last of the survivalist freaks came out of the woods about two years ago. I talk real quiet and slow, like to a little kid.

"They're explorers. They travel around to different planets and learn things, remember? Live in different places and help people out for a while. That's how they know so much. They been doing it a long time. Remember how they told all this right at the start? Dave? You remember?"

Dave walks over and grabs his notebook off the table in front of me like he don't trust me around it anymore. "Yeah, and remember how it only took them eight months to hammer out a deal with every country on earth to sell them information on their own terms? Every country! When were humans ever that cooperative? Never, that's when, not unless they're scared. Those Greenies did something, Lenny, something to the brains of every single government in the world. They got secrets, and they've got us at their mercy, and don't you forget it."

Dave just stands there then, and I can see he expects me to leave. He don't look deep to me anymore, staring down at me like I was a Greenie myself. He just looks stupid and mean and—can I believe it?—scared.

I stand up. "I think we got in over our heads here, Dave," I say. "I think some stupid talk got taken too far and now we're up the creek without even a boat, let alone a paddle."

"I mean to find out what those green bastards are hiding," Dave says, poking one finger out like he's going to push it into my chest.

I don't move. "What if they ain't hiding nothing?"

Dave kind of smiles, an old-Dave smile like he's going to say it's all a joke. "Then they got nothing to fear from Dave Gorman, do they?"

I realize then that the smile don't go nowhere near his eyes, and before I can stop them the words are coming out. Words about the Thing I Never Talk About.

"I hope and pray to God nothing ever happens to your Ellen, Dave," I say, feeling like my mouth ain't even moving, "But if they ever come to tell you that she's got a tumor where her breast used to be, and it's going to eat away at her until it takes her from you for good, and then the same doctors turn around and tell you that the Greenie cure is going to work and she'll be coming home in a few days without even a cut, then maybe you'll understand why I say let the Greenies be, and why I say whatever we paid for that cure was worth it."

And I can't help myself, I swat that goddamn notebook out of his hand and it sails across the room. A page falls out and flutters onto the carpet like a bird with a wing full of buckshot. "Now I'm going home to Beth, where I ought to be, 'cause I still got her to go home to. You think about that when you're out pestering Greenies, Dave. Think about that."

Whatever Dave's going to say, he don't get the chance, 'cause when I get to the door and open it there's five Greenies standing on Dave Gorman's front porch.

"Mr. King, Mr. Gorman," the one in front says, real pleasant like a friend just introduced us. "We should talk."

"You've developed an interest in us, Mr. Gorman," says the same one when we're all sitting nice and comfortable back in Dave's living room. Dave hasn't picked up the notebook where I sent it flying but he can't keep his eyes from glancing over at it. Something in me, something mean I guess, is glad to see him worried.

He's not letting on, though. "Maybe," he says.

The Greenie nods. "It's all right, Mr. Gorman. You are certainly not the only one. Many people have been interested in us at various times over the past seven years."

And it ain't at all hard to see that Dave don't like that. I can see him getting all puffed up like he does when we're down by a run in the slo-pitch tournament and it's his turn at bat, and Mick Stenko who Dave never got a hit off of yet is on the mound.

"Maybe I just think it's time we got to know you folks a little better." I know Dave is looking at me to back him up but I keep my mouth shut. Dave's my friend, but in this particular company I don't owe him nothing.

"You believe you're uncovering secrets about us. You believe we have something to hide. You want to be the one to 'expose' us." The Greenie doesn't sound mad at all. He's just telling it like it is.

"I think," says Dave, finally letting the anger in his voice match the look on his face, "That you haven't been straight with us. I think you pulled a fast one on 'most everybody, got them all glassy-eyed over the stuff you were selling to them, and you're just biding your time all these years." He sits back on the sofa and crosses his arms. "That's what I think."

The Greenie turns to look at me. "And is that what you think, as well, Mr. King?"

I know there's a word for the way that little green man's eyes look. Big, flat, black eyes that there's no understanding, no matter how long Greenies live on Earth. Inscrutable, that's the word. I never look away from him. I just tell the truth. "I don't know what to think."

He stares at me and nods a little, and then the Greenie

turns back to Dave. "I doubt you would believe me, Mr. Gorman, if I assured you that we are precisely what we say we are, travelling peddlers of a sort, and that we will be leaving Earth peacefully and completely once we have exhausted our supply of goods to sell."

"Maybe I would," says Dave, "if you weren't here right now trying to convince me."

"You think we have an ulterior motive. What might it be?"

"Maybe you want to conquer Earth."

"We have only a fraction of your population. We have been here seven years and have initiated no hostilities."

"Maybe we have something you want. Water. Resources. Food."

The Greenie shrugs, bony shoulders rising and falling like a wave. "We cannot drink your water without additives. We can eat only certain types of Earth food. Again, seven years without animosity. We have paid for everything we have used or taken."

Dave jumps up, fists hard, then sits back down again. He ain't used to backtalk. Then he gets up, goes over and gets the notebook and brings it back to the sofa. He waves it at the Greenie. "Well then, Mr. Smarts, you tell me this. You tell me what you're hiding. You tell me why you and your kind don't run, don't dance, don't ever make a fast move without a light flashing or glowing." He tosses the book down on the coffee table. "You tell me that."

I'm glad that if the Greenie opens that book, he won't see none of my handwriting in it.

The Greenie don't even look at the book. "Tomorrow morning," he says slowly, "we will begin our departure from this planet. It will take approximately four days. Your governments will want to discuss our leaving; some will plead with us to stay. To all we will say that it is simply time for us to choose a new destination, a new exploration and a new home for a time. We will thank you for your hospitality and we will leave."

Dave's starting to look pretty pleased with himself. Even the Greenie notices.

"No, Mr. King, it is not due to your exertions that we are leaving. We have learned much from our visit here, and have left you with knowledge that we hope will be of assistance to your race. This visit is one of many we are conducting as part of a pre-departure survey."

All I can think is *Thank God they stayed long enough. Thank God they saved Beth.* I never really thought about it that way before today, not in those exact words, that the Greenies had really saved her. But suddenly I know it's true. I stand up to go, because now I know for sure that I don't want no more part of what Dave Gorman's doing or already done.

The Greenie puts a hand on my arm. None of them ever touched me before. It don't feel weird at all, just a hand on your arm. That surprises me more than anything else.

"Please stay another moment, Mr. King. You can be of some assistance to us."

So I sit back down, but not next to Dave. I go over and sit on the wobbly little prissy chair that Ellen keeps by the telephone table.

"Your race has an interesting history of belief in intelligent beings originating outside your own solar system," the Greenie says, looking at me. "It has been part of your culture for a comparatively long time."

"Yeah, so? We were right," says Dave, "I guess that counts for something."

I just nod, not at Dave, whether Dave realizes it or not.

"It was a matter of some discussion among us when we were preparing to visit your planet, how we should...present ourselves to you."

"Since you had the whole goddamn planet eating out of your hands in eight months I guess you figured something out." Dave can't seem to shut up, and it's pissing me off. I shoot him a look, but he ain't looking at me.

"I'm sorry, Mr. Gorman, that isn't what I meant. We had to decide whether to look like this," and he nods to the other Greenies, "or to show our natural appearance, like this."

All of them fiddle some little switch on their belts then, and there's a big shimmer that I have to bet is nothing like anything Dave saw in all his Greenie testing.

Then the Greenies are gone, and there's just five other humans standing in Dave Gorman's living room.

Dave's so stupefied he don't even get up off the couch. I don't hardly think about it, I just get up and walk over to them for a good look and of course I see it then. The eyes. They ain't no human eyes, and they're not as big as they looked on Greenies, but they're eyes that grew up under a different sun. Except for that, they look exactly like us. The head guy gives me a nod.

"You see our dilemma."

Dave jumps up then. "What the hell is wrong with you? Why would you go around looking like a bunch of goddamn alien freaks when you could have looked like this? People wouldn't have hardly known the difference!"

The Greenie who's been doing all the talking looks at me.

I'm thinking I know the answer, but I'm scared shitless I'll get it wrong. I don't want to look like an idiot in front of these aliens, or even Dave Gorman, although that don't matter too much to me any more.

"You did right. We wouldn't have trusted you at all," I say slowly.

"Of course we did encounter problems. Our technology could not adapt quickly enough to the characteristics of light and vision on your world. Hence our difficulties with quick movements. Our illusion was unreliable under those circumstances, so we tried to avoid them."

"Are you crazy, Lenny?" Dave's not listening to the Greenie, he's looking at me like I'm an idiot again. "They could have changed just their eyes with that light thing, and we would have thought they were just like us."

I turn around, and I guess that look of Dave's is going right back at him this time. "Yeah, Dave, we got a great record dealing with people who look just like us, but we think they're stronger or smarter. You big dumbass, the only reason Greenies got along here was that every one of us was laughing inside at them all the time. We can handle someone being smarter than us, long as they look funny or different.

"We couldn't've handled aliens who looked just like us, 'cause we'd drive ourselves crazy looking at people and thinking, 'Is that one? Is she one? Are you one?' People would go berserk."

Dave looks like I just stabbed him in the back but the alien who's done all the talking is nodding. "That was our assessment as well, Mr. King. Thank you for your insights. I'm very pleased we caught up with you here."

The others turn and head for the door, but the talker ain't finished. "We'll be leaving several archives of information with the various governments," he says, looking me straight in the eye with his shiny dark ones. "You'll need conscientious and sensible representatives to ensure it's used well and properly."

There's another flash of light and zap! they're all Greenies again, and the talker follows the others out and shuts the door behind himself real quiet. And it's just me and Dave left in Dave's living room again.

"Hell of a thing," Dave says finally. He don't sound mad anymore, and he don't look right at me. He sits down on the couch. The notebook is still there on the coffee table where Dave threw it. He tries a grin on me. "Guess they didn't count on us bein' smart enough to figure out they didn't move right."

I don't answer, 'cause I'm too busy thinkin'. No more Greenies helping us poor stupid humans out. Not at any price. Just us, probably fighting over their leavings. I gotta get home to Beth.

"What'd he mean by that?" Dave says finally.

"I'm going home."

"You think he was talking about us running for the government? 'Cause that's what it sounded like to me."

Yeah, right. I don't think the alien meant Dave, but I don't say nothing, because what would be the use? Dave Gorman's gonna think what he wants to think and do what he wants to do. And so am I.

"Lenny? We're going to be looking for a new mayor next year. And a new Congressman the year after, if Phil

Kauptmann gets any sicker. I could do that. I could do that, Lenny."

I can hear the way he's talking better already, just thinking about it. In a way he's right—the Greenie as good as said the power's going to be with whoever controls that Greenie knowledge.

I don't say too much more, just leave thinking Dave can do whatever he wants. I'm already wishing I'd asked the Greenie if they have to do that with a lot of the planets they visit, make themselves look a certain way because of the assholes who live there. That's the one thing I'd like to know—are we any worse than anyone else out there? But I didn't think of it in time, and now I'll never know, 'cause I can't see them coming back here in my lifetime. Not with so many places to go. All them stars.

As I'm walking home I'm making plans of my own. Like try to get a better job, for Beth's sake, and maybe when the doctors give us the okay on it, we'll start a family. I figure I'm through talking about Greenies, although I know I'll never get through thinking about them.

But like I said at the beginning, I don't hold with the way Dave Gorman is telling this story, like he's Greenie-Approved Congressman material or something, and like I started sticking my nose where it didn't belong and maybe made the Greenies leave. You can think what you like after this and I'll just keep my mouth shut. I'm gonna be too busy to care, anyway, 'cause I got a new job and a new baby on the way. I just had to tell it like this, just one time, 'cause this is how it really happened.

If you haven't heard Dave's side yet, he tells it a little different.

The Goddess Problem

The moment she walked into my office, limned in a faint silver sheen, with that grinning, lupine dog at her heel, I knew she was no ordinary client. She didn't proffer a hand, just sat down in the blue leather chair opposite my desk, and said, "Hello, Ms. Sheridan. My name is Selene. Do you find missing persons?" Her eyes were very serious, very blue, and very fixed on mine. They shimmered a little with unshed tears.

She'd made it past the reception desk and Oliver, my often-annoying assistant and cousin, so he must think I should hear her story. Despite our frequent personality clashes, Oliver had developed a keen proficiency at weeding out the cases I'd absolutely hate. I gave Selene my most professional and sympathetic smile, and met those unnerving, if lovely, blue eyes. They were hard as sapphires; old as the sky.

"I do my best for every client, but I won't make any promises beyond that," I told her. "I've had some success with missing persons cases in the past."

The dog, rangy and shaggy as a wolf—maybe it was a wolf?—settled on its haunches beside her and panted lightly, tongue lolling. Selene stroked the creature's head with gentle fingers, never breaking our eye contact. "This will be a difficult case, Ms. Sheridan, and I may prove to be a difficult client. I will tell you some things that you may find challenging to accept."

I leaned back in my chair, which protested with a squeak. I was suddenly intensely aware of the dust in the corners of the room, the scratched and scabbed surface of my desk, the faint layer of windswept grime on the window behind me, and the lingering scent of tuna sandwich from my lunch. Oliver had been pestering me to repaint the place and freshen it up, but I'd resisted. Maybe he had a point.

"I'll try to keep an open mind," I said. "Challenging clients are a bit of a specialty here at Olympia Investigations, which is probably why you chose me."

She smiled a little, and didn't deny it. I'm the person to see when a non-human client needs help, and I rely on a lot of supernatural word-of-mouth.

"So, will you be explaining why your skin seems to glow? And I don't mean the kind of glow they promise in tv commercials."

She lowered her head in a slow nod. "I will. What you make of that explanation will be up to you."

I was intrigued, and business had been—let's face it, boring—the past two weeks. Too many mundane insurance investigations and spousal surveillances, and I start to wonder why I wanted to be a private investigator in the first place. A faintly glowing woman with a half-wolf for a pet promised to be, at the very least, not boring.

"Fair enough," I told her. "Two hundred a day plus expenses, I report to you at least twice a week, stop when you're satisfied with the results or don't want to pursue it any further. If that's agreeable?"

She shrugged elegantly, nodded, and held out a hand. I shook it, her skin pale and cool and luminescent against mine.

And that's how I first met Selene, Greek goddess of the moon.

The missing person in question, she told me, was her...hmmm. Not husband, because they'd never married, although according to legend he had fathered some fifty daughters for her. Consort, perhaps? I put him down on my information sheet as "significant other." Endymion, the man who, either at Selene's request or his own (reports varied), and by the acquiescence of Zeus himself, slept eternally in order to avoid growing old and dying.

I didn't know that it was much of a trade-off, but there were those fifty daughters to consider.

We'd made it only that far when Oliver knocked on the door and bustled in without waiting for me to answer, even though he knows I hate it when he does that. He was the picture of the efficient assistant—ebony hair slicked to one side, not a strand out of place, lint-free black turtleneck with the sleeves pushed up just so, and charcoal grey trousers pressed with a crease sharp enough to cut paper. And a mild, disinterested smile, camouflaging his raging curiosity.

Oliver carried a tray bearing two steaming mugs; sweet black coffee for me, and something pale and floral-smelling for Selene. She accepted it with a smile so I assumed he'd asked her in the waiting room what she'd like. He looked a question at me with raised eyebrows—anything else? want me to stay?—and when I shook my head minutely he left us again. To listen at the door, I had no doubt. Oliver could play the detached professional but it was all an act.

Anyway, Selene's story went something like this: after hundreds of years of peaceful slumber in a secret cavern, where Selene joined him every night, Endymion had somehow disappeared. A week ago, Selene arrived at the cave on a Tuesday night and found it inexplicably empty. Although she'd searched for him herself and questioned her fellow divine and semi-divine colleagues, she'd found no sign of him and uncovered no clues to his whereabouts. That's when she decided to hire me.

As I said, Olympia Investigations is rather singularly placed to handle cases for non-humans. I have no superpowers or special abilities save one: thanks to some ancestral quirk or covert dalliance, my mother and her siblings, and now their children, are able to see, communicate, and interact with all manner of beings. Ghosts, vampires, werewolves, demons, fae...the list goes on. I hadn't even realized until I was about seven that not everyone could see these beings. And now I could add "displaced deities" to that list. Anyway, having grown up with the ability to see the non-standard, it doesn't faze us. Which is why my cousin Oliver was practically my only choice when I decided I needed an assistant. I'd named my detective agency after my (100% mortal, as far as I knew) maternal grandmother Olympia, since the family quirk was generally acknowledged to have started with her. I kept a low profile so that my "special" clients knew they could count on my discretion.

Initially, of course, I had no proof beyond my own intuition that Selene was who she claimed to be. She might be completely human, if slightly delusional and operating in a self-defined alternate reality; the faint glow of her skin could have been some kind of paint or dye she bought over the Internet. But she paid me cash up front for the first week and I was willing to play along.

After all, the Greek pantheon boasted a considerable history of interacting with we mere mortals.

She'd left the blue leather chair and paced the room slowly while she detailed the background of the case. Her pale blue silk blouse fell open at the throat and tucked neatly into a charcoal broomstick skirt that swirled around her ankles as she walked. I caught the flash of tiny silver crescent earrings peeking out from her masses of night-black hair. The wolf-dog, whom she'd called Kyon, lay belly-down on the braided rug, head resting on massive paws, and watched her progress back and forth across the room as if she were the only thing in the room. Perhaps, for him, she was. She moved with grace and precision, as if movement helped marshal her thoughts and words. Her summary of the facts was concise and unemotional.

"Okay, I think I get it," I said finally, putting down my pen. "Now, I have a question for you."

She stopped moving and turned to face me, her head tilted to one side in anticipation.

"What do you think happened?" I asked.

She frowned, delicate creases tracing her pale brow, and shifted her gaze to stare at Kyon, or perhaps past him. The tears, resolutely denied, glistened in her eyes again and she swallowed a few times before she answered. "I think someone has taken him away," she said finally.

"Why? I mean, for what purpose?"

Selene pursed her lips. "I don't know."

"I can think of a few possibilities," I told her, and ticked them off on my fingers. "One, financial gain. Someone found him, realized who he was, and figured there was money to be made selling him or his story to the news media—or selling him back to you for ransom. Two, personal gain. Someone wanted to disrupt your relationship with him for their own reasons, which could be legion—lust, spite, revenge, who knows what else. Three, curiosity. Again, someone found him, and then had questions they wanted answered. Four—" I broke off. The last possibility could trigger the goddess' tears—or anger.

"Go on," she urged.

I licked my lips. "Four, he left on his own, for his own reasons. I'm sorry, Selene, but it is a possibility."

She pressed her lips together in a thin line, made her way back to the blue leather armchair and lowered herself into it. One tear escaped and trickled down a cheek, but she didn't raise a hand to dash it away, refusing to acknowledge its existence.

"I doubt it's number one or number three," she said finally in a controlled voice. "The chances of a human stumbling into the cave and thinking they could turn a profit from it are remote—it's sealed off entirely. And while curiosity is a great motivator, I think a person would be more inclined to bring someone else there, instead of trying to remove Endymion from the cave." She paused. "Which leaves numbers two and four. Either of which is entirely possible, if they found some way to get inside the cave. But even one of the other gods should have trouble doing that."

"Would someone have had to wake him first, before he could leave of his own volition?" I asked her, acutely aware that we were discussing the possibility that she'd been effectively dumped.

She nodded. "I believe so. But I don't know who could do either—get into the cave or wake Endymion—apart from Zeus."

"So no human could wake him, even if they'd found him?" I pressed.

She thought for a moment and then shook her head. "No. Zeus himself put Endymion to sleep, so it would take at least a modicum of magic to wake him."

"You suspect anyone in particular?"

"Not really," she said. "It's been so long...it's hard to imagine why anyone would bother with us now."

"Well," I said with a grin, "if it can't be a human, that eliminates a few billion suspects. I'll want to talk with Zeus for a start, and have a look at the cave, too."

"Whenever you're ready," she agreed.

"Meet me here in the morning, and we'll get underway," I told her. I wanted at least a few hours to do my homework. Before I met any other gods—or supposed gods.

Selene nodded. "Thank you, Ms. Sheridan."

"Please, call me Acacia. If I can call a goddess by her first name..." I said with a grin.

She smiled. "See you tomorrow, Acacia." Now that she'd revealed her true identity, Selene didn't bother using the door to leave. Instead she and Kyon simply shimmered out of my office.

The intercom had been broken for three weeks now, and Oliver and I had defaulted to texting each other between the offices. It seemed to work just fine, so I'd shelved the idea of even fixing the thing.

Could you come in here? I sent.

I could, but do you want me to? he responded. That's Oliver.

However, he did knock once and then open the door. He looked momentarily surprised that my client wasn't there any longer.

"Yeah, I guess she's the real thing," I said. "Just disappeared when we were done talking."

"I knew it!" he said, grinning. "Missing persons case, she said. I want details." He dropped into the blue leather chair and rubbed his hands together in anticipation, propping his loafer-clad feet on my desk. I'm not entirely sure Oliver understands the difference between the words 'assistant' and 'partner,' but we're working on it. I glared silently at his feet and he put them back on the floor with a sigh.

I briefly told him Selene's story. "Can you help me research the Greek gods before we finish up for the day?" I asked. "I might have to tread carefully on this one."

His dark eyes brightened and he raised an eyebrow. "True. I think they had a penchant for dealing with humans who got in their way in very inventive ways. Flaying them alive, turning them into plants or animals— or monsters—and boy, could they hold a grudge—"

I held up a hand. "Enough. That's why I want to do the research, right?"

"And I don't want to be out of a job, dear cousin, if you get transformed into a spider or a pig or something. I'll get my laptop," Oliver assured me with another grin.

It was going to be a long afternoon.

By the time Selene showed up punctually in the morning, Kyon by her side, I'd had a crash course in Greek mythology. I now knew, for instance, that Kyon was named for a dog who had guarded Zeus in his infancy, and later been placed among the stars as Canis Major. I knew that Selene's love, Endymion, had likely been a shepherd, and that only Selene, among several moon-goddesses, was thought to be the personification of the moon itself. Today the moon looked a little less contemporary urbanite and a little more Greek-goddess, in a white, belted tunic dress and metallic gold sandals. A silver crescent clasp tamed her fall of dark hair. I felt underdressed in denim capris, Skechers, and a pale green blouse, but I wasn't going to a fashion show.

"How about you show me the cave first?" I asked her. "Then I can get a feel for the possibilities."

Okay, I might have been putting off the audience with Zeus. Despite his supposed paternal interest and fondness for mortals, I wasn't quite ready to tackle him.

"Certainly." There was no trace of the tears this morning. She must have given herself a little goddess pep-talk the night before, and today would be all stiff upper lip and head held high.

"So, how far is it? I can get my car out of the parking garage," I offered, but she raised a hand. A faint smile quirked one corner of her mouth.

"We'll need something more efficient," she told me. "Will your assistant be coming with us?"

I knew Oliver wasn't listening right outside the door, because he would have flung himself into the room with a breathless "yes" if he'd heard that.

"No, thanks, he'll be staying here to watch the office," I told her.

"All right then, are you ready?"

I nodded, slung my bag over my shoulder and stepped out from behind my desk. She surprised me by taking my hand.

And then the world folded. I shut my eyes involuntarily, dizziness buzzing my brain and threatening to buckle my knees. Selene's hand stayed tightly clasped around mine, though, and only an instant later I smelled cool, earth-scented air and a tang of fish and seawater. I shivered. Should have brought a sweater.

Cautiously I opened my eyes as I felt Selene release my hand. I blinked in the half-light to adjust my vision, but she whispered an unfamiliar word and torches flared to life atop elegant polished brass standards. The temperature rose a couple of degrees, too. I looked around.

It was a cave, but that word doesn't accurately describe the chamber where Endymion enjoyed his endless—at least until recently—slumber. Walls of pale-veined, rough-cut stone rose on all sides, swathed and partially masked by swags of soft fabric. Six fluted Ionic columns supported the ceiling. A polished marble floor, inlaid with Greek keys around the border of each tile, held richly woven scatter rugs. Kyon ambled over to one of the columns and sniffed around its base, then lay down and put his head on his paws. He was obviously comfortable here.

The bedstead was the centerpiece of the room. Larger than king-sized, it looked invitingly soft, with richly adorned carvings at each corner and gold tracery skimming the curves of the headboard. Hammered silver shod the foot of each post. Drifts of vividly-embroidered linens trailed off the sides, and thick pillows crowded against the head. As I stepped closer to it, faint scents of laurel and something I didn't recognize tickled my nose.

Grandeur aside, however, the most striking attribute of the bed was—it was empty.

I turned in a circle, taking in the chamber. It measured perhaps thirty feet by twenty. A chair, matching the bed in design and decoration, and a small table piled with books, occupied one corner. Since Endymion spent no waking time in the room, I assumed that sometimes Selene passed time here in pursuits other than assignations with her slumbering lover.

"I don't see an entrance."

Selene shook her head. "There is none. Some natural vents in the rock reach the surface, but I asked Zeus to close off the original opening decades ago, when humans began to get more...exploratory. It used to be open to the sea."

"Why even stay here?" I asked her. "I'm assuming you could have moved him anywhere, even up to Olympus."

She sighed. "I suppose. But this has been my—our—sanctuary for so long..." Her voice trailed off. Apparently, even goddesses could be sentimental.

I nodded. "So that's why you're ruling out human involvement in this. Humans couldn't get in here on their own unless they blasted the rock, and obviously, that hasn't happened."

Selene nodded.

"So, besides Endymion, anything else missing or

changed?"

Slowly she turned a full circle, casting her gaze around the room. When she finished, she crossed to the chair and the books, inspecting the stack.

"Huh," she said in a surprised tone. "A book is missing."

"You didn't notice it before?"

"I didn't look before."

"What's missing?"

She frowned. "A volume of poetry. The Complete Poetical Works of Wordsworth."

I made a note. "Anything significant about that particular volume?"

"No, I like the poetry, that's all. In some ways Wordsworth could have been Greek."

I like Wordsworth myself. Slowly I paced the perimeter of the room, observing it from all angles. Kyon got up and joined me, his nose to the floor. He broke away from my path as we neared the bed and followed his nose until it pushed beneath the edge of the counterpane trailing the floor.

I crossed to him and lifted the fabric. A small white feather lay against the base of the bed. I picked it up, and it seemed to radiate its own warmth against my hand. A shimmer rippled across the soft vane in the torchlight. I showed it to Selene. "Does this look familiar?"

She blanched, although it was barely noticeable beneath the luminescence of her skin. "No, it isn't mine."

I tilted my head and gave her a hard stare. "But you know whose it might be? Come on, Selene, you're the one who hired me."

She swallowed. "I can't be sure, and I don't want to influence you. It could belong to any number of people. Wings and feathers aren't rare in my circles. Or it could have come from one of the pillows."

I tucked it into a pocket. "Have it your way. But you might have to tell me at some point, if you want this case solved."

She nodded.

As I stepped away from the bed, something crunched

underfoot. I knelt to examine a small patch of crystals on the marble floor, and when I swept some up on one finger I caught the distinct scent of ammonia, and something else—cough drops? I scraped the crystals carefully into a small plastic bag and added it to my pocket. Then I called the wolf-dog and he padded over to me. "Sniff around, Kyon, there's a good boy. See if you can find anything else that doesn't belong."

As if he understood me, he put his nose to the floor again and worked his way around the room in an amazingly methodical manner. I suppose I shouldn't have been surprised: he was a goddess' companion. Not likely a "normal" animal on any level.

However, a few minutes later he returned to me and sat, tail sweeping a slow, elegant swath across the floor behind him. The look in his intelligent golden eyes said, nothing, sorry.

I patted his head awkwardly, hoping it wasn't an insult.

"All right, I'd better question some of your colleagues, Selene."

"Where do you want to start?" she asked, as she crossed to me and took my hand again. I steeled myself for the uncomfortable transport I knew would follow.

I took a breath. "Might as well start at the top. Take me to Zeus."

She nodded, and the cave folded, flattened, and vanished.

When the world stopped doing uncomfortable things around me, I stood in a courtyard so painfully bright, especially by comparison to the cave, that I squinted through tear-brimmed eyes and tried to focus.

"Knock it back a bit, would you, Father Zeus?" Selene asked. "I've brought a mortal with me, and you know they're extra-sensitive."

"Very well," a booming voice drawled, and the light dimmed to bearable. I managed to open my eyes and take in the area.

The classical Greek architecture got another workout here, with dazzling white columns ringing the plaza and apparently holding up nothing but bright blue sky. Everything seemed to be covered with gold leaf, intricate carvings, and delicate bas-relief. And that was just the throne. Something that looked like a lightning bolt leaned crookedly against one arm.

The owner of the booming voice sat on the throne, looking half-bored and half-peeved. He sported the iconic white beard and long white hair, but wore an incongruous navy polo shirt embroidered with a tiny thunderbolt logo, and slate grey khakis. "Another mortal, Selene?" he asked in a withering tone. "Tired of the other one already?"

"In case you've lost count, it's several hundred years since I brought Endymion to you," Selene said drily. "And in case you haven't noticed, this one's a girl."

Zeus shrugged. "Boy, girl, your tastes are no concern of mine," he said. "What do you want me to do with this one?"

Selene drew a breath and released it slowly. When she spoke, I thought her teeth might be clenched. "Zeus, this is Ms. Acacia Sheridan. Ms. Sheridan, meet Zeus, King of the Gods of Olympus. If you wouldn't mind, Zeus, Ms. Sheridan is conducting some investigations on my behalf and would like to ask you some questions."

He raised an extremely bushy and skeptical eyebrow. "Ms. Sheridan is going to ask me questions?" He sighed deeply, as if this were just another in a long line of trials he would have to bear.

"I won't take up much of your time, sir," I said politely.

He raised his eyes above my head and I looked up. Some skittish white clouds had appeared, scudding across the blue. In a mournful voice he said, *"Time drops in decay, / Like a candle burnt out, / And the mountains and woods / Have their day, have their day; / What one in the rout / Of the fire-born moods, / Has fallen away?"*

I glanced at Selene but she only shrugged. "Riiight," I said. "Yeats?"

"From 'The Moods,'" he said with an approving nod.

215

"Very nice, sir. Now, what can you tell me about Selene's...er...companion, Endymion of Elis?"

It was Zeus's turn to shrug. "What's to tell? She fell in love with him, he was mortal, she asked if I'd set him to sleep eternally and not age. She was a little smarter than her sister Eos, who forgot the whole 'not aging' clause with that fellow—what was his name, Selene?"

"Tithonus," she answered, tight-lipped. I made a mental note to look up that story when I got back home.

"All right, so do you know why anyone would want to tamper with your setup there? Wake Endymion, or take him away from the cave where he slept?"

Zeus closed his eyes, tilted his head to one side, and intoned, *"Celestial visitant, once more / Thy needful presence I implore. / In pity come, and ease my grief, / Bring my distempered soul relief, / Favour thy suppliant's hidden fires, / And give me all my heart desires."*

"Sappho? Seriously, Zeus?" Selene asked in an exasperated tone.

"You don't think 'Hymn to Venus' is appropriate in the circumstances?" he asked her with a smirk.

"Just yes or no would really be great, sir," I interjected. Maybe so much time on the Olympian throne in all this heat and bright light had made the great Zeus a little loopy.

He levelled a pair of steely blue eyes at me, and I swallowed. There was nothing crazy about those eyes, unless it was the insanity born of uselessness and a longing for past glories. "No," he said in a voice that reverberated around the walls that weren't there. "I do not know why anyone, save Selene herself, would wake or move Endymion."

"Me?" Selene practically squealed. "Why would I hire a private detective if I'd done it?"

He shook his head, his long white curls swinging. "I didn't say you did it, Selene. I meant I would understand if you wanted to, if you were tired of his long slumber and wanted him awake with you. That's all." Zeus slumped back in his throne. "I swear, you youngsters are so excitable."

She glared at him and turned away. "That's probably all we'll get out of him right now," she muttered.

"I heard that."

I stammered, "Thank you for your time, sir," and followed Selene. He might not wield the power he used to anymore, but I didn't think I'd want to get on his bad side.

"What's up with you and your father?" I asked when I'd caught up to her. She strode down a column-lined path that magically sprang into being about twenty yards ahead of where she trod.

"He's not my actual father," she said witheringly. "My father is the Titan, Hyperion. Everyone calls Zeus 'Father.' If you're going to figure this out, you might have to study your pantheons and time periods a bit. Next I suppose you'll be calling me Artemis."

"Uh, sorry. I've been trying to reacquaint myself with the history, but even the sources aren't definitive about everything. So you, Artemis, Diana—although you're all goddesses of the moon—are not the same person?"

She rolled her eyes and shook her head.

"Okay, got it. You have to go easy on us mere mortals," I said, and she threw me a grudging half-smile. "Next question: What's with Zeus quoting all the poetry?"

"Most of us do that. I don't know, it must be something in our makeup. You get used to it after a time. At least some of us keep up with modern poets so we're not spouting the same thing constantly." She huffed. "Sappho, for goodness' sake!"

I quirked a smile at her. "So I guess I'll be hearing Wordsworth from you at some point?" Not that I considered Wordsworth exactly modern, but perhaps from an Olympian perspective, he was.

She returned my smile. "I'll try to restrain myself."

"All right, give me the abridged guide to the gods, would you, so I don't mess up again? At least the one you're close to."

The columns ceased and the path opened up into a garden, complete with a small pond and white ducks paddling serenely. A pair of black swans floated, majestic and aloof, on the far side. A white marble bench coalesced to one side of what was now a well-tended garden path. She sat and motioned me to the space beside her.

"All right. What do you want to know?"

What did I want to know? I decided to treat this like any normal case. "Tell me about your family, friends, anyone you deal with on a regular basis. For most cases, the answers lie pretty close to home."

She raised her eyebrows but nodded. "Okay. My parents are the Titans Hyperion and Theia. I have a brother, Helios, and a sister, Eos, as Zeus mentioned. I hardly ever see Helios, because he's gone all day, every day, and I'm a night person. Zeus' parents are two other Titans, so I guess that would technically make us cousins, of a sort."

"Okay." I scribbled madly in my notebook as she spoke. It seemed important to get all the relationships straight. "Friends? Enemies? People you encounter a lot."

"Friends?" She gave a bitter little laugh. "You really don't know a lot about Olympus. There's constant competition for whatever attention humans will pay us these days, and everyone sleeps around a lot. I don't know that there are many real friendships here."

"Well, since we ruled out humans when we were talking in my office, I think it must be someone close to you. Let's just focus on the people you deal with most."

"Keep your friends close, and your enemies closer?" she asked with a smile.

"Exactly."

I held my pencil poised. I had to understand the interactions between the gods if I was going to solve this case. Gods or no, they acted and interacted remarkably like we poor powerless humans did.

"Well, besides family, I get along pretty well with Leto, Hermes, and Aphrodite. I'm not sure I can trust them all, but we're not enemies. Hermes is Zeus' son, and Leto is another cousin. Aphrodite—well, her origins have never been entirely clear."

"Goddess of Love, though, right?" I asked. "She could

be involved here."

Selene nodded. "Maybe. I don't think I have any actual enemies," she said, furrowing her brow. "Not obvious ones, I guess, despite what I said before."

"Okay. I'd like to talk to your sister, Eos, and those three you mentioned. Maybe one of them will give us an idea where to go next."

She looked off into the middle distance for a moment, and I had the distinct impression that she was communing with someone else. "I'll take you to see Eos first," she said. "I doubt my sister could have anything to do with this without my knowledge, but you never know."

She laid a cool hand on mine and, bench and all, we went.

Eos had created a home for herself in a clearing on a small island, ringed with sentinels of dark pine and spruce, where the dense, springy grass was sprigged with tiny white and purple flowers. Her home was completely unlike the classical Greek architecture of Zeus's abode. It was, instead, a well-appointed log cabin with tall windows and an inviting view of the nearby beach. I took in the vista while Selene knocked on the front door, but turned back when it was answered promptly.

The goddess of the dawn had unsurprisingly rosy cheeks and a warm smile. She wore a simple but elegant robe in saffron yellow, bearing intricately embroidered multicoloured flowers along the hem. Large, white-feathered wings sprouted from her back, but she carried herself as if they were weightless. Blonde hair, perfectly waved, had been pulled loosely back from her face and gathered in a low chignon. Eos had a matronly beauty that might once have been quite overpowering and supernatural, but had mellowed over the centuries. She held the door open for her sister and me and motioned us in towards a chunky but polished wooden table. The small house was cozy, decorated in a charming country-elegant style.

Selene went ahead of me into the room and her back

stiffened. Glancing past her shoulder, I saw another, older woman already seated at the table. She wore what I can only describe as a rusty-looking black toga. Her hair, braided and coiled in an intricate knot atop her head, shone the golden red of autumn leaves, and she fixed ancient but bright black eyes on us as we entered. The barest hint of a smile curved the very corners of her mouth. She sat with her hands curled around a steaming mug of dark liquid, as if to warm them. Her fingernails were long, slightly curved, and painted the colour of old blood. The word 'harpy' came to mind.

"Apate, what a surprise," Selene said. She didn't include the word *pleasant.*

The red-haired woman inclined her head a fraction of an inch. "Selene. So sorry to hear of your current troubles."

She didn't sound at all sorry.

The woman continued, "I'd just dropped in to say hello, but I offered to leave when I heard you were coming. Eos wouldn't hear of it until I'd finished my ambrosia."

"Smells like coffee," I observed with a smile.

Apate flashed me a smile that held no warmth. "It is coffee," she said. "Just a little joke we enjoy up here."

"What news, Selene?" Eos asked, turning to her sister, her face filled with empathy. "No word of Endymion?"

"None, but Ms. Sheridan has undertaken to try and locate him for me. She wished to speak with you, among others."

Eos raised her eyebrows in surprise. "With me? I'm afraid I know nothing of the matter, except what my sister has told me."

I nodded. "I understand. But the job of uncovering the truth often involves much work that is merely routine."

"Well, I'll help if I can," Eos said. "Will you take a cup of coffee while we talk?"

Selene acquiesced for both of us, and I was glad she had. I was secretly dying to try the coffee of the gods, because it smelled absolutely amazing. When Eos set mugs in front of us, I took a tentative sip and thought I could die happy. It was the best coffee I'd ever tasted. I wondered briefly if it did contain ambrosia, because my research had indicated that things often went badly for mortals who partook of the heavenly substance. After another mouthful, however, I decided I didn't care.

Eos joined us at the table and looked at me expectantly. I forced my attention away from my mug and back to the topic at hand.

"Have you ever had occasion to visit the cave where Endymion slept?"

She pursed her lips in thought. "You never took me there, did you, Selene?"

There might have been a hint of accusation in the words, and it wasn't really an answer.

The skin around Selene's eyes was tight. "No, I don't think so, sister."

"Do the two of you spend much time together?"

Eos and Selene both shook their heads, half-smiling. At that moment I could see a sisterly resemblance, despite their differences.

Selene said, "My sister and I get along well, Ms. Sheridan, but rather obviously, she's a morning person and I'm a night person, so we don't see all that much of each other."

"And yet you're alike in many ways," I said. "Both beautiful, powerful—and you both fell in love with mortal men. Selene with Endymion, and Eos with Tithonus." I watched Eos to see how she would react.

She smiled a thin smile that did not reach her eyes. "*Love is a breach in the walls, a broken gate, where that comes in that shall not go again; Love sells the proud heart's citadel to Fate.*"

I knew that one; "Love," by Rupert Brooke. I tried to catch Selene's eye, but she wasn't looking at me. She stared hard at her sister, who met her gaze evenly. I waited a moment, but neither goddess seemed inclined to break off first.

Apate suddenly glanced up at the ceiling and said in a faraway voice, "*What is the gift we have given thee, Sister? What is the trust we have laid in thy hand?*"

The two sister goddesses broke off their staring contest at the same moment and reached for the distraction of their drinks. I wasn't sure what had just happened, but this Apate, whoever she was, gave me the creeps.

I reached into my pocket for the white feather I'd found in the empty cavern and laid it on the table. "You wouldn't have lost this, would you, Eos?"

Even as I said it, I thought it must be hers. In close proximity to her beautiful wings, it held a minuscule echo of her magnificent plumage.

She had the grace to take it and examine it carefully, then raised her eyes to mine as she handed it back. Unlike Zeus's steely eyes, hers were violet-hued and warm, although at that moment they weren't the friendliest I'd ever seen pointed in my direction. "No, I don't believe I did," she said. "I would know in an instant if it were mine. It is not."

And despite what my eyes were telling me, I believed her. She likely wasn't the only person around here sporting a set of white-feathered wings.

Well, that was all I had for now, so I shot a glance at Selene and nodded. The goddess looked relieved.

"We won't keep you from your visit, then," Selene said, and we got up to leave, but only after I had gulped down the last of my coffee. I was not about to leave a drop behind, and I didn't care how it looked. Apate merely nodded at our departure and sipped nonchalantly from her own mug. The sister goddesses embraced briefly and Selene and I left the cabin.

We walked down to the beach, where the lapping waves hissed gently across the sand. An errant breeze lifted Selene's hair and she tilted her face up to it. The white sand felt invitingly warm and I slipped off my shoes, dangling them from one hand as we walked. Someone had built an intricate sand castle near the water's edge and then left it for the waves to erode. Glancing back at the cottage to be sure we were out of earshot—although with gods, who knew?—I said, "The feather. You thought it might be hers."

Selene looked at the sand her perfect feet trod and

shrugged. "I thought it was possible, although I didn't want to believe it." She glanced at me. "You believe Eos? That it wasn't hers?"

I sighed. "It might have made things easier if it were, but yes, I believe her."

The moon goddess nodded and we walked in silence. After a moment I asked, "What was Apate quoting, back there? I didn't recognize it."

"It's from a war poem by Frederick Scott," the moon goddess said absently. "'To France,' I think. 'Sorrow hath made thee more beautiful, Sister' and more cheery thoughts like that. An encounter with Apate is never what you need if your spirits are already low."

"She didn't exactly light up the room," I agreed. "But don't let her get you down. It's early days yet."

Her wan smile told me my advice might be a little late, but we pressed on.

We visited Leto, Hermes, and Aphrodite after that, all of whom Selene had said she got along with, but also wasn't sure she could trust. We were still stymied on a motive for whoever had tampered with Endymion, although having met several of the deities and demi-gods, I was of the opinion that in the end it would come down to jealousy. Either someone wanted Endymion, or someone wanted Endymion out of the way to free up Selene's affections. Maybe it was what happened to gods when they didn't matter anymore and wielded ever-diminishing power, but they seemed almost obsessively concerned with relationships. Love, friendship, alliances, enemies—little else seemed to matter.

We found Leto, a slender goddess with upswept dark hair, reading on a modern-looking chaise longue under an arch of fragrant climbing roses. She rose to wrap Selene in a quick, friendly hug, then settled herself back on the chaise. As we spoke, she smoothed the skirt of her pale sapphire dress absently with one hand, one finger of her other hand bookmarking her place. I surreptitiously noted the cover—it wasn't Wordsworth, but a recent academic title on feminism.

She answered my questions easily—had never been to

the cave, didn't know who might have wanted to break up Selene and Endymion—and seemed genuinely concerned for Selene. As we wrapped up the conversation she sympathetically quoted Keats to us, from "Endymion," no less: "*A thing of beauty is a joy for ever: / Its loveliness increases; it will never / Pass into nothingness; but still will keep / A bower quiet for us, and a sleep / Full of sweet dreams, and health, and quiet breathing.*"

Which was very pretty, but entirely useless.

When we caught up to Hermes not far from Zeus' throne room, he grinned at us and deftly caught a golden coin he'd been idly flipping.

"God of luck," Selene whispered to me as we approached. "Sometimes he's kind of cocky about that."

"What else?"

"Hmm...athletes, travellers, shepherds, thieves, and merchants," she said quickly. "And messengers, of course."

At my first question about Selene and Endymion, Hermes quoted Robert Frost to us:

Yet some say Love by being thrall
And simply staying possesses all
In several beauty that Thought fares far
To find fused in another star.

But I couldn't let Hermes off with a smile and a snatch of poetry. On his feet he wore the famous "winged sandals" that gave him his legendary speed. And those wings were adorned with pure, white feathers.

"You wouldn't recognize this, would you?" I asked innocently, displaying the white feather I'd found in the cave.

Unlike Eos, who'd stayed calm in the face of the feather, Hermes seemed startled by its appearance.

"No, that's not mine," he said, recovering his aplomb quickly. He didn't reach out to take it as Eos had done. Selene snatched the feather out of my hand and held it close to him, and it vibrated a little, despite the lack of any breeze. A faint hum whirred in the air around us.

"It is yours," Selene accused, frowning. "You don't think I'd be fooled, surely. Hermes, why are you lying?"

He looked uncomfortable. "All right, it's mine," he said finally. "But I don't know where you got it. I get around a lot, you know? The whole 'messenger of the gods' thing."

I reached out and retrieved the feather from Selene, sticking it back in my pocket. "Endymion's cave," I said. "Let me guess; you have no idea how it got there?"

Hermes shook his head. "No, I don't. I've never been inside that cave."

Selene looked at him as if she'd found something nasty on the bottom of her shoe. "Oh really, Hermes," she spat. "You expect us to believe that?"

Apparently even a god could look guilty as Hades, but he turned a resolute face to Selene. "I mean it, Selene. I've never been in that cave in my life."

I felt reasonably certain he was telling the truth—but maybe not the entirety of it.

Selene turned on her heel and stalked away. Hermes gave me an *I-don't-know-what-to-tell-you* look and said nothing more, so I followed the moon goddess down another seemingly interminable garden pathway.

When I caught up to her I said, "I thought you and Hermes got along well?"

She sighed and absently pulled a leaf off an exotic-looking shrub starred with tiny fuchsia flowers. "We do. But Hermes is a bit like a teenager. He's your friend one day, but the next he's hanging out with someone 'cooler.'"

"I think he's telling the truth about not being in the cave," I said cautiously. "But maybe not the whole truth."

Selene shredded the leaf, long fingers tearing at it while her eyes stayed on the path. "Maybe Zeus could make him tell us more."

"It's a little early for drastic measures," I said. "Let's keep that as a last resort."

She tossed the remainder of the leaf away. "We're almost at Aphrodite's bower," she said. "Maybe we'll have better luck there."

But we didn't. Aphrodite, ensconced in a much-decorated, flower-garlanded gazebo of pink marble and sipping what I was sure was a margarita, gave no impression of hiding anything. She was breathtakingly beautiful and expressed her sincere sympathy that Selene was experiencing relationship difficulties. With an artful half-smile and tilt of her head, though, she managed to convey the feeling that it was Selene's own fault, and concisely quoted Wordsworth: "She suffered, as Immortals sometimes do."

That, and her insouciance, gave me pause, considering the missing Wordsworth volume from Endymion's cave.

"Do you think she cared overly for Endymion, herself?" I asked Selene, as we left Aphrodite's rather overblown (in my opinion) bower. "She is the goddess of love, after all."

Selene fetched a deep breath and blew it out. "I don't truly suspect her, for that very reason. Although none of us retains the power we once did, when we had worshippers and supplicants in plenty, she still wields enough ability to take him and his heart much more directly if she wished; even, likely, to erode my own feelings, so that I wouldn't care as much."

The gentle thrum of a stringed instrument reached our ears and I turned, surveying the wide garden that surrounded Aphrodite's sanctuary. On a bench off to our left sat a man, strumming a lyre, not looking in our direction. Intuitively, I knew he was nonetheless acutely aware of our presence.

"Who's this?" I asked Selene.

She rolled her eyes. "Don't let him hear you ask that. Apollo, principally the god of music, but if you ask him he'll be sure to add prophecy, colonization, medicine, archery, poetry, dance, intellectual inquiry, sun, light, plague and the care of herds and flocks. And if his personality is any indication, vanity, manicures, and bio-lift facials."

I snickered quietly, as we'd begun walking in the god's direction. He pretended to just notice us.

"Ah, Selene," he said mournfully, accompanying his words with a minor chord. "No joy in finding your lost love?"

"Not yet," she said, "But Ms. Sheridan here is assisting

me now."

He stood and bowed dramatically over my hand, the folds of his robe falling equally dramatically around his muscled shoulders. The laurel crown that graced his curling brown hair stayed firmly fixed even when he bent over.

"Still putting her faith in mortals, that's our Selene," he said as he straightened, although the hint of a smile danced around the corners of his admittedly sensuous mouth. "I have no doubt she'll be better served by you than she ever was by Endymion, my dear."

"Thanks for the vote of confidence," I said drily. "Now, you wouldn't know anything about Endymion's disappearance yourself, would you, Apollo?"

"Alas, no," he said with fervour, hugging his lyre over his heart and tracing the thick strings with a finger. Faint notes floated in the air around us. "I never met the man, awake or asleep," he said. "Perhaps in light of Zeus' waning powers, he simply woke of his own accord and walked away?"

"He might have encountered a bit of difficulty leaving a sealed cave on a remote mountain," I said, "so if that weren't the case, you don't know of anyone who would want to...remove him?" I asked. I couldn't let him off easy just on account of his good looks.

He lifted his shoulders expressively. "'Tis said that some—well, that some of us have always been...competitive...when it comes to affairs of love and lust," he said. "And it must be a god, to access the hidden boudoir, correct? Find he—or she—who desires one or the other of the pair, and you'll find your answer, Acacia."

And softly playing a beautiful, melancholy air on his lyre, he meandered off down one of Aphrodite's garden paths. Neither Selene nor I had mentioned my first name, so I knew he'd thrown it out there to put me off-balance. I narrowed my eyes at his over-confident back.

Selene wasn't watching him go. She stared off in another direction, her eyes probably not even registering the stunning blooms arrayed all around us. "If only I knew where he was," she said. "And that he was all right."

Her voice was so wistful...so human...that I knew it didn't matter that she was a goddess; she was in love, no matter how strangely that love had manifested itself across the many years, and her pain was as real as the pain of any human who has loved and lost.

Selene took me home when it was obvious I was too tired to do anything else just then. I was surprised to learn that I'd been away only a few hours by earthside reckoning, and fell into bed anyway. I was asleep almost before my head hit the pillow, Apollo's soothing music still echoing in my mind.

I slept the rest of the day and through the night, in deep, dreamless repose. In the morning, I sat at my computer and typed up my notes from the day before, adding my own impressions of the gods we'd spoken with and the things they'd said. When I got to work, I recruited Oliver again and we turned to the Internet again. Together we looked up every scrap of poetry they'd quoted to me, and did some more research into the gods' areas of influence and relationships. After a couple of hours, I closed the browser and rubbed a hand across my eyes.

"Everyone has at least two names and scores of lovers. No-one bats an eye at adultery, incest, or consorting with animals," I complained. "I can't keep it all straight."

Oliver blinked at his screen. "I could set up some kind of mega-spreadsheet for reference."

I blew out a sigh. "No. Not worth the time and effort. I'll stick with the gods and goddesses I've already encountered, for now. Maybe we're missing something. I think I'll get Selene in here again this afternoon."

Oliver brightened. "I'll pick up refreshments on my lunch break."

I mentally rolled my eyes. I could understand Oliver being smitten with the beautiful moon goddess, but I didn't think she was currently open to being impressed. But I wasn't going to crush his dreams.

"That'd be great," I told him, and went back to the computer to read over my notes. If I did that enough times, maybe something would make sense.

"Okay, we have a few things to go over," I told Selene later that afternoon. We sat in my office, and Oliver unloaded steaming mugs of coffee and a plate of *loukoumades* onto my desk. He must have gone all the way to the Greek bakery across town. Since there were three mugs, I assumed my cousin had every intention of staying for this discussion, and I decided I'd let him. He took the other client chair, next to Selene, and popped a cinnamon-sprinkled honey puff into his mouth.

"After yesterday's interviews, Oliver and I did some research. Now I have more questions."

"All right," the moon goddess said, shifting nervously. She took a mug and sipped from it, but didn't reach for a pastry. I suppose earthly bakeries can't compete with the fare on Olympia, but it was thoughtful of Oliver to have made the effort. I took one myself to show him I appreciated it. They were delicious.

When I'd swallowed the two-bite confection, I began, "You said you usually get along well with Hermes. Why do you think he tried to lie about the feather?"

Selene's nervousness dissolved into exasperation. "I don't know. Hermes is hard to read sometimes. I often think he cares more about humans than he does about the rest of us—he's always been protective of humans and taken your part."

I nodded. I'd picked up that much in my research between last night and this morning.

"But I don't know why he'd be interested in Endymion particularly," she continued.

Oliver licked cinnamon from his fingers and said, "He's a bit of a trickster, right? And the second-youngest of the gods. Do you think he might get involved in something just for a bit of fun, or to flatter one of the older gods? Even if it meant someone—like you—might get hurt in the process?"

Selene pursed her lips, one hand absently stroking Kyon's fur. "It's definitely possible. You think maybe he was helping someone else?"

"I don't know. If he did," I mused, "Maybe he's feeling bad about it now. He quoted that Frost poem, and it's all about how love is, in the end, stronger than thought. Could that mean something?"

"Maybe, but what?" Selene asked.

Oliver looked at me, too. I didn't answer, because I didn't know. Yet.

"Next question." I fixed her with a steady stare. "Why didn't you tell me about your sister's extensive interest in men?" Apparently Aphrodite had, once upon a time, cursed Eos with an insatiable sexual desire, and she'd gone through—abducted, actually—a string of lovers, including the unfortunately long-lived Tithonus.

The moon goddess fidgeted in her chair. "I didn't want you to suspect her just because of that," she admitted finally. "I mean, I know it looks bad, but I really don't think she's involved."

"Well, I need to know these things when I'm questioning someone," I said. "I can't do this job if you're going to hold pertinent details back."

She looked suitably chastised, and I reminded myself silently that I was dealing with gods, here. Maybe I should take it easy with the scolding. However, I hadn't been kidding about needing to know things. "Who's Apate? She seemed to make you uncomfortable, and she certainly had the same effect on me.""

Selene shuddered. "I don't know what she was doing at Eos's place. She tends to keep to herself, and just as well. I find her creepy."

"She was unnerving," I admitted. "But what's her power? You're all gods of something or other. What's her area of influence?"

"She's not a goddess per se," Selene said, pursing her lips. "More of a spirit, or personification. And she's a fine one to toss around words like 'trust.' She's only the spirit of deception and lies. Did you hear how she said she was sorry about my trouble? No-one has ever sounded less sorry about anything."

I frowned and drummed my fingertips on my desk. "You didn't see any problem with my questioning Eos while the spirit of deceit sat at the same table, sipping coffee? Like maybe she could help Eos lie convincingly?"

"Um." She stroked Kyon's head, where the half-wolf had rested it in her lap. I noticed that contact with the creature seemed to calm her. The wolf seemed to be eying the plate of honey puffs and I wondered if I should offer him one. "I guess I didn't think of it that way."

I sighed. "All right, is there anything else you haven't told me?" I asked, while she still felt bad.

"I don't think so. I mean, I could go on and on to you about the other gods...but things that could be important to the investigation?" She shook her head. "I really don't know."

"All right, we'll drop that for now," I said. "Let's go and see Eos again. And hope she's alone this time."

Oliver's eyes widened in hope, but I had to disappoint him.

We caught the goddess of the dawn at a late breakfast, buttery fingers shredding a croissant, eating flakes of the pastry distractedly. Her blonde hair seemed mussed, as if she hadn't brushed it yet, and she'd wrapped herself in an incongruous fuzzy purple bathrobe.

"Late start to the day?" I asked with a smile when we entered.

She gave me a withering look, even as she nodded us into the other chairs at the table. "I've already been out and brought the dawn," she said. "I like to come home and relax some mornings." She smoothed a hand over her hair and it settled obediently into the shining waves of yesterday. "It was a bit windy out there this morning. Coffee?"

Oops. Perhaps an annoyed goddess would be less inclined to be intimidated by me.

Both Selene and I accepted the offer and I was soon sipping the wonderful liquid again. Selene and Eos chatted for a moment, and then I cleared my throat.

"I wanted to go over a few things from yesterday, if you don't mind," I said.

Eos inclined her head, licking butter from her fingers. She fed the last morsel of pastry to Kyon, who accepted it gravely.

"You're sure you've never visited Endymion's cavern?" I pressed.

"I answered that question yesterday," she reminded me lightly.

"Well, you didn't exactly answer it, and you also had Apate sitting at this table with you," I said, meeting her eyes. "I know her...influences might make it easier for you to deceive us."

She turned hurt eyes to Selene. "And you, Selene? You think I was lying?"

Selene bit her lip. "I don't know. I'm letting myself be guided in this by Acacia." Then she caught her sister's hand. "But I do want you to tell us the truth. Perhaps you think you have something to hide, but I know you would not willingly hurt me."

Eos turned her eyes to me, but I met them. She might be a goddess, but she'd have to bring more to this game than a piercing stare. Zeus had unnerved me, I'll admit, but Eos seemed less daunting. We locked eyes for a long moment, Selene still holding her sister's hand.

Amazingly, Eos looked away first. "All right. I have visited the cave," she said in a soft voice, "and not so long ago."

Selene looked surprised but, to her credit, didn't pull away. "Truly, sister? I was not aware."

"How could you access the cave?" I asked sharply. "I thought only Zeus or Selene could do that."

Eos raised her eyebrows. "I'm the goddess of the dawn," she said. "When the first rays of light touch the mountaintop above the cave, I'm able to enter."

I looked at Selene. "Did you know that?"

The moon goddess shook her head and narrowed her eyes at her sister. "No, it never occurred to me. And I'm not even sure how you'd figure that out, Eos."

A shadow of guilt flickered across Eos' face. "Zeus told me. I was complaining to him about Tithonus, and he told me to go and see Endymion and then come back if I still felt like whining." She sighed. "So I went to see him. I wanted to know what it could have been like for me and Tithonus if only Zeus hadn't tricked me so cruelly."

I nodded, knowing the story.

"I knew you were busy with your moon duties," she said to Selene, clutching at her sister's other hand. "I went and watched him for a long time. I sat in your chair. I rifled through your books." She chewed her lip in a most un-goddess-like fashion. "It crossed my mind to interrupt his slumber. After so much time, the spell could be weak. Jealousy is a bitter worm when it tunnels into the heart, and what you had...well. In the end, I did nothing, and crept away, leaving him snoring in peace."

"He doesn't snore," Selene muttered.

"Did you see anyone else while you were there?" I asked. "Or evidence that anyone else had been there recently?"

Eos shook her head. "No, nothing, else I would have said so," she said. "I am sorry, sister."

I could almost feel the internal struggle Selene fought, but in the end she squeezed her sister's hands and said, "Thank you for telling us. But you could have come to me about this sooner."

Eos nodded. "Miss Sheridan, if there's any way I can help you with your investigations, please let me know. I have a debt to repay for lying to you, and to my sister. I'll assist you if I can."

"All right, let's put our heads together," I said, pulling out my notebook and looking over my notes. "What about Apollo? He was the only person we ran into yesterday who didn't quote poetry at me, although I thought he started to. And he definitely had an attitude when we spoke to him. He was trying to put me—maybe both of us —off-balance. Why?"

Selene splayed her hands. "I don't know Apollo that well. I avoid him, most of the time." She reached down and stroked Kyon's head, as if for reassurance. "I turned him down once—well, more than once, if I'm going to be honest."

"Turned him down as in, wouldn't sleep with him?" I

asked bluntly.

"One of the few who've said no to him, I'd say," Eos said, then blushed a deep pink. On the goddess, it was beautiful.

Selene nodded diffidently. "It seems like everybody on Olympia sleeps with everybody else eventually, and it's no big deal. But I just never felt that way about Apollo. And I had Endymion. I didn't want anybody else." Her blue eyes sparkled with unshed tears for a moment.

"Hmm. So that does give Apollo a motive," I said. "If he still wants you, he might see Endymion as the biggest obstacle. And he strikes me as a god who usually gets what he wants."

Selene sighed. "You could be right. He does think he's god's gift to...er, the gods. And mortals too."

"I've seen him watching you, Selene," Eos said, pursing her lips in thought. "I didn't read any particular meaning in it before."

"And," I said, the wheels turning faster now, "you're the moon. He's the sun. If he believes in the old 'opposites attract' thing, he's probably miffed that you weren't open to his attentions. That would hurt his pride, which he seems to have in abundance."

"But I don't see how even he could have managed it."

"If some gods' special abilities allow them to interact with the cave, as mine did..." Eos said, then trailed off. "I can't think of anything in particular about Apollo that would apply, though."

"Maybe Zeus can tell us something about that," Selene said in a grim voice. "Come on, Acacia, we're going to go ask him."

"Remember my offer," Eos said, and hugged her sister.

"We will, and thanks," Selene told her, and we took our leave of the cottage. From outside, she, Kyon and I made the transition back to the throne plaza. It was getting a little easier to take. I didn't feel physically sick this time, at any rate.

Selene marched up to Zeus' throne and he lifted his head to watch her approach. He seemed more annoyed than apprehensive.

"Back so—"

"You told Eos how she could get into Endymion's cave." Selene cut him off. No "Father Zeus" or "King of the Gods" this time. "Who else did you tip off?"

"'Tip off'? How very 'pulp detective,' Selene," Zeus drawled.

"Don't avoid the question. You should have told us earlier who else could access the cave, and if they knew that." Selene had stopped in front of the throne, glaring up at Zeus with her hands on her hips. Kyon stood next to her, his own yellow eyes fixed on the elder god, just the hint of a low growl rumbling in his throat.

Zeus flipped a casual hand at the moon goddess. "Almost anyone could access the cave, if they thought about applying their abilities in creative ways. That's not up to me, and despite my wide-ranging abilities, I can't yet read the minds of other gods."

"Apollo hinted that your abilities are waning," I said, keeping my voice polite. Selene might not be afraid of Zeus, but I wasn't ready to tackle him quite so head-on.

Zeus' face clouded for an instant, but then he quirked his mouth in a wry smile. "We don't wield much power in the 'real world,' as you humans like to call it, these days," he said. "We're the stuff of myths and legends. But there's a certain amount of residual power; quite enough to keep me—us—going for a while yet. Apollo can say what he likes—and look to his own eroded influence. But low-level celestial interventions still aren't difficult for most of us."

"So you didn't directly tell anyone else that they might be able to access the cave?" Selene asked doggedly.

Zeus bent forward and fixed his grey eyes on her. "No," he said, "I did not. But I can't swear that no-one overheard me talking to Eos, or followed her there, or that she didn't tell anyone else. I'm afraid I have no further clues to offer, you, Selene. As I've said before."

He leaned back and looked away, obviously signalling the end of the audience. Selene pressed her lips together in wordless rage for a moment, then turned and stalked out of the courtyard, catching my arm and dragging me with her. Kyon followed us, nails clicking softly on the polished marble.

Once outside, I tugged my arm out of Selene's grip. "Okay, okay, calm down. First rule of the detective business: not every lead turns into something useful."

"He drives me crazy!" She balled up her fists and then let them relax, blowing out a long sigh. Kyon nudged her hand with his head and she stroked one silky ear. "Okay. Where do we go from here?"

"I think we need to go back to the cave," I said after a moment's thought. "Maybe there's something we're missing."

She didn't look any more hopeful than I felt, but she nodded, took my hand, and we went.

The cave looked exactly the way it had the last time we'd been here. I knelt to speak to the shaggy half-wolf, stroking his soft head tentatively. "Sniff around some, boy, see if there's anything different, or anything we didn't find the last time." He put his wet black nose to the floor and began to snuffle around.

I walked the perimeter of the room again, looking for any signs that the walls had been physically tampered with. I tapped the wall in a couple of places and was rewarded with scuffed knuckles. Then I went to sit in the big reading chair, tapping my fingers on the arm. Selene stood motionless, staring at the empty bed.

"Do you have any regrets?" I asked her.

She turned to me and smiled. "It was an odd relationship, I know," she said. "Him asleep all the time. But when we were together, we...communed. Communicated in a way that didn't have words or actual conversation, but felt very real."

"Telepathy?"

Selene shook her head, dark hair swishing. "Nothing so crude, or definitive. I guess I can't explain it. But he was the one who chose to sleep, and within the confines of that choice, we had something."

I'd still never asked about the fifty daughters, and the time still didn't seem right.

"You never got the feeling that he'd changed his mind, or was having second thoughts? That he might be wishing things could change?"

"I never did," she said, "and even if I had...what could he have done about it? Call on Zeus?" she quirked an eyebrow at me. "You met him—do you think he'd care much about Endymion or what he was thinking down here? I can't see him making an intervention for that, even if he knew."

I nodded. Zeus had struck me as more bored and self-absorbed than interested in the foibles of either humans or the gods and goddesses who inhabited Olympus.

"But Eos thought she might be able to wake him," I mused. "Did you ever try?"

"No. This was his choice," she said simply. Selene moved to the bed, pulling the coverlet off and shaking it out. "Well, if I can do nothing else, I'm going to straighten things up a bit."

"Eos used her special ability to get in here, and considered waking Endymion," I said. "If she could do it, then other gods probably have powers they could use, too. To get inside, and maybe to wake him up. We just have to figure out who."

Selene flung the coverlet back onto the bed. She threw a wry glance at me. "Do you have any idea how many gods and goddesses are up there, and how many powers and abilities they have?"

I almost missed it, but something fluttered to the stone floor in the flickering torchlight. Kyon saw it too, and we both moved toward the small object. When he snuffled at it, it drifted under the bed.

"Kyon, no!" I scolded him, afraid he'd eat or destroy whatever it was before I could get a good look. "Get back, boy!" I forgot that I was talking to the half-wolf of a goddess, but lucky for me, he didn't bite my head off.

Kneeling, I felt under the bed until my questing fingers found it. I pulled the tiny, smooth thing out and held it up for Selene to see. I knew immediately what it was, and where I'd seen more just like it. "Maybe we just got a lucky break," I said.

It was a laurel leaf. And only one god had been wearing a crown of them when we'd talked.

Apollo.

I made Selene take me back to my office, having convinced her that there would be little use in going to confront Apollo just yet. He'd shrug off the leaf, correctly noting that it proved nothing, that anyone could have left it to point to him, and that they were plentiful both in Olympus and on Earth.

No, before we confronted the god of Music and Assorted Other Things, I wanted to have all the pieces of the puzzle firmly in place. I invited Selene to make herself comfortable in the blue leather chair while I asked her a question.

Oliver must have sensed our arrival because he came in without knocking and placed a steaming mug where Selene could reach it. Without catching my eye, he sat down in the other chair and crossed his arms. Message received—he wasn't leaving.

I ignored him and spoke to Selene. "I suspect that Hermes was involved somehow, as well as Apollo. And he did give us a clue."

"He did?"

I nodded. "He quoted Robert Frost's poem that pits Love and Thought against each other. And Apollo is the god of intellectual inquiry—or thought. I think Hermes knows more than he feels comfortable saying."

"But why would Hermes help Apollo?" Selene asked.

"I was hoping you might have some ideas about that."

The goddess got up and paced behind the blue leather chair, tapping a long, slender finger against her lips. The wolf-dog raised his head and watched her progress, but didn't rise to follow her. "He is a younger god," Selene mused. "And I think sometimes he gets weary of being ordered around by all the others. He might have welcomed a chance to do a real favor for an older god, one that might benefit him later."

"He might have thought he was helping Endymion," Oliver suggested. "He's the god of shepherds, right? And Endymion was one."

"The problem is, how to get Apollo to confess," I said. "It's still all circumstantial, unless Hermes tells us everything, which I don't think is likely."

"If we could find Endymion, he might be able to confirm that it was Apollo," Selene said, but then she slumped down in the chair again. "But if I could find him, I wouldn't have had to come to you."

"I don't think Apollo would have harmed Endymion," I mused. "He's certainly done some nasty things to people —humans and gods alike—who opposed or harmed him, but he'd have no particular grudge against Endymion. He wanted him out of the way, sure, but I don't think there was a lot of malice in it."

"That's true," Selene said, a note of hope in her voice. "Apollo's got a mean streak, and a narcissistic one, but he has no reason to hate Endymion."

I stood and paced. "So that means he sent Endymion— somewhere. Somewhere he'd be safe, but out of the way."

Selene looked skeptical. "Endymion has been asleep for centuries," she said. "The modern world is going to be a confusing bedlam for him. Where's he going to be safe on his own?"

"Let me sleep on that," I said. "The answer's got to be in Apollo's character, and Endymion's. Hermes might have had a hand in it. And Apollo might even have asked Endymion where he'd like to go."

"I'll think about it, too," Selene offered, but her voice was dubious.

"Come and get me first thing in the morning," I told her. "One way or another, we'll go and confront Apollo."

With a sad smile, she left, and I sat down at my desk, booted up my computer, and went online.

"Go get your laptop," I told Oliver. "We've got more research to do."

I'd like to say that I was waiting at the office for Selene the next morning, ready to go and pin the disappearance of her lover on Apollo, but I can't. The truth is, I was up half the night hashing over the case, our possible avenues of inquiry, and the various abilities and influences of Greek gods, with Oliver. He kept us going by uncomplainingly refilling the coffeemaker—but that meant I didn't sleep well the other half of the night. Selene actually came to my apartment to rouse me, which was more embarrassing than I can say. If you don't habitually wake up looking like a goddess yourself, you might have some inkling of what I mean. However, I was glad to see her.

"Can you get in touch with Eos and ask her to come see me?" I asked Selene as I filled the coffeemaker. "She said she'd help, right?"

She frowned. "Yes. But what can she do that I can't?"

"Your job is to get everyone together on Olympus."

"Aren't we going to confront Apollo?"

"Absolutely." I pulled a mug from the cupboard and offered her one, but she shook her head. No doubt what I called coffee—even my good, fair trade variety—was unpalatable to the gods. "But I don't want Apollo to squirm out of this. I have a job for Eos and Oliver, and I have this job for you. Can you do it?"

She looked affronted. "Of course. And what are you going to do?"

I filled my mug and added a dollop of cream. "Drink a coffee, and get a shower," I said with a grin. "I can't go to Olympus looking like this. Come back for me when you have everyone rounded up."

The moon goddess looked like she wanted to ask more, but did as I asked. She sent out some kind of wordless message to Eos and disappeared. Eos arrived in response to her sister's call and I outlined her task, giving her directions to go and collect Oliver to help. He knew the plan we'd worked out last night. If it didn't work, I had an Alternate Plan B in mind, but I hoped it wouldn't come to that.

I had time for the shower and two cups of coffee before Selene returned for me. We arrived on Mount Olympus and found an impressive array of deities awaiting us. Impressive, and intimidating. I was glad I'd taken a little extra time to shed my scruffy-detective persona, and dress in a black pantsuit with a brilliant red power-blouse. This is my sole 'impressing-people' outfit, and I hoped it was up to the task.

I'd left Selene to figure out a way to gather them all together, and she in turn had recruited Zeus to assist. From the sour and sullen looks on some of the beautiful faces gathered in Zeus' throne room, they'd been ordered to attend and weren't happy about it. I sought out one face in particular and soon spotted Apollo, lounging on a marble chaise longue, plucking softly at his lyre and looking completely unconcerned. My heart faltered. What if I was wrong? It would be quite a stunning audience to have for an utter failure.

I steeled myself and approached Zeus. "Good morning, O Father of the Gods."

He granted me the merest of nods, but I thought he looked pleased. I turned to the assemblage and said, "Thank you all, for coming. You probably know that I am here to reveal what has happened to Selene's lover, Endymion."

"Finally woke up and bolted," someone said in a stage whisper, and some snickers stuttered around the room. Selene ignored it and I did the same.

"I won't bore you all by relating every step of my investigation," I said, "But I will tell you what evidence I've relied on in reaching my conclusion. In the cave where Endymion had previously slept, we found a single white feather and a laurel leaf. From that location, in addition to Endymion, a volume of poems by William Wordsworth had also gone missing."

There was some whispering at the mention of the poems, but the gods and godlings settled down at a glare from Zeus.

"You all know that the cave was sealed, and although Selene had freedom of passage in and out, it would not have been so easy for anyone else, even an immortal. Some of you could do it, yes, but you'd have to know how to utilize your particular influences or abilities to visit the cave."

I saw Zeus turn an interested look on me, but I pretended not to notice. Let him ask me, if he wanted to know everyone I'd pegged as possibilities.

"Are we going to be here all day? Because I didn't bring enough wine for that," a rotund little god yelled from his seat next to a marble column. A lithe goddess with long auburn hair and sheaves of grain embroidered on her robe nudged him in irritation.

"Stow it, Bacchus," Apollo said, coaxing a languid chord from his lyre. "Let the mortal spin her tale. At least it's something different."

Bacchus stuck his tongue out at Apollo, but subsided.

"All of this suggests to me that more than one perpetrator was involved," I continued. "And I've concluded that one of those was Hermes."

Hermes jumped to his feet. In fact, he jumped higher than that, and hovered a few feet above the floor, the wings on his sandals and helmet beating furiously. "Outrageous!" he cried, face flushed. "Why would I do such a thing, and why would any other god need my help?"

I waved my notebook (containing my Wikipedia notes) in his direction, "One of your spheres of influence is described as 'transitions and boundaries,'" I reminded him. "That would presumably give you the ability to gain access to the cave, or to manipulate things so that someone else could go inside. And possibly pass out again."

Hermes scowled at me, but said nothing.

"I did believe you when you said you'd never been inside it yourself," I added. "I'm willing to accept that you were tricked or coerced into helping." Hermes had helped me, however circumspectly, and I wanted him to know I wasn't throwing him to the wolves.

"I believed him, too," Selene breathed. "So are you saying maybe the feather was planted there?"

I pointed at her. "Exactly what I was thinking. The feather definitely belongs to Hermes, and it's possible that it came to be in the cave by accident. But it's also possible that whoever really took Endymion planted that feather to implicate Hermes, or at least to throw us off the track. The person may have given Hermes a perfectly understandable reason why he or she wanted access to the cave—but now Hermes is afraid to confess that he helped."

Hermes remained silent, but his wingbeats subsided and he let himself sink gently back to floor level. He didn't say anything, but he looked relieved.

"The laurel leaf," I continued, "leads me to believe that Apollo was also involved in Endymion's disappearance."

The beautiful god struck a horror-movie chord but smiled languidly. "Shocking! Of course, if Hermes' feather was planted in the cave, then a single laurel leaf could have been, too. I'm not sure your evidence adds up to anything yet, dear Acacia."

"Granted, but there is still the volume of poetry," I said. "I've noticed that all of you have a penchant for working verse into your conversations, and Selene confirms that this is true."

"TRUTH, so far, in my book," someone piped up with a laugh. I thought the quote might be Browning, but I wasn't as fluent in poetry as the rest of the assembled company.

Someone else recited in a booming voice, "*And truth, you say, is all divine; 'T is truth we live by; let her drench / The shuddering heart like potent wine; No matter how she wreck or wrench.*"

I held up a hand. "Lovely, and thanks for verifying that for me, but if everyone has to get a verse in, this will take all day. What actually struck me about the poetry thing was that Apollo was the only god I spoke with who didn't quote verse to me—especially notable since he is the god of poetry."

Apollo rolled his eyes. "I don't always quote poetry. Perhaps the mood simply didn't strike me when we were speaking. You might ask them about that," he added, nodding to a group of nine young women who seemed to move as a unit. Seven had their shining heads bent over what looked like smartphones, the eighth stared dreamily into space, and the ninth regarded Apollo with a strange mix of amusement and adoration. The Muses, I guessed. But I wasn't going to let Apollo distract me.

"You almost did," I said, shaking an admonitory finger at him. "I'm sure you thought I didn't notice, but you began to say, 'Tis said that some—and then you changed tack, talking about the competitiveness of gods in the arena of love. It was very smooth, and I almost didn't catch it. However, there's a Wordsworth poem, "'Tis Said That Some Have Died For Love," that begins exactly that way, and I think you caught yourself just in time. If you'd simply quoted it, I might not have thought anything of it —everyone up here does that. But you changed your mind, because you didn't want to be caught quoting Wordsworth—of all poets, considering the book missing from the cave as well—to me at that moment."

Apollo raised his eyebrows. "A fascinating theory," he said, "but perhaps 'not quoting poetry' doesn't quite meet the evidentiary standard you're hoping for, either."

"There's also this." I pulled out the plastic bag containing a few white crystals. "When I found these, next to Endymion's bed, they smelled like ammonia and eucalyptus—a strange combination, I thought. Cleaner and cough drops? However, I discovered that ammonium carbonate, often in combination with another aromatic substance, is smelling salts. It occurred to me that the powers of a god of medicine, using a chemical compound for arousing consciousness, could have been just the ticket to wake Endymion."

Apollo strummed another lazy minor chord. "Fantastic detective work, Miss Sheridan. But pure speculation, nonetheless."

It was my turn to shrug. "I could put Hermes on the spot, and perhaps Zeus could force him to tell the truth, but I don't think I'll need to."

While I'd been laying out my evidence, Eos had discreetly joined the gathering and now sat, her ankles crossed demurely, watching the proceedings. Today she wore a fire-yellow dress with tiny flames embroidered at the hem. She'd piled her hair into a practical twist atop her head, no doubt to keep it out of the way whilst tackling the job I'd given her. When I caught her eye, she nodded once, stood, and disappeared.

A mighty whispering broke out among the gods, and Selene looked puzzled. I hadn't disclosed to the moon goddess the task I'd set Eos and Oliver, in case it didn't pan out. But that nod told me that it had.

Before the whispering could grow to full-blown speculation, Eos reappeared, holding hands with Oliver on one side and a young man I'd never seen before on the other. Oliver staggered and then caught his balance. His mouth slowly opened as he looked around the opulent throne room at the assembled deities, but no words escaped. I didn't waste too much time worrying about him—he'd recover his aplomb quickly, because he was Oliver. Instead I studied the other young man. A mop of dark curly hair cascaded below his shoulders. He wore a somewhat vacant expression, jeans a size too big, and a Proclaimers t-shirt. In his other hand, he still held a beer mug, half-full of foamy amber ale. He looked around the assemblage of gods and saw Apollo. His face split in a somewhat goofy grin.

"Hey, Paul," he said, his words slow and thick from the ale, apparently not his first of the day. His brow furrowed into a frown and he added, "You shaid you'd come back for me. You din't."

Apollo fidgeted and wouldn't meet Endymion's eyes. "Sorry, pal, I, er...got a little tied up."

Endymion burped and quirked a half-smile. "'S'no problem. Good pub you left me in, anyway." He took a pull from his mug and surveyed the group again. This time he saw Selene. She smiled meltingly and took a step toward him, but Endymion's posture changed. He stiffened almost imperceptibly, then affected extreme casualness, glancing away. "Oh, hey, Selene."

The goddess faltered, her smile fading. I thought I should come to her rescue.

"As you can all see," I said to the assemblage, "Endymion himself is here. I think we should listen to what he has to say."

Eos led Endymion to a chair and urged him into it. He sort of fell the last few inches, but didn't slop out a drop of his beer. He took another swig and fixed his eyes on

Oliver.

"Now?"

Oliver nodded. "Now, buddy. Just tell everyone what happened."

Endymion sighed, and suddenly he looked very young. "I don't 'member everything," he started, "but Paul came to see me—"

"And this is 'Paul'?" I interrupted, pointing to Apollo.

Endymion nodded. "Yup, but I think that's not his full name, you know? More like a nickname." He belched again. "So Paul came and woke me up, and I was like, whoa, what's going on? Because I haven't had anyone...much...to talk to for a long time." He didn't look at Selene when he said that.

I suddenly wished that I'd talked to Endymion in private instead of setting up the big reveal this way. Selene looked pale, even for a goddess of the moon, and I hadn't meant to subject her to such a public embarrassment. But I'd been afraid that Apollo would need a very public unmasking for it to make any impression. It was too late now. Once he was started, Endymion plowed on.

"So we talked and Paul said the world had changed a lot while I was asleep, and wouldn't I like to get out for a bit? Just a breath of fresh air and a drink, and catch up on things. And I said sure, now that I thought about it, it was a long time since the last Harvest and by Demeter, I'd love a beer."

The harvest goddess perked up at the mention of her name. She was the redhead who'd nudged Bacchus earlier, and the god of wine snorted. "Beer! Peasant."

"So Paul said he knew a place where I could get some beer and conversation, and I've been there ever since." He took a swallow and regarded the now-empty glass with regret. "Nice people," he said. "Know a lot about sheep."

Selene looked at me in confusion and I put up a hand. "I knew that Apollo wouldn't take Endymion anywhere in Greece," I said. "Too easy. First place you'd look, right? And then I got to thinking that Endymion had been a shepherd, and that Hermes, who's got a reputation as a trickster, might have been in on the decision about what to do with him..."

Hermes wouldn't meet my eyes now, although I could see that his ducked head hid a smile.

"So where was he?" Selene asked. Her voice was admirably controlled.

"Scotland," I said succinctly. "At a pub called the Shepherd's Rest."

"You would not believe how many pubs in Scotland are named after shepherds or sheep," Oliver groused. "Took us almost all night to find him." Then he seemed to remember where he was and fell silent.

"Eos and Oliver tracked him down and brought him here," I explained. "So all that's left to talk about is—" I turned and caught Apollo's eye and held his gaze, "Why?"

The sun god pulled his face into a haughty pout. "Can't you figure that part out, too, Acacia? Since you've proven yourself to be so clever."

I tilted my head at him. "I have some ideas. You're the sun, Selene is the moon. You probably have some notion that she should be attracted to you. She's one of the few females up here that you haven't slept with."

Muffled giggles erupted from the cluster of Muses and elsewhere around the room, but I ignored them. "You saw it as a challenge," I said. "You took the book of Wordsworth to study up on what might appeal to her—or simply because you could."

I turned to Hermes. "And you helped, maybe because you're a younger god and wanted to ingratiate yourself with Big Brother, or maybe just because it appealed to your mischievous nature. Maybe Apollo wasn't completely truthful about why he wanted access to the cave. Or maybe," I added, "you did it because you've always had a soft spot for humans, and you thought Endymion might enjoy a bit of freedom. I have no doubt Scotland and shepherds was your idea, a place where he'd fit in."

Hermes looked abashed.

I turned to Selene and continued, "At any rate, there's your answer. Endymion himself has identified Apollo— nicknames notwithstanding—as the person who woke him and took him from the cave. And he's no longer missing. I think my job is done." I didn't add, *although he may not want to go back to that cave.* He and Selene would have to figure out that part on their own. I'd had my fill of gods for a while.

The crowd dispersed fairly quickly after that, and, after thanking me distractedly, Selene went off with Endymion to talk. I thought she'd have to get him sobered up quite a bit before they could have any meaningful conversation, but I expected she might be able to bring some divine ability to bear on that front. Eos kindly offered to take me and Oliver home, to which I agreed. Oliver whispered that he would have liked a chance to look around a little more, but I deemed it wiser to get out of Apollo's sight as quickly as possible. I don't think Selene ever would have given him the dalliance he wanted, Endymion or no, but to all appearances I was the one who'd spoiled his plans.

Eos took us to my office and looked around with a puzzled air. "This is where you work?" was all she said, but I was acutely aware of the shabby surroundings. Maybe Oliver was right, and I should invest a little money in sprucing the place up.

"Well, thank you for helping my sister," she said, beaming a sunny smile at me. "We're not always the best of friends, but I do love her."

"Thanks for your help," I returned. "I don't think we would have gotten anywhere with Apollo if you and Oliver hadn't found Endymion. And that was really what Selene wanted, anyway."

The goddess' smile faltered a little. "I don't know how that's going to work out for her."

I nodded. "It'll be better than not knowing, anyway. Maybe you and she will end up with something to commiserate over."

"Well, thanks again," she said. "If I ever need an investigator, I'll come to you, Acacia."

I rather hoped she wouldn't. Dealing with gods was exhausting. But I smiled and shook her hand. She tipped

Oliver a wink, and disappeared.

I raised an eyebrow. "I saw that. Did it really take you two that entire time to find Endymion?"

"Of course! It was completely business. Although," he mused, looking at the spot where she'd been. "We did get along. Maybe there was a little bit of chemistry there."

"Don't read too much into it," I told Oliver. "You know what we learned about how she goes through men."

"Yeah, I know," Oliver said speculatively. "Still, she's very attractive."

I let it go. If Oliver got involved with Eos, it would be his goddess problem, not mine.

About the Author

Sherry D. Ramsey is a speculative fiction writer, editor, publisher, creativity addict and self-confessed internet geek. When she's not writing, she makes jewelry, gardens, hones her creative procrastination skills on social media, and consumes far more coffee and chocolate than is likely good for her.

Her books include the middle-grade fantasy, *The Seventh Crow*; two books in the Nearspace series, *One's Aspect to the Sun* and *Dark Beneath the Moon*, with the third, *Beyond the Sentinel Stars* due out in late 2017; the urban fantasy *The Murder Prophet*; and an earlier short story collection, *To Unimagined Shores—Collected Stories*. With her partners at Third Person Press she has co-edited six anthologies of regional short fiction. Every November she disappears into the strange realm of National Novel Writing Month and emerges gasping at the end, clutching something resembling a novel.

A member of the Writer's Federation of Nova Scotia Writer's Council, Sherry is also a past Vice-President and Secretary-Treasurer of SF Canada, Canada's national association for Speculative Fiction Pro-fessionals, and is SFC's long-serving web administrator.

You can visit Sherry online to find free stories, subscribe to her erratically monthly newsletter, and follow her blog at www.sherrydramsey.com.

Connect with her on Facebook at Sherry D. Ramsey Writing News, and follow her much more pithy musings and glimpses into her life on Twitter and Instagram @sdramsey.

Nearspace

Follow Captain Luta Paixon and her crew as they search the wormhole-riddled reaches of Nearspace for the truth about immortality, greed, and what makes us family.

One's Aspect to the Sun
Tyche Books
ISBN 978-0-9918369-5-6
getBook.at/onesaspecttothesun

Dark Beneath the Moon
Tyche Books
ISBN 978-1-928025-31-3
getBook.at/darkbeneaththemoon

Beyond the Sentinel Stars
Tyche Books
Forthcoming, 2017

The Seventh Crow

When you can't remember most of your life, you have to be prepared for anything...

A talking crow, a forgotten world, and a young girl's quest to regain her memory, find her power, and protect those she cares about.

The Seventh Crow
Dreaming Robot Press
ISBN 978-1-940924-08-3
getBook.at/theseventhcrow

Magica Incognita

Magic, murder, and a goose with attitude...urban fantasy with a twist.

The Murder Prophet
ISBN (Print): 978-0-9938973-0-6
ISBN (Ebook): 978-0-9938973-1-3
getBook.at/murderprophet

Coming soon:
The Chaos Assassin

www.ingramcontent.com/pod-product-compliance
Lightning Source LLC
Chambersburg PA
CBHW072211170626
46813CB00003B/895